The men and women who fought and won World War II, and truly made the world safe for democracy, come together in these thrilling stories of war as it was really fought by these great and bestselling military writers:

Stephen Coonts
Ralph Peters
Harold Coyle
Harold Robbins
R. J. Pineiro
David Hagberg
Jim DeFelice
James Cobb
Barrett Tillman
Dean Ing

VICTORY

INTO THE FIRE

EDITED AND INTRODUCED BY
STEPHEN COONTS

HAROLD COYLE

HAROLD ROBBINS

R. J. PINEIRO

FORGE®

A TOM DOHERTY ASSOCIATES BOOK
NEW YORK

This is a work of fiction. All the characters and events portrayed in this book are either fictitious or are used fictitiously.

VICTORY: INTO THE FIRE

Copyright © 2003 by Stephen Coonts
Introduction copyright © 2003 by Stephen Coonts
"Breakthrough on Bloody Ridge" copyright © 2003 by Harold W. Coyle
"Blood Bond" copyright © 2003 by Jann Robbins.
"The Eagle and the Cross" copyright © 2003 by Rogelio J. Pineiro

A Forge Book
Published by Tom Doherty Associates, LLC
175 Fifth Avenue
New York, NY 10010

www.tor.com

Forge® is a registered trademark of Tom Doherty Associates, LLC.

ISBN 0-812-56168-6
EAN 978-0812-56168-5

First edition: May 2003
First mass market edition: May 2004

Printed in the United States of America

0 9 8 7 6 5 4 3 2 1

To all the men and women who fought for Liberty
during World War II

CONTENTS

INTRODUCTION

I was born in 1946 on the leading edge of the baby boomer generation, one of the sons and daughters of the men and women who fought and survived the greatest war the humans on this planet have yet experienced, World War II.

Early in the twentieth century Winston Churchill noted that the wars of the people were going to be worse than the wars of the kings—which was prophecy. There have been other wars since World War II, horrific wars such as Korea and Vietnam. And yet, terrible as they were, they did not become the defining experience for an entire generation, as did World War II, World War I, and the American Civil War. At the dawn of the twenty-first century our wars are fought by volunteers, professional soldiers, and not very many of them. There are those who say that this is progress. In any event, it insulates the vast bulk of the population from the rigors and emotions and risks that define war.

I don't think that the age of general warfare is

over. The biblical admonition to be fruitful and multiply has been blindly obeyed by the world's poorest people. There are now over six billion people on this modest planet, one that must provide the wherewithal to support all the creatures that live upon it, including the humans. Too many people and not enough land, food, and jobs has always been a prescription for disaster.

Today nations around the world are busy developing weapons of mass destruction, a handy term to describe nuclear, chemical, and biological weapons that kill indiscriminately. In the early months of 2002, India and Pakistan, two of the world's poorest, most populous nations, went to the brink of nuclear war and stared into the abyss before backing away. As I write this in the final month of 2002, United Nations' weapons inspectors are again searching for weapons of mass destruction in Iraq, an outlaw nation led by one of the worst despots on the planet. What will happen next in Iraq is anyone's guess.

If that weren't enough, one of the world's major religions, Islam, has grown a perverted branch that holds that murdering those who don't believe as you do is a holy duty. Worse, some of the clergy of this religion teach their acolytes that suicide while committing mass murder is martyrdom that earns the criminal a ticket to paradise. This isn't a new thing—Islam has gone through these paroxysms before. Mercifully, most of the other religions that demand human sacrifice are no longer practiced on this planet.

And finally, there is the planet itself. These six billion people have arrived on earth during what many climatologists feel is a rare period of unusual warmth. The only thing we can say for certain about climates is that they change. If the world cools or suffers an extended drought, the planet's ability to support its present population will be severely impaired. But we don't have to wait that long for disaster to strike: If a supervolcano (such as Yellowstone) blows, or major earthquakes inundate populated coastal regions, or a cosmological disaster (such as a meteor) strikes, our happy, peaceful, post–World War II age will come to an abrupt end. Man may survive, but not six billion of us.

And man may not survive. Despite our best efforts our species may well go the way of the dinosaur and the woolly mammoth. The tale has yet to be written. In any event, armed conflict will probably be a part of man's experience as long as there are men.

As I write this fifty-seven years after the Japanese surrender aboard USS *Missouri* in Tokyo Bay, World War II is fading from our collective memories. Currently about one thousand veterans of World War II pass on every day. All too soon World War II will be only museum exhibits, history books that are read only in colleges and universities, black-and-white footage of Nazi troops, and thundering *Victory at Sea* movies that run late at night on the cable channels. Some of us also have knickknacks that our parents kept to remind them of those days when they were young and the world was on fire, yet all too soon old medals and fading photographs become merely artifacts of a bygone age.

The sons and daughters of the veterans understand that they are losing something important when their fathers pass on. Many have approached me, asking if I know of anyone who would help them write down their father's memories while he is still able to voice them, capture them for the generations yet unborn. Alas, except for a few underfunded oral history programs, these personal

memories usually go unrecorded. Diaries have long
been out of fashion, and the elderly veterans and
their children are usually not writers. Even those
who could write down their memory of their expe-
riences often get so caught up in the business of
living through each day that they think no one cares
about their past.

Perhaps it has always been so. From the Trojan
War to date, personal accounts by warriors are few
and far between. Other than the occasional memoir
by a famous general (often one out to polish his
military reputation), the task of preserving the past
is usually left to historians who weren't there . . . and
to writers of fiction.

Historians write of decisions of state, of fleets and
armies and the strategy of generals and great battles
that brought victory or defeat. Fiction writers work
on a smaller scale—they write about individuals.

Only in fiction can the essence of the human experience of war be laid bare. Only from fiction can
we learn what it might have been like to survive the
crucible, or to die in it. Only through fiction can we
come to grips with the ultimate human challenge—
kill or be killed. Only through fiction can we prepare ourselves for the trial by fire, when our turn
comes.

STEPHEN COONTS

BREAKTHROUGH ON BLOODY RIDGE

HAROLD COYLE

HAROLD COYLE graduated from the Virginia Military Institute in 1974, with a B.A. in history and a commission as a second lieutenant in Armor. His first assignment was in Germany, where he served for five years as a tank platoon leader, a tank company executive officer, a tank battalion assistant operations officer, and as a tank company commander. Following that he attended the Infantry Officers Advanced Course at Fort Benning, Georgia, became a branch chief in the Armor School's Weapons Department at Fort Knox, Kentucky, worked with the National Guard in New England, spent a year in the Republic of Korea as an assistant operations officer, and went to Fort Hood, Texas, for a tour of duty as the G-3 training officer of the 1st Cavalry Division and the operations officer of Task Force 1-32 Armor, a combined arms maneuver task force.

His last assignment with the Army was at the Command and General Staff College at Fort Leavenworth, Kansas. In January 1991, he reported to the 3rd Army, with which he served during Desert Storm. Resigning his commission after returning from the Gulf in the spring of 1991, he continues to serve as a lieutenant colonel in the Army's Individual Ready Reserve. He writes full time and has produced the following novels: *Team Yankee, Sword Point, Bright Star, Trial by Fire, The Ten Thousand, Code of Honor, Look Away, Until the End, Savage Wilderness, God's Children, Against All Enemies,* and *More Than Courage.*

PROLOGUE

August 1942

On August 7, 1942, men of the Fifth Marines climbed over the sides of their landing craft and dropped into the shallow surf. Before them lay a picture-postcard view of a tropical island. From a distance the sandy beach, the lush green jungle, and the prominent hill that was their first day's objective seemed more like paradise than a battlefield. Only slowly would this and so many other illusions entertained by soldiers and leaders of both sides die on an island that would become known as Starvation Island.

This event also set into motion an advance that would end three years and eight days later with the complete and utter defeat of the Japanese Empire. The young Marines making their first amphibious assault of the war that morning had no way of knowing that their efforts here would lead to such a victory. The cruel fact was that since the Japanese attack on Pearl Harbor on December 7, 1941, American ground forces had known nothing but defeat. The only success of note that the American Army and Marines had managed to achieve at a terrible price during those eight months was to delay the advance of Japanese forces in the Philippines and Wake Island. While those feats demonstrated that the Americans could fight, no event to date provided any proof that during the course of a campaign American troops could prevail over Japanese soldiers, who had been raised since childhood to serve and die for their Emperor.

It is all too easy for historians tucked safely away in their studies or standing behind a podium in cool, clean classrooms to pontificate on how American military might have made victory in World War II a foregone conclusion. Nothing can be further from the truth. Anyone who has taken the time to study war realizes that it is the soldier, the man charged with closing with the enemy and destroying him by use of firepower, maneuver, and shock effect, that decides battles. Even the most lavishly equipped army is of no value if its soldiers and the men selected to lead them do not have the courage and will to go eye to eye with their foe. In World War II, battles were often won not because one side or the other had superior weaponry or greater numbers, but because the men on the firing line and those who commanded them refused to be beaten.

The battle for Guadalcanal is well worth studying in detail because it is one of those rare occasions in military history that the fate of nations rested squarely upon the shoulders of a few good men. Decisions by the leaders on both sides during this campaign were made under combat conditions that are all but impossible to image. More often than not they were based upon fragmentary and erroneous information. Sometimes a leader had little to go on but his gut instinct. The decisions they made had a bearing on more than the outcome of the battle in which they were engaged. Their efforts would determine the course of the war in the Pacific Theater, for the fight for Guadalcanal was a campaign that could have easily gone either way. American commanders would not be confident of eventual victory until mid-November, while the Japanese did not face up to failure until late December. During that time American Marines and soldiers grappled with Japanese soldiers in a tropical hell. It was a battle that was brutal and uncompromising. In numerous small encounters and the heat of massive attacks, soldiers of both sides were pushed beyond the limits of human endurance and asked time and time again to go further. One such encounter took place in mid-September, when a brigade-sized unit under the command of Major General Kiyotake Kawaguchi met two understrength battalions commanded by Lieutenant Colonel Merritt A. Edson on a barren spine of land that would forever be known as Bloody Ridge.

ONE

SEPTEMBER 8, 1942

Shortly after 0430 hours, Lieutenant Francis J. Pearson gave up the relative safety of the ancient destroyer transport and started to make his way down into the Higgins Boat tied alongside. While he grappled with the thick knotted rope of the cargo net, Pearson could feel other Marine Raiders who belonged to the platoon he commanded struggling to find footing or a handhold. Like their platoon commander, they were doing their best to clear the way for those behind them while at the same time taking care that they did not miss the Higgins Boat which rose and fell with each passing wave. Even when he felt his left foot make contact with the gunwale of the landing craft, Pearson knew this first challenge of the day was not over. One had to be careful to make sure not to let go of the cargo net before he had both feet firmly planted. To misjudge would either send him pitching backwards into the small craft and on top of those already aboard it or down into the sea between the steel sides of the fast transport and the Higgins Boat. The former would be embarrassing, the latter fatal.

Once aboard, Pearson made for the front of the boat as best he could. As an officer, that was where he belonged. Farthest forward and first out. Only when he shared a boat with his company commander or a battalion staff officer did he find he needed to yield this "honor." Today he would have it all to himself. In a few minutes, when the shallow-bottomed craft nudged its prow into the sand of the distant shore, Pearson would spring up and over the side of the Higgins Boat like a jack-in-the-box and into the shallow surf, ready to lead his platoon into whatever hell the Japanese had waiting for them.

But that was still in the future. For the next few minutes there would be little for him to do. Both Pearson and his men would be in the hands of the landing craft's coxswain and at the mercy of the Fates who governed the destiny of mere morals such as they with a capriciousness that was as outrageous as it was frightful. Francis J. Pearson had seen those fickle goddesses at work on Tulagi. While hunkered on the ground next to one of his BAR gunners, pointing out a target he wanted the man to take out, Pearson noticed that the man was making no effort to bring his weapon to bear. Angered, the young officer turned to face the man. Only then did Pearson notice that the BAR gunner's head was slumped over to one side. Aside from the glassy-eyed stare that saw nothing, only a small bright red dimple square in the middle of the man's forehead betrayed his fate. Though he was to see many other men die that day, that one particular incident spooked Pearson. Whoever had fired the shot that killed the BAR gunner had taken his time and aimed well. Pearson could not but help thinking that the same Jap could just as easily have dispatched him. Though he tried to tell himself such were the fortunes of war, the young Marine officer could not but help feel that no matter how good he was or how hard he tried, when the Fates decided that a man's time was up, there was nothing he could do to stop it.

The run in to the beach seemed to take forever. No one in the Higgins boat spoke as the huddled Marines crammed into the craft that swayed to and fro. There were no mysteries to ponder this time, no great unknowns to overcome. All their curiosity as to what would happen once they landed had been put to rest on Tulagi. On this day the only question that remained to be answered was how bad would it be?

There had been little time to prepare for this raid. Some of Pearson's men had even found it necessary to abandon meals they had been preparing. For men who were surviving on meager rations drawn mainly from captured Japanese stocks, that was a great sacrifice. Few took comfort in the rumor that the enemy they were expecting to encounter were poorly armed, starving, and war-weary. Such rumors could not make the hunger a man felt disappear or allay the fears that threatened to rob him of his senses.

A sudden lurch forward telegraphed the news to all in the landing craft that it had taken them as far as it could to the beach. As one, the men along the gunwales leaped up and over the side, into the surf. Pearson was among the first to get his feet wet. After pausing only long enough to be sure of his footing, adjust his gear, and bring his .45 caliber. Reising up

to the ready, the young Marine platoon leader
flipped the safety off and charged headlong for the
first patch of cover he caught sight of.

In this endeavor he was not alone. To his left
and right men who were a bit more fleet of foot and
equally concerned about their vulnerability splashed
past him as they madly dashed forward. Throughout
the furious race to negotiate the surf and get clear
of the open beach, not a word was uttered. Every
man present had done this so many times before,
back at Quantico, Virginia, and on Samoa during
training, that nothing needed to be said. Yet even
the seemingly routine manner with which his men
deployed and the eerie absence of enemy fire could
not disguise the fact that this was not a training exercise. To a man, the Marines around Pearson
waited for the first shot to be fired. Everyone expected it. The young platoon commander even
found himself praying for it. Only then, when there
was a clearly identified enemy against whom he
could lash out, would he be freed from the awful
tension that gripped him so tightly that he feared
he would choke on his own bile.

But there was no enemy fire to greet them. The
only noise that disturbed the predawn darkness was
the splash of hundreds of feet sloshing through the
surf and a hoarse chorus of gasping men driven by
fear and physical exertion to gulp down mouthfuls
of air while running forward for all they were worth.
He was still in the water when Pearson saw that the
spot he had chosen to head for was already being
occupied by members of his platoon who had managed to dash past him. Having made no plans beyond exiting the Higgins Boat and going for that
one piece of cover, the platoon commander slowed
his pace, then stopped as soon as he was out of the

surf. Looking this way and that, he scanned the beach for someplace that afforded any sort of cover.

He was in the midst of his search for sanctuary when he saw the tracks. At first he didn't see them for what they were. Only when he spotted a line of backpacks neatly laid out in rows just beyond the high-tide line did it dawn upon Pearson that his men and the other Marine Raiders were not the first soldiers to cross this particular strip of beach that night. The realization that fresh Japanese reinforcements were close at hand sent a chill down his spine. In an instant, he abandoned all thought of finding a place where he could hunker down and wait until the entire company was assembled and turned instead to find his company commander.

Pearson found that his superior, Major Nickerson, had already stumbled upon the fresh enemy tracks and jettisoned field packs. Both men agreed on what this meant. What the major didn't know with any degree of certainty was what impact their discovery would have on the raid that they were supposed to mount against Tasimboko, a village that lay about four thousand yards or so to the west along the same strip of beach they were standing on. For that decision, they would have to wait for their commander, Colonel Merritt A. Edson, who was coming ashore with the second wave. Until then, all Pearson and the other Raiders belonging to Company B could do was sit tight, keep their eyes and ears open, and pray for all they were worth.

By the time he made his way back to where his platoon had deployed to cover the shallow beachhead, Pearson found that some of the more stalwart individuals in his command had managed to shed their preassault willies and allow their curiosity to get the better of them. Despite the specter of im-

minent combat, a few were already busy poking
about, examining the contents of the discarded
packs and looking over an antitank gun that had
also been abandoned. Pearson himself found that
he could not resist the temptation to join his men
in this impromptu inspection of their most unusual
find. The scene reminded the young officer of the
manner in which the Raiders themselves set aside
their field packs at a rifle range they had marched
to for training. Even the small gun had the look of
a piece that was ready for a parade ground inspection and not a weapon that had endured the ravages
of combat and the miserable tropical humidity that
turned any uncared-for metal to rust.

The appearance of their battalion commander
put an end to the sight-seeing and redirected Pearson's full attention back to the tactical situation that
confronted his platoon. The examination of the
abandoned equipment was now taken up by the battalion's Intel section, which included one of the
least likely Marines in the entire Corps. Wearing
thick glasses and skinny as a rail, John Erskine was
initially rejected by the Marines because of his
height. It was said that even if he stood on his toes
he didn't reach the minimum required. But the
man had one thing that the Marines needed desperately in 1941, the ability to read and write Japanese and an intimate knowledge of their culture. In
short order, the son of a missionary who had spent
his first sixteen years living in Japan was able to as-
certain that the packs that had been discarded on
the beach belonged to the Second Artillery Regiment of the Sendai Division, a unit that wasn't even
supposed to be on Guadalcanal.

Yet as bad as this bit of information was, the sudden appearance of warships and a pair of transports

emerging from the early-morning gloom just off Taivu Point sent a wave of alarm through the entire command. At that moment there were but three hundred Raiders ashore. The APD transports had yet to return with Company C and the under-strength Paramarine battalion. No one needed to explain to Pearson or his men what it would mean if those warships and transports turned out to be Japanese. "Well, sir," one of Pearson's more cynical squad leaders said as he looked first at the uniden-tified vessels, then peered off into the jungle, "now I know what they mean when they say between a rock and a hard place."

Luck, however, was running with the Raiders that morning. Not only had their timetable delivered them at Taivu Point after the Japanese flotilla had brought in the Japanese gunners and departed, but the unexpected appearance of an American cruiser and pair of destroyers escorting two transports con-vinced the Japanese troops in the area that they were facing a major invasion. Though he did not know it, Edson and his small band of Raiders had been given a period of grace and a powerful psy-chological edge. This was further reinforced by the APD destroyer transports that had delivered the Raiders. On their way back to pick up the rest of Edson's force, the commanders of the USS *Manley* and USS *McKean* shelled the village of Tasimboko with their three-inch guns. Though the damage was minimal, this action served to enhance the impres-sion that the one-day raid was actually a full-scale invasion. For a moment some of the defenders even managed to set aside the bushido code under which all Japanese soldiers lived and seek safety farther in-land. Some, but not all.

Not wanting to wait until he had his entire com-

mand ashore, Edson began his march on Tasimboko, the objective of the raid. Although his
battalion was already split, with only three companies ashore and the rest in transit, the bold and re-
sourceful commander of the First Marine Raiders
further divided it for this movement forward. While
Company C, under the command of Captain Bob
Thomas, held the beach and awaited the arrived of
the rest of the battalion and the Paramarines, Captain John Antonelli's Company A struck inland in
an effort to get around the flank of any resistance
the Japanese might offer. Company B remained
within sight of the coast throughout their westward
movement. The lead platoon of this company was
commanded by John Sweeney, an officer who had
recently been promoted to captain but remained
with his platoon. Pearson and his men followed.

The advance of Company B was slow, but not because of the terrain the Marine Raiders encoun-
tered. Along the coast the ground was quite level
and the vegetation far less imposing than that found
little more than a few hundred yards farther inland.
There was even an occasional clearing in the undergrowth, a rarity on Guadalcanal. Pearson figured
the reason for such a cautious pace was due to their
commanding officer's being as spooked by the abandoned equipment and tracks they had found on the
beach as he was. As if to reinforce his supposition,
every few yards additional caches of backpacks as
well as hundreds of discarded life preservers were
spotted. They even came upon another antitank
gun sitting out in plain view, as if waiting for inspection. All of this added up to something, something that even the dullest man in Pearson's platoon
could tell was not at all favorable to them. After
pausing but a moment to study the assortment of

first-rate equipment trailing off in the direction of Tasimboko like bread crumbs dropped by Hansel and Gretel, Pearson took in a deep breath, tightened his grip on his Reising submachine gun, and pressed on. With each step he found himself wishing for something to happen, a wish not at all uncommon at such times but seldom fulfilled in a manner that is desirable.

The shot that shattered the dreadful silence wasn't recognized at first for what it was. Pearson was facing toward the rear of the column, checking to make sure his men were maintaining their proper distance, when something shrieked past him, cutting through leaves and branches and scattering their fragments behind. Before he could turn to look, a sharp crack from somewhere up near the front of the column shattered the early-morning stillness. It was followed by a detonation someplace in the rear of the column. Utterly confused, Pearson continued to look this way then that, trying to sort out what, exactly, was going on.

Gunnery Sergeant Karl Jacobi, his platoon sergeant, didn't need anyone to tell him what was going on or what he needed to do. Even as he dived for cover, he bellowed in his best drill sergeant voice, *"Hit the deck!"*

Responding to the order rather than the actual danger that had motivated it, Pearson complied. He dropped to the ground with such force that he all but bounced up. From somewhere behind him one of his men put in words the same thought that he himself was entertaining. "What the hell was that?"

Again it was Jacobi, known to all as Gunny Jay, who supplied the answer. "A Jap field gun. Now keep your head down and listen up for the lewtenant's orders."

The last part of Jacobi's response struck Pearson.
What orders? What was he suppose to be ordering
his men to do? Hesitantly, he lifted his head just in
time to witness the explosion of a second round,
which impacted near the front of the column
among Sweeney's lead platoon. Not until he heard
the familiar crack of '03 Springfields and the deep
hammering of a BAR returning fire did Pearson finally lift himself up off the ground a few inches and
gaze at the line of prone Marines, who were looking
back at him. "Stay low, keep your eyes open, and
listen up." What he wanted them to listen for was
beyond him. But given the present circumstances,
Pearson figured it was the best he could do until he
received an order from the C.O. to do something
that fit the situation as it developed or deteriorated
a bit further.

The engagement was taking place not more than
a hundred yards ahead, yet it was completely out of
sight, making the entire experience quite nerve-
racking. Pearson could hear every shot as Sweeney's
men deployed and brought more fire to bear on the
enemy gun emplacement. The spattering of small-
arms fire was punctuated every few seconds by other
rounds from the enemy field gun, some of which
found their mark among Sweeney's platoon and
others that flew overhead as they went hunting for
a target farther back along the column.

Determined that he wasn't simply going to sit
there and wait for those damned Fates to draw his
name, Pearson continued to look about as his mind
raced to find something useful that he and his platoon could do. The obvious choice was a flanking
maneuver, either to the left or right and around
Sweeney's platoon. Since the beach was but a few
yards to the right and offered little cover or room

in which to maneuver, Pearson looked to the left, an option that would take them farther inland. Any effort on his part, he decided, would best be made by going that way. But how far he should go and when were questions he had no answers for. He wasn't even sure if he should take the initiative at all or simply wait for orders.

The young officer's tactical dilemma was resolved for him by the actions of the platoon in contact. Relying on good old-fashioned marksmanship, one of Sweeney's men managed to make his way forward to a spot from which he was able to put the enemy gunners under direct fire. After the young Marine fired two shots, each of which found its mark, a third Japanese gunner opted to seek safety in flight rather than die for the Emperor.

In the aftermath of the encounter that pitted a Marine Raider armed with a rifle type classified in 1903 against a 75mm regimental gun adopted into service in 1908, the rest of the day was a relative snap. In all, two Marines were killed and six wounded in sweeping aside what little resistance the Japanese rear guard offered in their defense of Tasimboko. For their efforts the Raiders were rewarded with a treasure trove of food, munitions, weapons, medical supplies, antitank mines, rubber boats with motors, communications equipment, and reams of raw intelligence left behind in what the Japanese had assumed was a safe rear area. Those Marines who managed to slip away from their squads and platoons for a few minutes helped themselves to tins of sliced beef and crab, while organized parties went about methodically destroying everything that could not be carried away. Even Richard Tregaskis, a war correspondent who was accompanying the Raiders that day, joined in by gathering up Japanese documents in a blanket and carrying them back to the First Marine Division's D-2.

Not every challenge a young officer is faced with in a combat zone involves life-or-death decisions. As soon as the officers were able to restore a modicum of order, Lieutenant Francis Pearson found himself charged with overseeing the destruction of the rice that was stockpiled throughout the area. This they accomplished in the most expedient way available. The Marines tore open the sacks of rice with their bayonets and spilled the contents onto the ground, where the mud, rain, insects, and incessant tromping of boots of other Marines in search of booty would do the rest.

While supervising his detail, Pearson could not help but notice that a number of his men not busy despoiling rice and other foodstuffs seemed to be sneaking about and darting behind corners of the native huts every time he glanced their way. At first he paid no attention to their behavior. It wasn't until he saw Gunnery Sergeant Jacobi leading three of the platoon's most notorious individuals down to the designated debarkation point on the beach along a rather circumspect route that Pearson became suspicious. Each man, including Jacobi, carried a partially filled rice sack close to his chest. Doing his best to act nonchalant, Pearson called out to his senior NCO, "Gunny Jay. Could I have a word with you?"

Like thieves caught in the beam of a policeman's flashlight, the four men stopped short and did their best to assume what they thought to be innocent poses. After whispering to his compatriots and handing one of them his rice sack, the gunnery sergeant shooed them along their way before jogging over to where Pearson was waiting. "Yes, sir. What can I do for you, sir."

"Dare I ask, Gunny, what's in those sacks?"

Straight-faced and without blinking, the twelve-year Marine veteran replied crisply. "No sir. You dare not."

"I see. Well, in that case, I find I have no choice but to rely upon your good judgment and common sense in ensuring that upon our return to Henderson things won't get out of hand."

Realizing that he was going to be allowed to keep the three cases of beer and half-gallon flask of sake that he had managed to secure, Jacobi smiled. "Oh, sir. You can bet your bars on that."

"Let's hope," Pearson replied dryly, "that it doesn't come to that."

"No, sir. I'll see to that."

"Okay, Gunny. Carry on."

Taking care to hide his joy, Jacobi took off at a trot to rejoin his foraging party. By 2200 hours that night, the tired but well-fed Raiders belonging to Pearson were enjoying the fruits of the day's labor in the relative security of the Marine lodgment at Henderson Field.

TWO

Unable to believe what he was seeing, sublieutenant Yoshio Sawa paused and blinked his eyes in an effort to clear them of sweat. When he had managed to refocus on the obstacle before him, the young officer examined the gigantic tree root that lay athwart his path. Still not sure that he was not imagining things, he looked back past the file of exhausted soldiers struggling under the weight of their equipment to catch up to him. Sure enough, not more than twenty meters back, Sawa caught sight of a tree root just like the one before him. Were it not for the fact that he could see the one he had just passed over mere moments before, he would have sworn that they were going about in circles and stumbling over the same damned tree root over and over again. Like everything else about the tangled jungle they had been moving through for days, nothing seemed to change. Each step just took them a little farther along, a little deeper into a labyrinth made up of gigantic trees that blocked the sun and nurtured a tangled chaos of vines, brambles, and thornbushes along the ground that seemed to reach out and snag anyone foolish enough to pass their way.

The young officer did not bother wasting his time scrutinizing the men behind him in an effort to gauge their condition. He had no need to. He knew how he felt, both physically and mentally, and didn't imagine that they could have been much better off. Instead, he returned to his examination of the root that blocked the trail before him.

Why, he found himself wondering, hadn't those leading the column simply gone around this obstacle? Why had they insisted upon plowing straight ahead without any regard to what lay in their path? A quick inspection of the terrain to his left and right quickly provided Sawa with an answer to those questions. It would not have made a bit of difference how the guides had gone. No matter which way he turned, his eyes were greeted with the same unimaginable morass of vegetation, rot, and stagnant pools. If anything, Sawa appreciated the fact that if the guides had attempted to bypass each and every obstruction, like this root, they would simply have added to the misery of those who followed by making an already meandering trail longer.

Resigned to the fact that he had no choice but to take on the offending tree root Yoshio Sawa once more stared at the obstacle before him. In the process of mustering the strength the task would require, the young sublieutenant found himself unable to keep his mind from drifting off in other directions. Along with his physical strength, his ability to maintain a sharp focus on the matter at hand was oozing away like the sweat that drenched him from head to toe. It has been a strange and twisting trail, he found himself thinking, that had led him to this wretched place.

Less than two years before he had been facing other barriers of an entirely different nature. In the summer of 1940, when he should have been preparing for his last year of law school, Sawa had found that the world he had been expected to enter no longer existed. It was as if he and his classmates suddenly were shaken out of a deep sleep only to find that everything they knew and understood no longer applied. Up until then the war in China had been the concern of the militarists. That all changed in the twinkling of an eye. Suddenly it was everyone's war. Events in Europe that had seemed so far away and of no interest to a student of the law were having very real and unpredictable effects on each and every citizen of Japan. Even his chosen profession no longer seemed to be relevant, as the national emergency that Japan faced caused the government to rewrite the law and the manner in which it dealt with its own people.

As with the tree root before him, Sawa and his friends had tried to find a way around the new hurdles being thrown before them on an almost daily basis. Only when it became clear that it would be impossible to follow the path he had set out upon did he face up to the reality of his times. With great temerity, not at all like that which he now felt, Sawa set aside his law books and took up the sword of an officer. It was, given his options, the only wise thing to do.

Wisdom and sanity, like circumstances, tend to change as time passes and one's place in the world drifts away from the known path of civilized man and into the dark wastelands of war. The young officer was reflecting upon this philosophical issue when he became conscious of the another's presence. Pushing aside his deep and misplaced thoughts, Sawa turned to notice that one of his soldiers was standing next to him, staring at the great tree root in much the same way that he had when he first came across it. Because the man was so close, Sawa found it necessary to crane his head back in order to focus on the soldier. When he took note of his officer's actions the man misunderstood them and jumped back, coming to a rigid position of attention as he did so. In anticipation of the blow he believed his officer was about to deliver, the soldier closed his eyes and braced himself to be slapped for being so impertinent as to stand shoulder to shoulder with a superior.

Like so many of those in his platoon, the man standing before Sawa was a simple farmer. Just as Sawa had been uprooted from all he knew, the former peasant had been swept way by the tides of war that had carried them all away and to this wretched place. Sawa imagined that while he had been plowing through books that codified the laws of civilized man, this poor fellow had spent his days tending to his pigs, chickens, and crops, day in and day out. Now the two of them stood in a place neither could have imagined in his worst nightmares, joined by the common goal of finding other young men like themselves and killing them.

Sawa's conscious mind turned upon itself, admonishing him for allowing such whimsical thoughts to keep him from his duty. *You must not think such thoughts.* With the same strident tone that his training officers and his company commander used, this ever-vigilant voice from within reminded the former student of law that he was an officer in the Imperial

Army, bound by the code of bushido. He had no time to entertain such irrelevant thoughts. Duty and the will of the Emperor were his masters now. Everything else meant nothing. Everything else had to be set aside until victory had been achieved.

In an effort to regain a correct posture Sawa made a threatening gesture that caused the soldier before him to recoil. Sawa had no intention of striking the man. He simply needed to make the man think he was going to do so in order to maintain the strict discipline that his commanding officer expected. Having thus reasserted himself and put the private in his place, Sawa turned, preparing to continue on. Then, as quickly as his sudden burst of martial spirit had appeared, it evaporated. The tree root was still there. It still needed to be surmounted.

Resigning himself to this sorry fact, Sawa slowly lifted his left leg and threw it over the root. Not only did this simple task take far more energy than it should have, but the need to take care as to where he placed his hands, feet, and legs during the maneuver complicated the seemingly simple task. Already he had fallen victim to a centipede during a similar crossing. Like every other inhabitant of this green hell, the nasty little creatures left their mark on the unwary. In the case of the centipede, its particular signature was a series of tiny yet painful wounds where every one of its tiny legs came into contact with human flesh.

Once he was fairly sure that the surface he would be straddling was clear of bugs and such, Sawa pulled himself up and over, ever conscious that the eyes of his peasant soldiers behind him were fixed upon him. It was times like this that the old Army saw, "Duty is heavier than a mountain," rang true. Duty was indeed heavy. If that were so, Sawa thought as he eased himself down onto the ground on the other side of the root, was the second half of the saying also true? Was death lighter than a feather?

Not wanting to ponder this grim thought and anxious to close up the gap in the column that his tarrying had created before his commanding officer noticed, Sawa brushed aside his foolish ruminations and mustered enough strength to break out into a trot. Like a senior sergeant calling cadence, the young Imperial officer took up repeating his own personal cadence under his breath with each footfall, "Duty—is—heavy. Duty—is—heavy. Duty—is—heavy."

Yoshio Sawa was not the only officer in the long serpentine column agonizing over his current plight. Though he did his best to maintain a calm demeanor, Major General Kiyotake Kawaguchi was beginning to have doubts about his ability to meet his own timetable for launching his attack against the Marine toehold as planned. Already many key elements of the plan he had laid out four days prior had either gone awry or failed to unfold as he expected. As if the destruction of so much of his supplies and the loss of valuable field pieces at Tasimboko weren't enough, the scattering of one of the battalions that he had insisted be brought to this island by barge further weakened his force. That unexpected development had forced him to acquiesce to an offer of additional troops that he had once refused. The experience had been a humbling one, like the struggle his brigade was currently engaged in against the jungle they were pushing through. Humiliating and frustrating.

The man who commanded the brigade comprised of units from the Kurame Division had expected the going to be both slow and arduous. Lack of local air superiority dictated that Kawaguchi move his main force deep into the jungle in order to avoid detection and attack from the air. This meant that every round of ammunition that would be used in the attack, every piece of the mountain guns tasked to support it, and every mouthful of rice needed to sustain his soldiers until they reached their objective had to be carried on the backs of his men. Such demands were part of every soldier's life. Kawaguchi expected those he led to meet every challenge without complaint, without question, and go on until victory was achieved. It was their duty to endure all the hardships that came their way and overcome every obstacle placed before them. But of late, Kawaguchi found himself wondering if perhaps there were simply too many obstacles being tossed into his path. Perhaps there was a point when neither will nor courage would be enough.

While making his way along the narrow jungle track in silence, the man charged with defeating the American Marines on this miserable island had a great deal of time to reflect upon these foreboding thoughts. While in Rubal he had exuded confidence as casually as the staff of the Seventeenth Area Army had. Both they and Kawaguchi had good reason to be sure of victory. In Borneo, Kawaguchi had met with nothing but success.

But this was not Borneo, the general reminded himself as he trudged along through the mud and stifling heat. There he had enjoyed easy victories against a pathetic foe who lacked everything, including overwhelming air and naval support. While it was true that the Imperial Navy controlled the seas around Guadalcanal by night, without air cover the Navy, like his command, had no choice but to scurry for shelter every morning when the sun appeared on the eastern horizon.

This pathetic state of affairs would not be corrected until the Rising Sun fell upon an airfield that was once more controlled by the Emperor's troops. Only then would the fleet be free to make good the losses in matériel and supplies that had been sustained at Tasimboko. Even more importantly, once Japanese aircraft were operating off the landing strip that the Americans had completed at Lunga Point, the Seventeenth Area Army would be able to return to its primary mission of seizing Port Moresby, New Caledonia, Fiji, and Samoa. Until then, both he and his men would have to slither about in the primordial muck, much like the deadly snakes and vicious insects that seemed to lie under every log.

THREE

Frustrated with his efforts to dig deeper into the coral crust he had spent the last hour gnawing away at, Francis Pearson rose on his knees, straightened his back, and looked about. Setting the entrenching tool he had been using on the tip of its dulled blade, the young Marine officer cupped his hands one over the other on the end of the handle before setting his chin on top of them. Ignoring the sweat that ran down his brow and into his eye sockets, Pearson gazed off into the jungle below.

Except for a think blanket of razor-sharp Kunai grass, the hogback or ridge their battalion commander had brought them to was bare. While following the narrow trail that ran along its crest one was treated to something that was rare on Guadalcanal, a view. Ranging in width from as little as fifty yards but never more than three hundred, the coral spine, which was shaped like a lazy *S*, stretched a thousand yards from the edge of Henderson Field in the north to where Pearson's platoon was digging in along its southern edge. After a brief interlude in a coconut grove near Lunga Point on the tenth of the month, this dominant piece of ground had become the home for the combined Raider and Paramarine battalion.

Well, at least for most of the Raiders. Some, like those belonging to Thomas's Company C, were off to the right, stretched out along a line that cut through a particularly nasty patch of jungle that lay between the lagoon where Company B's right flank was anchored and the Lunga River. While those poor souls had a much easier time as far as digging was concerned, the dense vegetation blocked even the slightest hint of a breeze. Besides exacerbating the stifling heat, the jungle down there left them with virtually no fields of fire except those the Raiders could clear with a handful of machetes and their bayonets. Lifting his chin off the handle upon which he had propped it, Pearson stared up into the sky.

Of course, Pearson concluded as he continued to look back at the top of the ridge, this was no heaven on earth either. Twice since their arrival Japanese bombers had paid them a visit, giving the lie to Colonel Edson's claim that this was a rest area. Even his dullest rifleman could see that this was, militarily speaking, prime real estate. And if he and the members of his platoon could see it, Pearson had little doubt that the commanding officer of those unseen Japanese whose supplies they had destroyed back at Tasimboko had to see it, too.

While he was pondering these troubling matters, Pearson felt a hand on his shoulder. Looking about he saw PFC William Sterling, his platoon runner, standing over him. "If you need a break, Lieutenant, I'll take a turn on the E-tool for a bit."

Rocking back on his heels, then onto his feet, Pearson grasped the shovel and turned it over to Sterling. "Be my guest. Just don't dig it too deep."

Kicking at the solid coral with the toe of his boot, Sterling grinned. "I'll keep that in mind, sir."

With that the young Marine officer set off on a tour of his line. The left of his platoon was held by First Squad leader Sergeant Russell Smith, a man who was not much older than he. Whether it was their similarity in age or the fact that they were, relatively speaking, new to the Corps, Pearson felt closer to Smith than to any of his other NCOs. Like Gunny Jay, the sergeants who led Pearson's Second and Third Squads were career Marines, men who had been busy learning their trade in the jungles of Nicaragua while Pearson was in high school trying to capitalize on his recent discovery that boys and girls were different. Perhaps that was why he kept the First Squad close at hand and sent one of the others whenever he had the need to send a squad farther afield. Since Gunny Jay said nothing about this particular habit, Pearson assumed that he was doing right.

The First Squad's left ended at the trail that ran down the spine of the ridge. Over on the eastern side of the trail was Company A of the Paramarines commanded by Captain William McKennen. To the right of the First Squad, occupying a spot that was about as commanding as any on the ridge, was a machine gun section that belonged to the Raider's Company E led by Corporal Allen Malin. In addition to the air-cooled .30 caliber machine gun, the section leader who was damned with an unfortunate name combination had managed to arm one of his men with a .30 caliber BAR and another with a Reising M-50 .45 caliber submachine gun. This additional firepower, the young officer reasoned, helped make up for the thinness of his line.

The center of the platoon's territory was held by Perry Mitchal's Second Squad. He was the quietest NCO in the unit. Not only did the man keep his own counsel unless he had something important to say, but even when angered, he never spoke above a whisper. Just that morning Pearson had witnessed that apparent contradiction when one of Mitchal's men, flustered by his inability to carve out a decent foxhole in the coral, threw down his entrenching tool and screamed that he wasn't going to waste another second trying. Without batting an eye, Mitchal laid aside his own E-tool, calmly walked over to where the enraged Marine stood, and grabbed the man by the collar of his shirt. In one smooth, deliberate motion, Mitchal lifted the Marine off his feet and held the astonished man inches from his face for several long seconds before the crusty NCO whispered, "Dig." With that, Mitchal put the man back down, watched as the stunned Marine retrieved his shovel, and waited until the man was back in his hole digging for all he was worth before returning to his own labors. Mitchal was a rock. If anyone could hold the center against the storm that Pearson expected to break upon them, it was Mitchal.

Pearson's westernmost positions were manned by Staff Sergeant Ken Carroll's Third Squad. Carroll felt that it was his purpose in life to make up for Mitchal when it came to gabbing. In civilian life Kenny Carroll would had been a con man. In the Marines he was one of those colorful characters who had bounced back and forth between private and sergeant so many times that some of the old hands joked he should use zippers to attach his stripes instead of stitches. Yet in a fight Carroll had the reputation for being a real no-holds-barred brawler. It was this particular characteristic that caused the commander of the Third Squad so much grief over his career and had led Pearson to select him to secure the platoon's critical right flank.

It wasn't until he had reached Carroll's squad that Pearson ran into Gunny Jay. The platoon sergeant had just come back from coordinating with the next platoon over, something Pearson had intended to do himself. Gunny Jay greeted his platoon leader with a nod. "Well, by tonight, we're going to be as ready as we're going to be."

Pearson didn't reply at first. Instead, he looked down at the foxhole belonging to two men in Carroll's squad. "I want the men to go deeper."

Jacobi didn't bother inspecting that hole or any of the others. He already knew how deep they were. "Lew-tenant, I would like nothing better myself. But we can't keep going without a break. Unless you want every man jack among us to fall asleep by midnight and let the Nips come walking through here like nobody's business, they need time to sleep."

After a moment of halfhearted reflection, Pearson nodded. "Pass the word down the line. Have the men settle in, eat something, then rotate. Half awake, half resting."

Making no effort to hide his own weariness, Jacobi slowly nodded. "Aye aye, sir." With that, the two parted.

Pacing like an impatient cat, General Kawaguchi waited to hear from the three battalions that had made the long, arduous trek from Taivu Point to their designated assembly areas south of a ridge his

staff called the Centipede. With night fast approaching and none of them where they were supposed to
be, the only solace Kawaguchi managed to find in
the pathetic state of affairs was the fact that he had,
against his own better judgment, stayed with his decision to attack on the night of September 13 and
not the twelfth as he had originally intended.*

This had not been an easy thing for Kawaguchi
to admit. When he had departed Rubal, he had
been so confident of victory that he had turned
down an offer by the staff of the Seventeenth Area
Army of an additional battalion. Only after he had
arrived on this forsaken island did he discover that
he had taken his task far too lightly. One by one,
problems and misjudgments made by him and by
the staff on Rubal conspired against him. Nothing
was as easy as it had been imagined. His entire command lacked proper maps. The frightening nature
of the jungle was unlike anything he had ever en-
counted. Even the incessant rain that pelted his
command during a time of year that was supposed
to be the dry season came as something of a shook.

Yet it wasn't until they were already committed to
his plan of operation that Kawaguchi realized just
how badly he had miscalculated the time it would
take his units to cover the distance from the coast
to the point from which he wished to launch his
attack. His decision on the sixth to delay the attack
by twenty-four hours had been a difficult one to
make at the time in light of his boasts back on
Rubal. But it had been a correct one, even in the
face of a September 7 report disclosing that a convoy of troop transports bearing Marines had arrived
in Fiji.

Now, after having endured a trek that would have
broken lesser men, Kawaguchi was certain that he

had made the right choice. He was just as certain of this as he was that his plan would succeed. Already embarrassed by the scattering of a battalion that had tried to reach the island by barge, a mode of transportation he himself had insisted upon, as well as the destruction of his base at Tasimboko, Kawaguchi had to succeed. Having overcome so many obstacles, he would let nothing stand in his way. Not the jungle, not the enemy air force, not even the two thousand Marines holding the airfield would keep him from securing a complete and crushing victory.

Exhausted, hungry, and completely disheartened, Sublieutenant Yoshio Sawa was far less sanguine than Kawaguchi was about their prospects of inflicting a smashing defeat upon the American Marines. He and his men would do well, he began to find himself thinking, simply to survive in this hellish place. After endless days of struggling with the jungle, Sawa felt as if he was nearing the end of his tether. *How can they keep going on like this?* he found himself wondering. His men were tough, as stoic and determined as any man in the Imperial Army. Yet there was only so much that a man could endure. There was only so much, Sawa reasoned, that one could ask.

But no one was asking anymore. From their commanding general all the way down the chain of command, every officer and NCO was *demanding* that their men keep going. All Sawa heard now up and down the line were admonishments to keep pressing on, keep marching, keep moving. And they did, one step at a time. Across countless rivers, along trails that did not deserve that title, and through torrential downpours. Together with his men, Sawa marched ever deeper into the all-consuming jungle.

"Ignore the hunger," a staff officer advised his men every time he passed Sawa's struggling platoon. "We will feast upon the food we take from the Marines."

"You have no need to rest now," Sawa's company commander admonished. "We will have plenty of time to rest once we have broken out of this jungle and reached the sea once more." That many of those men that he worked so hard to encourage would not find any rest here on earth was left unsaid.

Where the officers tended to use exhortations and promises to keep the men moving, the NCOs within Sawa's company relied on their sharp tongues and well-placed blows to drive their charges forward. Their exhortations had become so pervasive that the parrots perched in the trees above began to mimic the bellowing human taskmasters below. "Hay! Private! Keep Moving!" echoed through the jungle on the ground and from above. While some thought it funny, no one laughed when the annoying birds screeched out another common phrase, *"Hikoki!"* "Enemy Planes!" It did not matter what the source, this fearful warning sent officer and enlisted alike diving for the nearest cover, a fact that only added to the misery of all concerned and further slowed their advance.

On this day not even darkness brought an end to their struggles. In the jungle, where light was a rarity, the moonless night of September 12 turned the horrific march into an absolute nightmare. Men no longer marched because they had to, they did so out of habit. Sawa's world slowly shrank until it was reduced to an area no greater than the length of his own arms. Sometimes he went for an hour or more unable to see the back of the man who was not more than a meter before him. Only the sound of that man's labored breathing and his struggle to push through the jungle kept Sawa on the path along which his battalion was traveling.

What thoughts the former law student entertained during those endless hours of unspeakable suffering were almost as dark as the jungle that engulfed him. How was it possible that he had come to such a pathetic end? What great force had upended the neat, orderly world that he had worked so hard to become a part of? Surely this wasn't the work of his own people? While there were hotheads who dreamed of conquest and empires, the Emperor would not, could not allow them to lead his people into a war such as this.

No, Sawa told himself. It had not been his people who had brought this war on. Then and there he decided it had been the Americans. Had they not been so unreasonable, war would not have come. Had they simply understood and accepted the role that Japan played in the affairs of China, both nations would still be at peace. It was the Americans. *They* were the ones who were determined to deny Japan its rightful place in the world by insisting that Japan's army withdraw from China. *They* had been the ones who had imposed the embargo on steel and oil when his nation's leaders had refused to bow to the Americans' unreasonable demands. *They* were the ones who had left their homes and crossed the Pacific to take this island away from the Emperor. *They* were responsible for all of this. So, *They* would have to pay. Sooner or later Sawa knew this trail of misery would lead him to this unreasonable and barbaric foe. Soon the marching would be over and the fighting would begin. When that time came, Sawa pledged as he clutched his sword, *They* would be the ones who would die.

FOUR

MIDMORNING, SEPTEMBER 13, 1942

The quiet and uneventful passing of night was greeted with a mixture of joy and foreboding by Company B. The seemingly endless hours spent alternating between fighting bouts of fear that the night jungle inspires and shaking off an all-consuming exhaustion that eroded one's vigilance were over for now. The Japanese had not come. Though no man doubted that they were out there and that in their own good time they would come, for the moment the world the Marine Raiders lived in was at peace.

That this tranquil interlude would not last long was a given. Even before the sun had crested the eastern horizon, the privates and lance corporals had collectively seen and heard enough to know that this day would not pass quietly. "Something" was up. Knowing their battalion commander, they had no doubt that this "Something" meant only one thing—they were going after the Japs.

The Marine Raiders, both Edson's First Battalion and Carlson's Second, had been organized, equipped, and trained to be elite strike forces. President Roosevelt himself had envisioned them as nothing less than an American version of England's famed commando units that had played hell with the Germans during Britain's darkest hours. Members of the fledging Raider battalions were even dispatched to England to observe commando training. But the Raiders evolved into something that was uniquely American. In part this was due to the men who commanded the first two units, and in part their final form and use emerged as a result of the debate within the Corps over the necessity of having units such as the Raiders. Many within the Fleet Marine Force saw the Raiders as nothing more than a publicity stunt, an effort to boost civilian morale in much the same way that Doolittle had in April of '42. According to them, any properly trained Marine could execute the sort of raids and special recon missions the supporters of Raider concept were envisioning. The creation of special formations, armed with exotic weapons and manned with the pick of the litter, was seen as wasteful and out of step with the true, long-term goals of the Corps.

Merritt A. Edson, nicknamed Red Mike because of the color of a beard he had once sported during the Banana Wars, understood the politics of the issue. He was astute enough to know that he needed to be flexible while keeping faithful to his vision. A true member of the Old Breed and a Marine through and through, Edson insisted that his battalion maintain the strict protocol and smartness that were hallmarks of the Corps. He was also a team player. These qualities muted much of the criticism opponents leveled at the Raider concept. They also allowed him to wield more influence than he might otherwise have.

Intelligence the First Marine Division's D-2 had garnered from Tasimboko and reports from native scouts led Edson to the conclusion that the next Japanese effort would come from the interior of the island. That view was shared by Colonel Gerald Thomas, the operations officer or D-3. Unfortunately, Major General Vandergrift did not concur with this assessment. He saw a counterlanding by the Japanese at Lunga Point or a major thrust along the coast from the east or west against the Marine perimeter as posing the greatest threat to the American lodgement on Guadalcanal. Since Vandergrift was the commanding general in both name and habit, he had deployed five of his six infantry battalions on either side of Lunga Point and along the narrow coastal plain. The sixth unit, Second Battalion, Fifth Marines was held back as a divisional reserve.

That left only the First Engineer Battalion, First Amphibious Tractor Battalion, and the First Pioneer Battalion to cover the southern portion of the perimeter. Surprisingly, none of those units occupied the centipede-shaped ridge that rose out of the jungle and pointed due north like a dagger at the center of Henderson Field. When Edson and Thomas presented to Vandergrift their operational estimate as to where the Japanese would attack together with the recommendation that Edson move his combined Raider-Paramarine Battalion up onto the ridge, the commanding general grudgingly agreed. In this manner a terrain feature that would have served the Japanese as an unimpeded highway right into the heart of the Marine perimeter on the ninth of September became a strongpoint that they would need to storm on the thirteenth.

Placing his combined battalion in a position where it would do the most good was not enough for Edson. His command was organized and trained to carry the war to the enemy, not simply to hold ground. Therefore, on the evening of the twelfth he gathered his company commanders together and laid out his plan for a spoiling attack to the south, an attack whose aim was to find and strike the Japanese before they had a chance to do the same to him. In the parlance of the day it was a "gutsy move," especially when one considered that it would pit Edson's eight hundred Raiders and Paramarines against more than twenty-five hundred Imperial soldiers that Major General Kawaguchi had gathered just south of the centipede-shaped ridge.

At first Yoshio Sawa took the crack of scattered rifle fire to be nothing more than random jungle noises. Only when the rip of machine guns and the thud of grenades joined in did he realize that the enemy was close at hand. Scrambling to his feet, he trotted toward a gaggle of anxious soldiers who had been stirred from their sleep by the growing sounds of battle. Like him, they were milling about and peering north into the jungle in an effort to see beyond the dense vegetation.

"Are we attacking already?" a bold private mused in a tone he was sure his officer could hear as both he and Sawa continued to stare at the unyielding jungle.

"No," Sawa snapped without having to weigh the question. "We attack tonight. It must be an enemy patrol that has run afoul of one of our outposts."

The private thought for a moment before nodding. "Ah, yes. I see."

Of course, like his platoon leader he didn't really see. No one who was with Sawa could see a damned thing. He was just accepting his officer's opinion as he continued to watch, listen, and wait.

Neither Sawa nor the private had long to wait. When it became clear that the engagement that had stirred them all from their fitful rest was more than a patrol brushing up against an outpost, the former law student stepped back from the group of soldiers he had been standing with and wearily looked to his left, then his right, in search of his company commander, Captain Tetsuzan Oyama. Sawa both feared and respected the captain, a professional soldier who had first seen action in China. Oyama would know what to do. He always seemed to know.

As if the mere act of thinking about him was enough to conjure up his superior, Oyama appeared. Walking calmly through the brush, Sawa's commanding officer clutched the scabbard of his sword as he slowly moved among his men and peered intently in the direction of the gunfire. When he was within a meter of Sawa, Oyama turned his gaze upon his worried subordinate. "Form your men into line of battle," he ordered with a casualness that belied his concern. "Be prepared to move forward on order. If we go in, the First Platoon will be on your right, Second to the left."

Snapping to attention, Sawa bowed his head slightly. "Yes, sir."

With that, Oyama continued on, moving off to the left, where he would repeat his order to the lieutenant commanding the Second Platoon. He showed no interest in explaining what was going on, and Sawa made no effort to inquire. The former student of law had his orders and something to do, which was good enough for him.

At some point during their move forward, Pearson had expected to come into contact with enemy outposts. These small clusters of lightly armed soldiers were a universal feature in war, deployed forward of a main line of resistance or assembly area to provide early warning and fend off small enemy patrols. When faced with a superior force, the soldiers manning such outposts are normally charged with firing a few rounds in an effort to cause the approaching enemy to hit the dirt and deploy. Having achieved that, in most cases the intrepid occupants of the outpost were free to slip away and make their way back to rejoin their now alert and well-prepared comrades before their foe was able to recover from their surprise and overwhelm them with superior fire or numbers.

The Marines leading Russell Smith's First Squad didn't give the Japanese they stumbled upon that option. Seeing no need to wait for a BAR gunner to come forward, the pair drew a bead on their foe and dropped them before they had a chance to make good their escape. By the time Pearson was able to make his way up along his platoon's line of march to a point where he could assess the situation, the one-sided firefight was over.

It quickly became apparent to Pearson that not every platoon was enjoying the same sort of luck his had just experienced. At the same time his point element made contact, the unit to Pearson's right hit another Japanese outpost. From the sounds of the incessant firing, that one was not only better manned, but seemed to be supported by at least one, and perhaps two 6.5mm Nambu light machine guns. Rather than diminishing, the fire grew in both intensity and volume. Even more ominous to the young Marine platoon commander was the fact that it seemed to be spreading.

Unsure of what to do next, Pearson listened for several minutes. Every now and then a voice could be heard above the growing din of battle. Most of the shouts he was able to make out were orders, quick sharp commands barked out by officers and NCOs struggling to deploy their men as quickly as possible. Mixed in with the orders bellowed by anxious and excited commanders were shrill screams of pain and desperate pleas for help from the wounded. When Pearson began to hear commands being given in Japanese, he realized that it was time for him to join the chorus, shake out his platoon, and brace for the coming storm.

Leaving his First Squad where it was since it was already partially deployed, Pearson started back along his platoon's line of march, issuing orders to his squad leaders as he came across them. When he came upon his Second Squad, which had been next in the line of march, the young Marine officer ordered its squad leader, Staff Sergeant Perry Mitchal, to move his squad off to the right, where the fighting seemed to be the heaviest. Not knowing what exactly was going on over there, he warned Mitchal to refuse his right and have his men hold their fire unless they had a good target. After Mitchal took off to place his men, Pearson continued on down the line, ordering Corporal Malin to take his machine gun section up to join the First Squad, where he was to orient his gun in the direction of where the Japanese outpost had been. He had just reached Sergeant Ken Carroll, who was in the rear of the platoon column with Gunnery Sergeant Jacobi,

when a spate of fire erupted at the head of the column. The distinctive crack of '03 Springfields accompanied by the quick, short bursts of BARs
contrasted with the snap of the Japanese 6.5mm Ar-
isaka rifles. Taking only a moment to point Carroll
off to the left, Pearson turned and ran as quickly as
he could back to where the First Squad was engaging the enemy. Never more than a few steps behind
him all the way was Gunny Jay.

Just before he reached Smith's squad, Pearson
stumbled upon one of Malin's men lying in the middle of the fresh trail that the movement of his platoon had created during their advance. At first the
young officer thought the man at his feet had gone
to ground rather than continuing forward. Angered
by the apparent act of cowardliness, Pearson kicked
him with his boot, and yelled, "On your feet, Marine!"

When the figure didn't respond to his prodding,
the young officer drew back. Bending, Pearson
reached out, grabbed the man by his shoulder, and
rolled him over. The lifeless Marine's mouth hung
open as if frozen in the middle of a scream. His un-
seeing eyes gazed up into Pearson's. Unhinged by
this sight and his unkindness to the dead, Pearson
pulled away, stood up, and stared down at the dead
Marine for a second. Only when the spreading
sound of gunfire became too much for him to ignore did Pearson step over the corpse and continue on.

By the time he caught sight of Mitchal's First
Squad, the exchange of fire was steady. Doing his
best to ignore the distinctive *zing* of near misses that
sailed past his head or smacked into nearby trees,
Pearson peered over one of his own men lying
prone on the ground in an effort to catch sight of

the enemy. After several seconds of searching without seeing anything that remotely resembled a Japanese soldier, the young officer dropped to the ground and made his way over to where Mitchal was busily working the bolt of his rifle. "What the hell are your people shooting at?"

Stunned by this question, the veteran Marine rolled over onto his side and looked at his platoon commander. "Japs!"

"Where?"

Flopping back down onto his stomach, Mitchel cradled his rifle in one hand and pointed at a clump of vegetation not more that thirty yards distant. "Watch."

At first Pearson saw nothing. Then, after taking the time to concentrate on the spot that his squad leader had indicated, he saw a rustling of leaves followed by a muzzle flash. While he had been watching this, Mitchal had brought his own rifle up, aimed it, and fired. Remaining motionless the squad leader tried to determine if he had hit anything. Only after he was sure that the Jap he had been firing at was either dead or had moved to another spot did Mitchal slap the bolt of his Springfield with the palm of his right, grasp it, and jerk it back, sending a spent cartridge case sailing through the air.

"It ain't like banging away at the targets on a range, but it's better than sitting here with our thumbs up our asses."

Looking down the staggered line of Marines under Mitchal's command Pearson saw that they were doing just as their squad leader was. Only Malin, hammering away with his machine gun, made little effort to seek out discrete targets. Instead, he was relying on the traverse and elevation mechanism to control a grazing fire with which he was sweeping

the area to his front. With his right hand he grasped
his M1919 Browning light machine gun and fired a
series of short bursts. After each burst, Malin twisted
the traverse knob a bit to the left with his other
hand before squeezing the trigger again. When
Malin reached the limit of his sector of fire, he began to turn the traverse knob to the right. In this
manner he put out a steady stream of fire that never
rose more than a foot off the ground and saturated
the entire area to his front with .30 caliber slugs.
Snuggled up next to his corporal was the assistant
gunner, feeding the belted ammo into the gun. To
either side of this pair were the ammo bearers, both
armed with automatic weapons they used to aug-
ment their section leader's awesome firepower while
waiting to pass another box of ammunition to the
assistant gunner. Only the persistent zing of enemy
fire flying overhead and the dead Marine back on
the trail served to remind the young officer that this
was real combat and not just another live-fire exercise.

He was still huddled up behind Mitchal when two
figures coming from opposite directions dropped
on the ground to either side of him. To his left was
Gunny Jay, coming over from where he had just finished watching Carroll deploy his squad. On the
right was Captain John Sweeney, the former platoon
leader who had taken over Company B when Major
Lloyd Nickerson proved to be too ill to carry on.
Without preamble Sweeney asked Pearson for an
update on his situation. Not having had an opportunity to make his way along the entire length of his
line, Pearson did the best he could. "I've got all
three squads up in line, with this being the center.
So far enemy fire is light, but it seems to be along

the entire line. This is either a really big outpost or their main line."

Sweeney nodded. "Yeah, it's more than an outpost. We're to hold here and keep them occupied while Bob Thomas and Company C find a flank."

The first sensation that Pearson felt when he heard his company commander's orders was a sense of relief. They would not have to rise from the relative safety of the ground and go forward into the enemy fire. All his platoon had to do was continue just as they were. That other Marines led by young officers like himself would have to expose themselves to enemy fire didn't matter at the moment. Guilt over harboring such selfish thoughts only comes later, after the firing has faded.

Forlorn and seemingly isolated in the midst of the growing storm over which he had no control, Major General Kawaguchi's response to the unexpected confrontation between the three battalions that made up his central attack force and a large force of Marines ranged from anger to utter frustration to downright despair. As a professional soldier, he knew that war was not easy, that often battle was little more than an affair of chance. But in all his years he had never experienced anything like this. At every turn during the campaign all of his plans and efforts had been frustrated. Despite his best efforts, every time it seemed as if he had finally managed to master the situation, something unexpected occurred that caused it to slip away from him. *And now this!*

After storming forward a few meters, Kawaguchi stopped and peered off in the direction of the firing, which had matured into a general engagement. That he had lost the element of surprise, a key component in his plan of attack, was quite obvious. That the enemy force that had slammed into his slumbering command was no mere patrol was equally clear. Aside from that, Kawaguchi knew nothing with any degree of certainty. Unable to contact his battalion commanders, he could only guess as to what his subordinates would do in response to this latest turn of events.

Turning sharply upon his heels, Kawaguchi stormed back to where his staff stood waiting for his orders. Like him, they were of little value at the moment. Only after the situation had resolved itself one way or the other would the general have an opportunity to sort out the mess and begin the process of salvaging what he could of his plan.

With a suddenness that startled even the crustiest of Pearson's NCOs, a wave of Japanese emerged from the jungle before them with bayonets leveled. Accompanied by the shrilled scream of *"Totsugeki!"* the irresistible mass swept forward, giving the thin line of Marines facing it little time to rise off the ground and meet it.

Fighting an urge to recoil from the surging wall of humanity, Pearson somehow managed to make it to his feet and hold his ground. Tucking his submachine gun into his side, he aimed his weapon by turning his body and cutting loose with a steady burst at a group of three Japanese soldiers who seemed to have singled him out as their target. Gunny Jay, who had remained with him after Captain Sweeney had moved on, fished a grenade from one of his pockets, jerked the pin, and tossed it into the middle of another group off to the left. Corporal Malin, still working his machine gun, disconnected the traverse and elevation mechanism. Using the sight of the weapon itself to lay it, he methodically turned it on successive groups of Japanese as they rushed into his line of fire. Throughout these first frenzied moments the machine gunner continued to exercise great restraint as he unleashed quick, well-measured killing bursts.

Yet despite the best efforts of Pearson, Gunny Jay, Corporal Malin, and every Marine on the firing line, the Japanese could not be stopped. They were simply too close and too numerous. Stepping over and on the bodies of those who had been cut down before their very eyes, the following waves of Imperial soldiers surged forward and closed with Pearson's platoon. This collision of determined men gave rise to new sounds. Along with the crack of rifle fire and eruption of grenades a cacophony of human screams, shrill cries, angry epithets, and desperate pleas, mixed with the chilling crunch of bone being smashed by rifle butts.

Pearson was no longer able to piece together a comprehensive picture of what was going on around him. The best he could manage was a series of quick, seemingly disjointed images to which he responded. To his right he caught sight of a Japanese soldier impaling one of his men. Pinned to the ground by the long bayonet, the Marine wrapped his hands about the front hand grips of his foe's rifle as he bellowed, kicked, and twitched about violently. Swinging the muzzle of his Reising about, Pearson cut loose with a burst that caught the Japanese soldier square in the chest, throwing him back and away from his rifle, which remained firmly implanted in the stricken Marine.

Before he could do anything to aid the wounded Marine he had just saved, something else caught Pearson's attention. Bracing himself for a threat

that he had yet to clearly identify, the young Marine
officer spun about, firing blindly as he did. That
seemingly rash response saved Pearson from being
hacked to death by an enraged Japanese officer who
was closing with him at a dead run. The enemy officer was so committed to his attack and so determined to kill Pearson that the .45 caliber slugs that
ripped into him had no apparent effect. As the Japanese officer grasped the hilt of his razor-sharp
sword high above his head, his momentum propelled him into Pearson, bowling the Marine over.

The blow of the enemy officer colliding with him
and their uncontrolled impact on the ground
knocked Pearson's Reising from his hand. Though
stunned and pinned beneath his assailant, the
young Marine officer somehow managed to pull his
.45 pistol from its holster, jam it into the stomach
of the man on top of him, and fire three quick
rounds. With each discharge Pearson could feel the
midsection of the Japanese officer jerk up for a moment before flopping back down onto the muzzle
of Pearson's pistol. Only when he was positive that
his foe was no longer able to harm him did Pearson
cease fire.

"Lew-tenant! Are you alright?"

The distinctive pronouncement of his title and
the sudden image of Gunny Jay standing above him
as the Marine NCO pulled the body of the dead
Japanese officer away was the first proof Pearson
had that he had somehow managed to survive.
Reaching up, he grasped the hand Gunny Jay was
offering him.

Even before he was on his feet, his senior NCO
stepped back and looked Pearson over. "Jesus
Christ, sir! Are you alright?"

Looking down Pearson saw that he was covered

in blood. Still badly shaken by his struggle with the crazed Japanese officer, he nodded. "Yeah, I think so."

Then, realizing that he was standing upright, the startled Marine officer jerked his head to the right, then to his left, searching for whatever new threat that might be coming his way. It took him a second or two to realize that the Japanese were gone. Well, he reflected as he cast his eyes upon the tangle of bodies strewn about at his feet, at least those who had survived were gone.

Sensing that his platoon commander was a bit confused and shaken, Jacobi reached out, put his hand on Pearson's shoulder, and explained the situation as it stood. "I don't know how, but we threw them back. As suddenly as they appeared, they were gone. We're still sorting out our own dead and wounded and taking fire, but I don't think it was too bad."

From where he stood Pearson could see three Marines lying on the ground, unattended and not moving. Despite the precarious position his platoon was still in and the incessant zing of bullets whizzing by, the young officer found himself wondering just exactly what Gunny Jay meant by "too bad."

"The captain said we're to stand fast and cover the withdrawal of the rest of the company," Gunny Jay added. "We're going back to the ridge."

To this, Pearson said nothing. In comparison to their current plight, he now saw the precarious line of defenses they had worked two days preparing as a veritable sanctuary. He would be glad to go back there, he found himself thinking as he collected himself and prepared to reassume command of his platoon. *Anywhere,* he figured, *has to be better than this spot.*

FIVE

The events of the afternoon were still fresh as Yoshio Sawa led his platoon forward to their final attack position. The brief but violent confrontation with the American Marines earlier that day had cast a pall upon an enterprise that in retrospect seemed to have been doomed before it had begun. The former law student could not imagine how the tired, hungry men who followed him, armed with little more than rifles and their courage, would be able to overcome the brutal firepower that had thrown their attack back that morning. While it was true that the mad rush they had made at the Marines was poorly organized, it was equally true that the Marines had been unprepared to receive it. Yet they had thrown his men back. If the Americans could achieve that while out in the open, what chance would his men have against Marines who were dug in?

Once more shrouded by the moonless night, the depleted ranks of Sawa's platoon crept on, following the lead of their company guide, who had scouted the route to their attack position before the sunset. They would not spend much time in that position. It was meant only as a control measure, a place where the company commander could organize his platoons into a proper offensive position and they could wait under cover until their battalion commander gave the signal to attack.

Sawa, however, had no desire to stop and wait. The events of the past few days had worn upon him, physically and mentally. He found that he no longer cringed every time he heard equipment being carried by one of his men bang together. The Marines had to know they were coming. Sawa was positive of that. No one was that stupid. Surely, American staff officers had managed to pull together enough evidence that the large force of which he was a part was about to fall upon them. They had to know that their ill-advised seizure of the airfield would not be allowed to go unchallenged forever.

So the young Imperial officer found himself chafing at the idea of sneaking about, the prospect of holding at the attack position angered him. Now that they were committed to this offensive, now that they were finally going forward, Sawa didn't want to stop. He wanted to keep going. If that meant that he would die, so be it. That sad fate was part of his duty, a burden that all Imperial soldiers must be prepared to shoulder. If anything, death would come as a blessing, one that promised to bring an end to a miserable existence. Duty, after all, was heavier than a mountain. Death, lighter than a feather.

Young Yoshio would have been startled by how similar his thoughts were to those his commanding general was entertaining at that very moment. Like his humblest of platoon leaders, Kawaguchi was also anxious to get on with the enterprise. Rocked by one unforeseen incident after another, the general had no longer any desire to hold back. Everything, he felt, had come down to nothing more than a simple roll of the dice. All his careful planning, all his meticulous preparation, all his insistence that they maintain the strictest of secrecy had been for naught. When the Americans weren't doing their utmost to frustrate his efforts, nature itself had done all it could to thwart him. Even now, the very darkness which he had counted on to cover his attack worried Kawaguchi. Darkness was an advantage. The pitch-blackness that engulfed them was not. Cowed by so many disappointments over the past few days, the general began to wonder how many of his units would become lost en route to their final attack positions. That, he mused, would be the final insult.

Casting aside those grim thoughts, thoughts matched only by the darkness of the night, Kawaguchi turned his mind to his plan. Closing his eyes, he envisioned a map that outlined all of the objectives his scattered battalions would soon be rushing forward to seize. With him, facing the southern rim of the Marine lodgement, were three battalions that comprised the main force of his command. Arrayed from right to left, this central group was made up of the Third Battalion of the 124th Infantry Regiment, the Second Battalion of the Fourth Infantry Regiment, and the First Battalion of the 124th Infantry Regiment. At 2200 hours the Third of the 124th would push north, moving along the eastern slopes of the centipede ridge to secure an objective

at the northeastern end of the airfield's runway,
which he dubbed "NI." They would then continue to
the beach midway between Lunga Point and the Ilu
River. Second of the Fourth would assault the centipede head-on, sweeping up onto the ridge and using
it for the axis of their advance onto the center of the
runway and beyond to two objectives designed "HE"
and "NU" before going on to the sea. First of the
124th would follow the Lunga River until it broke
out of the dense jungle that lay west of the centipede and struck the southwestern end of the runway. After securing a piece of high ground known
as 15 Meter Height and marked as Objective "R,"
the First of the 124th would continue its advance to
35 Meter Height. There another of Kawaguchi's battalions, attacking from the west, would link up with
the Central group. A fifth battalion, known as the
Kuma or Bear Battalion, would attack from the east
at the same time as all the others to pin and then
roll up the Marines defending along the Ilu River.
By dawn, if all went as he expected it would, the
airfield would be cleared and ready to receive aircraft flown down from bases at Rubal.

None of his plans allowed for a reserve force. Kawaguchi had five battalions, each with eight hundred men. All five would go forward at the same
time. Even before he had tried to take the jungle
head-on, Kawaguchi had concluded that his opportunity to commit a reserve force at the right time
and place during a night attack would be all but nil.
So he made no provisions for one. Nothing would
be held back. Every man would go forward at once.

All of that, of course, was now out of his hands.
The time for him to influence the battle that was
about to erupt was over. Having made his final dispositions after shaking off the effects of that morn-

ing's brief but bloody run-in with the Marines, Kawaguchi was prepared to step aside and allow his battalion, company, and platoon officers to secure the victory he had worked so hard to achieve.

Not far from where Major General Kawaguchi awaited the appointed hour of attack, another major general was also keeping his own lonely vigil. Having become painfully aware of just how right both Edson and his own operations officer had been, Major General Alexander Vandergrift used every precious minute his opponent and daylight gave him to brace his command for the coming storm. Leaving Edson's combined Raider-Paramarine Battalion on the centipede ridge, he ordered his reserve battalion, Second of the Fifth Marines commanded by Colonel William J. Whaling, to take up blocking positions south of Henderson Field between the runway itself and the northern edge of the centipede. Their job would be to serve as a backstop should any Japanese forces make their way past Edson's positions and emerge to the north.

To support both Edson and the Second of the Fifth Marines, Colonel Pedro de Valle, commander of the Eleventh Marines, the divisional artillery unit for the First Marine Division, brought every gun he dared to bear. To direct their fire, forward observers were located with both Edson's command and the Second of the Fifth Marines.

One change that Vandergrift refused to make during the last frantic hours was the displacement of his headquarters. The divisional CP had originally been located near the airfield, a place where it was subjected to daily air attacks directed at the airfield. On the tenth of September, it had been shifted to a spot in the northeastern lee of the centipede ridge, a location selected because of its relative safety. It had been this move that had allowed Colonel Thomas and Edson to conspire and move the Raiders and Paramarines onto the centipede. Though he was now having second thoughts about the move, Vandergrift refused to back down now.

Not satisfied with these preparations, Thomas met with both Colonel Clifton Cates, the commanding officer of the First Marine Regiment, and Colonel Leroy P. Hunt, who had the Fifth Marines, to advise them of the situation. During his discussions with each of these men, Thomas asked that they be prepared to dispatch some of their units south to reinforce the Second of the Fifth Marines at the airfield if, as he said, "things don't go well tonight for Edson."

On the ridge itself Lieutenant Francis Pearson woke with a start. It took him a moment to orient himself and appreciate the fact that night had fallen. It took him a bit longer to realize that not only had he somehow managed to drift off to sleep, but his runner, who shared the foxhole with him, had as well. Reaching across the tight confines of their shallow defensive pit, Pearson shook Sterling.

In a flash the young PFC was wide-awake, gripping his weapon and leaning against the forward lip of the foxhole searching for targets. "Are they coming?" he whispered when he didn't see anything right off.

"No, not yet," Pearson replied in a low voice. "I was just waking you, that's all."

Sterling was the sort of Marine that didn't need to be yelled at. He was forever doing his utmost to please his superiors, doing things that needed to be done before having to be told to do so. That quality, together with his speed and agility, were what had recommended him to Pearson. Ashamed that he had been caught dozing off, Sterling bowed his head and sheepishly apologized. "I didn't mean to conk out like that, sir. I just sort of . . ."

"Don't sweat it, Sterling. So did I. Just make sure that neither one of us does it again, okay?"

Having settled that issue, Pearson hunkered down and resumed the vigil he had been keeping before it had been interrupted by his unplanned nap. He didn't have long to wait.

SIX

The drone of a single aircraft broke the eerie silence that had fallen over the Marine lodgement. The unmistakable chug of the plane's engine identified it as a Japanese float plane, the sort launched from cruisers and battleships for spotting and reconnaissance. To the Marines all such float planes were known collectively as "Louie the Louse." While its name was somewhat of a joke, the appearance of the float plane was not. Louie was the harbinger of death and destruction. As with so many other aspects of the struggle for Guadalcanal, the Marines could do little but endure Louie and the suffering that followed in its wake.

Traveling at a stately pace, the float plane made its way across the narrow strip of land controlled by the First Marine Division. As it approached the northern tip of the centipede ridge, it began to drop green parachute flares. Just offshore, gunnery officers aboard the light cruiser *Sendi* and destroyers *Shikinami, Fubukl,* and *Suzukaze* used the light thrown off by these illumination devices to lay the main batteries of their respective ships. At 2130 hours the command to fire was given, shattering the still night and initiating Kawaguchi's long-awaited counteroffensive.

During previous visits by the Imperial Navy, Henderson Field had been ground zero for these nocturnal bombardments. Tonight, however, the occupants of that contested strip of land were spared for the moment. Instead, the six-inch shells of the *Sendi* coursed their way to the ridge where Edson and his polyglot force of Raiders and Paramarines waited.

Unchallenged by American warships, the small Japanese flotilla brazenly paraded back and forth off Lunga Point, spewing out shells at a steady cadence. Aboard each ship sailors toiled belowdecks in powder magazines, manhandling projectiles onto mechanical elevators that hoisted them to the sweltering confines of the gun turrets. There, their shipmates rammed the shells home into the waiting maws of their ship's guns before bracing themselves for firing. On the ridge, Lieutenant Francis Pearson and his platoon were utterly powerless to stop them. Their only recourse was to seek what safety they could in the shallow holes they had scraped into the coral hide of the centipede. None of the Marines took much solace when any Japanese shell missed the ridge completely and sailed harmlessly overhead into the jungle, causing much grief to the Japanese infantry massing for attack.

All told, the naval bombardment lasted twenty minutes. This preliminary to Kawaguchi's ground attack was immediately followed by a second barrage from six 75mm howitzers that Kawaguchi's gunners had managed to haul forward from Taivu Point. In conjunction with this renewed shelling, a shower of smaller flares were launched skyward from the ground just south of the Marines' positions on the centipede-shaped ridge. Unlike those dropped by the float plane during the course of the naval shelling, these were signal flares sent aloft by battalion commanders to alert their subordinates that the time to go forward had come.

At first there was nothing resembling a coherent or overwhelming attack. Rather than coming forward en masse, the attack began with gibbering voices and shouts that pierced the darkness. Some of these noisy assailants used broken English to hurl defiant oaths or challenges at the nervous Marines. Knowing full well that the purpose of these random and seemingly ill-advised outbursts was to draw fire and thereby give away their positions, the Raiders simply watched, listened, and waited.

From his foxhole, Pearson peered over the edge into the jungle below, straining his eyes in an effort to catch a glimpse of the enemy host that was by then close at hand. During this strange interlude, a spattering of small-arms fire broke out along the line of outposts each Marine company had sent forward. Sometimes the exchange was fitful, almost hesitant, as single rifle shots were traded back and forth. Other confrontations between the Marines manning the outposts and the Japanese soldiers easing their way forward erupted with a sudden and all-consuming violence. Eventually these little pitched battles faded as the Marines occupying the outpost line withdrew to the main line of resistance, hid in the dense undergrowth to avoid detection, or were overwhelmed and dispatched by their assailants.

Sensing that their moment was at hand, Pearson passed the word to his left and right. "Get ready. They're coming." Turning to the forward observer from the Eleventh Marines, who had scraped out a position just behind Pearson's, the Marine lieutenant ordered him to alert the 105mm howitzer batteries that he would soon have a target for them. "Don't wait for me to ask," Pearson told the FO. "Feel free to lay it on as thick as you please."

The young Marine officer had no sooner finished making this statement than a fresh volley of ground-launched flares lit the sky above his position. Unlike those which had preceded it, this shower of flares elicited an immediate and stunning response. From the jungle below and across the entire front of Pearson's platoon half a dozen voices rose up as one with the shrilled cry of *"Banzai!"* In response to this call to battle, hundreds of excited voices echoed the exhortation before stepping off into the attack at a dead run.

For a moment all Pearson could do was watch as he tried to shake off the shock that this ancient war cry evoked. Then, rising onto his knees and leaning out of his foxhole as far as he could, he leveled his Reising submachine gun and flipped off the safety while he bellowed out his own response. *"Open fire! Open fire!"*

There had been no need to repeat the command. His second "Open fire," was drowned out by a hail of fire all along Company B's front. The report of no individual weapon could be heard, not even the Reising he himself was firing. Detonations of grenades, both those tossed downhill by his men and the grenades launched by the Japanese in return, using their strange 50mm knee mortars, were masked by the pulsating din of battle. Only the whine of 105mm shells passing overhead cut through the cacophony. When he heard the shriek of friendly artillery overhead, Pearson held his fire so as to observe its effects. In awe, the young Marine officer watched the impacting shells light up the jungle below, silhouetting the waves of screaming Japanese soldiers surging forward toward his position. When he saw that the leading edge of the enemy formation closing on his platoon's positions had not been affected by this initial volley, Pearson spun about and yelled to the FO behind him. *"Drop one hundred! Fire for effect!"*

The Marine artillery spotter had also observed what Pearson had and understood what was happening. And while he would have made a less radical shift in fire for fear that it would hit some of Pearson's own men, the artilleryman passed on the command.

Having done all he needed there, Pearson turned his attention back to the front. The Japanese were closer now, alarmingly close, and coming on without any sign of letup or hesitation. Even in front of Malin's machine gun, where the soldiers of the second wave were stepping on the backs of those cut down before them, the Japanese were gaining ground. With his men already firing as fast as they could work the actions on their rifles or feed more rounds into their automatic weapons, Pearson had nothing to do other than keeping the trigger of his own gun down and feeding it fresh magazines as quickly as his fingers allowed. He had no interest in counting the number of men he cut down. Once they were down, the dead and dying were unimportant, no longer a threat. It was the ones who were still on their feet, still screaming like lunatics as they pressed forward brandishing bayonet-tipped rifles and howling incessantly all the way, who mattered. "Just keep firing," he shouted over and over again, not knowing if he was admonishing his men, talking to himself, or simply pleading with his submachine gun. "Just keep firing."

Then, in the twinkling of an eye, the entire landscape before him was torn apart in a sheet of flame that rocked both him and PFC Sterling back on their heels. Stunned by the effects of his own artillery, Pearson was tempted to dive for the bottom of his foxhole and safety. He didn't. Instead, he managed to turn once more to where the shocked FO was reeling from the effects of the 105mm rounds that had barely missed them. Reaching out of his own foxhole Pearson grabbed the man by the arm. "That's perfect! Repeat! I say again repeat! Tell them back there to keep marching it back and forth just like that!"

Within seconds of commencing their advance, Sawa's company was raked by a storm of enemy small-arms fire that carried away the man who had been standing right next to him. This calamity made no difference to the young officer. With sword held high above his head and waving madly about in the air, he repeated his commanding officer's cry of *Banzai* and threw himself forward without a second thought.

The immediate aim of Captain Oyama's company was to pierce the enemy defensive positions that lay in the low ground just east of the centipede ridge. Oyama instructed his lieutenants to use the high ground to their left as a guide. "If you keep the ridge in sight as you go forward, you will not get lost." Having spent endless days moving through the jungle without having any clear idea where he was,

Sawa was pleased that they would have a landmark such as the centipede during the course of the attack. After all, he told himself, he would have far more important things to worry about when they went forward.

It wasn't until they were actually committed to the attack that Sawa discovered how quickly all of the worldly concerns and trepidation he had been harboring for days simply evaporated like the morning mist. There was nothing that he needed to do. All the decisions had been made for him. He had no need to direct his men or tell them where they were to go or what was expected. Just as he was following Captain Oyama, they were following him, screaming as loudly and lustily as he was. It was as simple as that.

It was also very deadly. Their forward movement unleashed a barrage of enemy fire that was devastating and continuous. Up ahead, beyond his commanding officer Sawa could see a line of flashes that lit up the enemy positions like a string of animated fireflies. Even in his excited state he could hear and almost feel the zing of enemy rounds as they whirled past his head. Somehow in the midst of everything going on around him, the distinctive thud that fast-moving lead bullets make when they slam into human flesh and bone managed to penetrate the deafening roar of battle.

On they went. Men all around him were hit by enemy fire and thrown back as if they had been punched by a great invisible fist. Perhaps Sawa found himself thinking he could be next. It did not matter, he told himself. He was doing his duty in a manner befitting a servant of the Emperor. If he were to die here and now, he would take an honored place among his ancestors. It was in the midst of this chaos that Sawa realized that the old saying was true. Death was lighter than a feather.

Up ahead, Captain Oyama continued to set the pace for his company. Turning his head without making any effort to slow his pace, Sawa's commanding officer lowered his sword and pointed it back at the mass of soldiers following him. Holding his arm straight out and at his side, he made a wide sweeping motion until he had brought his sword back around to his front. Pointing it at a gap where there seemed to be no enemy fire, he yelled to all who could hear to make for that point. While he was unable to hear Oyama's orders, Sawa understood the significance of his commanding officer's action. Repeating his captain's gesture, Sawa angled off in that direction and, taking care not to hit any of his men with his sword, he pointed for the point at which they were to penetrate the enemy positions. "Over there!" he yelled as loud as he could. "Follow me over there!"

In his excitement, Sawa took scant notice of the deafening explosions that tore through the ranks of the company following his. The screams of men being torn to shreds by tiny shards of steel shell fragments was drowned out by the thunderous crash of high explosives. Even Sawa's own words, *"Totsugeki!"* (*"Charge!"*) and *"Banzai!"* repeated again and again were swallowed up by the clamor and tumult of battle. From out of the green hell that had dominated his every waking hour since arriving on this godforsaken island, the former law student continued his unflinching advance into a man-made one.

From his forward command post just behind his Company A, Colonel Merritt Edson was able to monitor the flow of the battle. With great satisfaction he took John Sweeney's report that Company B had thrown back the first massive attack with heavy losses to the enemy. Company A of the Paramarines also was able to communicate that they were managing to keep the enemy at arm's length. Unfortunately, both the commander of that unit and that of Company C Paramarines deployed down in the jungle to the east of the ridge relayed their fear that large numbers of enemy soldiers were finding gaps between their platoons. Hammered by repeated attacks and fearing that his two companies holding the left of the line would be isolated by enemy troops who were pouring through those gaps, the commander of the Paramarines ordered both Company A and Company C back.

Successfully withdrawing under pressure at night is extremely difficult. Doing so while enemy troops are in the process of penetrating your lines makes it all but impossible. The second line of positions that Edson had established in the middle of the centipede ridge were there to keep the whole line from collapsing if the first line could not hold. In theory, the Marines from the forward-deployed units would pass through the units manning the second line. Once in the rear and out of the immediate line of fire, the officers and NCOs of the withdrawing units would rally their men, reorganize them as best they could, and stand by to go forward either as reinforcements or as part of a counterattack. That was what Torgerson intended to do with companies A and B.

No sooner was the American withdrawal getting under way than a Japanese soldier threw a smoke grenade among the Paramarines. Already teetering on the edge, some of the Paramarines were panicked by the sudden and inexplicable appearance of a dense cloud of smoke. When someone yelled "GAS!" a stampede of terrified men all but swept away Edson's entire left flank. Eventually Paramarine officers and the heroic efforts of Major Kenneth D. Bailey of the Raiders brought an end to the rout and restored order within the ranks of the Paramarines. Unfortunately, by the time they did, the damage had been done. For several precious moments, Lieutenant Colonel Kusukichi Watanabe's Third Battalion, 124th Infantry was left unchallenged and unchecked. Surging forward, they sideswiped Edson's second line and continued north toward their first objective of the night, the northeastern edge of the runway.

Nor was their breakthrough the only crisis facing Edson. Whereas his Company B on the ridge had comparatively good fields of fire, Company C of the Raiders, commanded by Captain Bob Thomas, had virtually none. Located on the extreme right of the line, Thomas's men were in the dense jungle that filled the area between the Lunga River and a small lagoon. The Japanese soldiers belonging to the First Battalion of the 124th Infantry were on top of Company C before the Marines were able to fire more than a few rounds. Though the fighting was vicious and heroic, the sheer number of attackers decided the issue. Three things kept the collapse of Company C from turning into a total disaster.

The first was the horrible price the Raiders extracted from their assailants for their success. Even when there was no longer a coherent front line, pockets of Raiders and individual Marines continued to fight where they stood. The cost of this stubbornness to the Japanese was counted in more than simple casualties. The First of the 124th began to lose its cohesion as companies, platoons, and small groups of soldiers ceased advancing and turned instead to eradicate pockets of resistance that lashed out at them.

The next obstacle the Japanese faced in the confined space between the Lunga River and the ridge was Marines belonging to Company D of the Raiders and the First Pioneer Battalion. In the Corps every Marine is a rifleman. The men of the First Pioneer Battalion were no exception, and they proved it that night. Together with the thirty-five Raiders of Company D, the First Pioneers continued the frightful attrition that Company C had begun, as contributing to the total loss of whatever structure the First of the 124th had managed to maintain up to that point.

The final factor that kept the First of the 124th from achieving anything of significance was the jungle itself. Within the Marine lodgement there was perhaps no place where the jungle was thicker and less navigable than in the low ground between the Lunga River, the lagoon, and the ridge. Already scattered by the vicious fight in which they were engaged, the Japanese became hopelessly lost in the tangle of vegetation made even more frightful by fierce Marine resistance. Though some Japanese officers finally did manage to make their way through this hell, they had few soldiers with them and absolutely no overall command structure. The Marines belonging to the reserve battalion deployed south of the airfield had no trouble driving those pitifully small groups back into the jungle from which they had emerged, one by one.

The same, however, could not be said over on the eastern side of the ridge, or even on the ridge itself.

It took Sergeant Russell Smith several minutes to realize what was wrong. Japanese soldiers who had been throwing themselves against his squad's position suddenly stopped coming at them head-on. Instead, he began to notice that they were sliding off to his left. Only when his men ran out of targets to their immediate front and ceased fire did it dawn upon the leader of Pearson's First Squad that there was no firing coming from the Paramarines dug in on the other side of the trails despite the number of Japs who were going over there. Fighting the urge to jump up and run over to the left to check things out himself, Smith called down the line to the two men he had posted over there. "Hill, Mossier! What's going on over there? Are the Paras still in their holes?"

After several long seconds Mossier called back, keeping his voice as low as he could while still being heard. "There ain't no one over there, Serge. They're gone!"

Stunned, Smith didn't know whether he should redeploy his men to cover his open flank or report this hideous piece of news to his lieutenant first. "Hill, Mossier! Watch your left. Everyone else, odd man face to the rear." Having done the best he could within his own squad, Smith crawled up out of his hole and headed off to find Pearson.

Both Smith and Captain Sweeney descended upon the young Marine officer within seconds of each other. Deferring to the breathless company commander, Smith held back as Sweeney informed Pearson that Company C of the Raiders had been broken. "There's Japs all over the place down there," he stated, doing his best to remain calm. "I'm refusing the right and bringing it back up onto the ridge."

Unable to hold back, Smith blurted out his news. "The left is gone, too. The Paramarines have pulled out."

Stunned, both company commander and platoon commander looked at Smith. Appreciating their state of mind, Smith reinforced the urgency of the situation his squad faced. "There ain't no one over there but Japs, and there's nothing I can do to stop 'em."

In the midst of this crisis a voice was heard coming from the direction of where Edson had his forward command post. "John Wolf, do you hear me?"

John Wolf was the code name that Sweeney had been assigned for use when communicating via radio, and the voice belonged to PFC Walter Burak, who was part of the battalion's communications section. Sweeney yelled back that he could. Burak then relayed his commander's message in the only way he knew how under the circumstances. "Red Mike says it's okay to withdraw."

Relieved by this timely intervention, Sweeney turned to Pearson. "Hold here while I get everyone else to the right on the move. Then break contact and follow as best you can."

Though he didn't much like the last part of his orders, the part that went "as best you can," Pearson had no choice but to respond, "Will do," and wait for his turn.

SEVEN

Pressing on, Yoshio Sawa paid no attention to how many of his men were still with him. His only concern at the moment was finding his company commander. To do so he needed to keep going forward as quickly as his ebbing strength and the jungle he was pushing his way through would let him. The young platoon leader had lost track of Captain Oyama when they had literally stumbled upon a lone Marine who had resolved to fight to the death.

The one-sided skirmish had been quick but vicious. One minute Sawa was making his way forward, the next a Marine jumped up from out of nowhere right in the middle of Sawa's platoon, firing his submachine gun. The exclamations of surprise mingled with the cries of those who were being cut down. Startled and enraged, Sawa spun about and pushed those who had been following out of his way. When he came face-to-face with the Marine, the man had just finished discarding an empty magazine and was reaching for another. Seizing his opportunity, Sawa brought his sword up over his head and rushed forward. Using every ounce of strength he could muster, the former law student brought his sword down, catching the Marine where the neck and the shoulder meet.

With an ease that seemed unreal, Sawa's blade cleaved its way through bone and flesh, sending the stricken Marine to his knees. Drawing his sword back, Sawa raised it and repeated his blow again, and again, and again. Even when the dead Marine toppled over onto the ground, Sawa continued to hack away at the corpse, propelled by an anger that he had never felt before. Only when he felt a hand on his shoulder did Sawa snap out of his fit of rage. "He is dead, sir," a voice whispered.

Shaken by his exertions and the frenzied attack, Sawa stepped back, still holding his sword above his head, ready to strike again. He did not know who had stopped him. For the longest time he didn't take notice of what was going on around him. He simply stood there with his ancient weapon held aloft, looking down upon the mutilated body of a man he had just butchered. Only slowly was he able to regain his composure, relax his stance, and turn his attention back to the tactical situation at hand. By then his company commander was nowhere in sight. In the brief span of two minutes, maybe less, Sawa and those men who were still with him had lost contact with everyone else in their company. It was only when he came to appreciate this that Sawa turned away from the slaughtered Marine and continued his advance north.

During the course of his search for Captain Oyama, Sawa could hear the sounds of other units moving about through the dense jungle. Whether they were Japanese or Marines was impossible to tell. Every now and then there would be a sudden eruption of small-arms fire as one party of soldiers ran into the enemy, much as had happened to Sawa and his small band of followers. Not knowing where to direct his men or their fire, Sawa chose to avoid any skirmishes and continue toward his objective.

His advance was brought to an abrupt halt when he came across a group of Japanese soldiers standing about in a small clearing. None of them paid him any attention. Instead, they continued to pick through a stack of boxes that littered the clearing. "What are you doing,?" Sawa demanded in his best officer's voice.

Like children caught making mischief, the soldiers nearest Sawa stepped away from him before snapping to attention. It took one of the bolder among them to explain. "Food, sir. We found this enemy food and were . . . we were eating, sir."

Stepping forward, Sawa looked into one of the open boxes. Reaching in, he retrieved a tin. Turning it this way and that, he studied it for a minute. Then, before he knew what he was doing Sawa laid aside his bloody sword and began searching his pockets for a small pocketknife he always carried.

Taking their cue from the platoon leader, the dozen or so men who were still with Sawa rushed in among the others already standing around the stack of boxes and grabbed what they could.

The three hundred Raiders and Paramarines Edson managed to rally around the portion of the ridge known as Hill 123 were in desperate straits. Ammunition was low, morale was sagging, and reinforcement was, under the circumstances, all but impossible. The only thing that there seemed to be plenty of was Japanese. Not only were they now pouring down the ridge from the vacated positions along the southern tip, but small groups kept popping up out of the jungle that covered the western slopes of the ridge.

Still, the Raiders and Paramarines fought on, resorting to bayonets and rifle butts when all else failed. In the effort to hang on to the ridge, they were supported throughout the night by the guns of the Eleventh Marines. When Colonel de Valle's batteries were no longer able to receive clear fire missions from forward observers who were either dead or fighting for their lives with Edson's men, the fire direction centers responded to whatever appeal for help they received, no matter how vague. One battery spent an hour simply sweeping the crest of the ridge back and forth. Its guns shifted a little to the left, then a little to the right, laying down a curtain of steel just south of where the Raiders stood. Those Japanese who were foolish enough to brave that fire found that personal courage was no match for high explosives.

Shortly after midnight even that support was threatened. Though bloodied and badly disorganized, the soldiers of Watanabe's Third Battalion, 124th Infantry were still advancing just east of the ridge. It wasn't long before scattered and determined clusters of Imperial soldiers began breaking free of the jungle. Often led by an officer, these ad hoc mobs fanned out, initiating a rampage that threw the rear areas behind Edson's embattled command into confusion. Gunners who had been diligently serving their howitzers one minute suddenly found themselves under assault from raging Japanese soldiers bent on revenge. Using anything they could lay their hands on, the men of the Eleventh Marines fought to save their guns as well as their own lives. Even the staff of the First Marine Division fell victim to a succession of marauding attackers. From the commanding general himself down to the most junior enlisted man present, members of the division headquarters left their posts, took up their weapons, and joined the fight. As noble and heroic as this may sound, when generals and colonels are forced to fight for their lives, they are no longer available to command or direct the battle. Nor are signal troops free to keep lines open or relay desperate pleas for help.

Having expended the last of the ammunition for his Reising, Lieutenant Francis Pearson policed up a Springfield. There were plenty of them scattered about, cast off by the wounded or still clutched tightly by lifeless hands. Finding a weapon wasn't a problem. Securing ammunition for it was. Everything was running out, including time and hope. When Captain John Sweeney grabbed Pearson by the arm and ordered him to pull his platoon out of the line facing south and shift it around to support the fight for the division headquarters, Pearson stared at his commander dumbfounded. "What platoon? There's me, Gunny Jay, and six men. That's it."

Not having taken the time to keep track of such things, Sweeney blinked twice as he considered what Pearson was saying. Then he repeated his order. "If that's all you have, then they'll have to do. Now move out."

By the time Pearson managed to back away and pull his men off the firing line, he had only himself,

Gunny Jay, and five men. "Follow me. We're going to save the division headquarters."

Exhausted but still able to find a touch of dark humor in their plight, Gunny Jay chuckled. "You've been in the sun too long, Lew-tenant. You're becoming delusional."

The best Pearson could manage was a weak smile. "I'm not delusional, Gunny. I'm a fucking Marine!"

Crouching low as they made their way to the rear, the Marines found progress arrested by a figure standing in the middle of the trail they had been following. "Where are you people going?"

From his knees, Pearson looked up at Colonel Merritt Edson himself. Edson had spent the entire night going from crisis to crisis, rounding up all the strays that he could find and dispatching them to where he thought they were needed the most while keeping the firing line supplied with ammunition as best he could. Realizing that this officer didn't know about his orders, Pearson told Edson what Sweeney had just finished telling him.

Edson shook his head. "They aren't there anymore. The general and what's left of his staff pulled out ten minutes ago, headed for Geiger's CP down at the airfield."

Given how confused things had become, Pearson wasn't the least bit surprised by this news. As in all battles, events often overtake the orders that are issued in an effort to control them. Looking back from where he had just come, Pearson wondered if he should simply backtrack or go elsewhere. Deciding that the former would only serve to confuse the men who had taken over their portion of the line, the young officer looked back up at Edson. "Where do you want us?"

While Pearson had been pondering what he

should do, Edson had been considering the same thing. Looking around, the Marine colonel hesitated before he spoke. When he did, Pearson could tell how much his words pained him. "We can't hold here any longer. They're getting around us, and there's no way to resupply up here." Then, casting his weary eyes down into Pearson's, Edson placed his hand upon the young officer's shoulder. "Son, spread your men out on either side of this trail and hold it. I'm going to start pulling everyone who can make it back. If anyone asks, tell them we're reforming behind the Second of the Fifth back at the southern end of the runway. Understood?"

Understood? What in the hell, Pearson wondered, was he asking him to understand? The order to hold there, which seemed to have no clear limit on how long he was to hold? Or his instructions to tell people where they were to rally? Only when he realized that it was neither the time nor the place to ask his commanding officer for clarification did Pearson nod. "Aye aye, sir."

With that Merritt Edson made his way forward to begin the tedious process of withdrawing his command while under attack.

Reinvigorated by the food he had managed to gulp down, Yoshio Sawa gathered up his own men and those he had stumbled upon in the small opening. After organizing them as best he could, he led them in the direction of the airfield.

Throughout their brief interlude and during their renewed advance, the fighting around them had continued unabated. The vicious and pervasive din of explosions, rifle fire, and the rattle of machine guns was just as fierce as it had been when the attack had begun. Surely, Sawa found himself thinking, the

Marines could not last much longer. How could they when there had only been two thousand of them on the entire island? Based upon what he had seen himself, the former law student reasoned, they had to be nearing collapse. Looking back at his pitifully small collection of men, Sawa repeated this last thought with greater emphasis. *They have to be.*

After so many hardships and so much frustration, Sawa was startled when he stepped out into the open and gazed upon the flat expanse before him. In an instant he realized that he was looking at the airfield. *They had made it!* They had reached their objective! Well, he corrected himself, they had almost reached their objective.

Spinning about, Sawa waved his sword once over his head and pointed its tip in the direction of the airfield. "There is our objective! There is our victory! *Banzai! Charge!*"

Without waiting to see if his men were following, Sawa began to make a headlong dash forward. In his excitement he failed to take into account that the airfield was a very large objective and his command was very, very small. Nor did he bother to inspect the ground that lay between where he had stood at the edge of the jungle and where the runway began. Even if he had, it is doubtful that he would have seen the hastily dug positions where the men of the Second of the Fifth Marines sat waiting. Not until those Marines opened fire did Lieutenant Yoshio Sawa realize that his trials were not yet at an end.

DAWN, SEPTEMBER, 14, 1942

Feeling like a man twice his age, Francis Pearson shuffled down the edge of the runway, ignoring the planes of the famous Cactus Air Force of Guadalcanal as they roared past him and leaped into the air. He was followed by all that remained of his platoon, some of whom had become lost during the night and had not found their way back to the fold until just before dawn. Together with this gaggle of ragged figures, Pearson trudged on toward a spot near the beach that Colonel Edson had picked as a place to collect his shattered command and rest them. When John Sweeney mentioned that they were headed for a rest area, Gunny Jay groaned. "Jesus, sir. Not another one! We can't take any more of the colonel's rest areas." Even Sweeney, shaken by the terrible cost that the previous night's fighting had taken on his company, couldn't help but laugh.

"A rest area," Pearson muttered as he looked about at the torn and battered landscape. "It'll be a cold day in hell before they find a rest area on this island."

That thought was still rattling about in his head when his eyes fell upon a curious sight. Stopping, Pearson gazed down at the lone body of a Japanese officer lying facedown in the mud at his feet. The man's arm, stretched out as far as it could, still clutched a sword whose tip touched the steel mats Marine engineers had used to reinforce the runway.

Coming up next to his platoon leader Gunnery Sergeant Jacobi looked down at the Japanese officer as well. "Gee," the Marine NCO mused, "some of the bastards actually did make it to the airfield."

"Yeah, Gunny, he made it." Pearson sighed. Then, without giving the body of Yoshio Sawa another thought, Lieutenant Francis Pearson continued on.

FACT AND FICTION

AUGUST, 2001

Despite numerous attempts, the Japanese never re-
captured Henderson Field. This story is based upon
what I considered their best opportunity to do so.

The two young lieutenants and everyone within
their platoons are fictional characters. Captain Tetsuzan Oyama is fictional. All other characters mentioned by name are real. Most of the actions taken
by these fictional characters are based upon actual
events and incidents that occurred on Guadalcanal
and within the ranks of the First Raider Battalion
USMC, and the Japanese forces commanded by
Major General Kiyotake Kawaguchi during the September campaign, including Edson's raid on Tasimboko.

I marked the place in the story where it takes its
"What if" turn with an asterik. When Major General
Kiyotake Kawaguchi left Rubal, he had intended to
make his attack at 2200 hours on the evening of the

twelfth. Upon arriving on Guadalcanal and assessing the reality of the situation, Kawaguchi postponed his attack until the thirteenth. When he received word of the troop convoy at Fiji, the Japanese general once more changed the date back to the original one, which he favored. With the destruction of his long-range transmitter by the Raiders during the September 8 raid, Kawaguchi lost all contact with Rubal, making any further changes impossible.

The dispositions of Marine forces to include the Raiders and Paramarines prior to the attack are based upon the defensive scheme of the twelfth. Changes were made during the thirteenth, but only in response to the aborted attack Kawaguchi launched on the night of the twelfth. Since that attack did not take place in this story, there is no reason to believe that Edson would have made any major shifts before the night of the thirteenth.

The reconnaissance in strength depicted in this story conducted by the Raiders on the thirteenth was planned by Edson. In fact, he had just finished issuing his orders to his company commanders for that foray when the Japanese bombardment began on the twelfth.

The naval bombardment and preliminaries described in the story are as they actually occurred. Kawaguchi's plan of attack, the axis of advance for each of his battalions, and their objectives are taken from the orders issued by Kawaguchi. When the Japanese tried to launch their attacks on the twelfth, they did so in a rather haphazard manner. Those units that managed to arrive in time went straight from the approach march into the assault. Without any reconnaissance of the Marine positions or routes forward, battalions and companies quickly lost their way. Most units never did attack that night. Things did not go much better on the thirteenth. The Japanese once more stumbled about and went in piecemeal while the Third Battalion, 124th Infantry failed to make any serious contribution to the effort. In the story I made the assumption that the battalions of Kawaguchi's central force adhered to Japanese tactical doctrine and, despite Edson's spoiling attack, made the necessary preparations for a proper night attack.

The results of that attack and the response of the defenders is a mix of what actually happened and what might have happened.

A FINAL WORD

In the story the Japanese fail, just as they did on the twelfth and thirteenth of September 1942. It is my considered opinion that even if things had gone exactly as Kawaguchi had planned and the Japanese had somehow managed to seize the airfield, they could not have held it. There were simply too many Marine infantry battalions on the island, and the Japanese losses, even under the best of circumstances, would have been too prohibitive for them to hold on. The Marine commanders of the First Marine Regiment and the Fifth Marine Regiment, after brushing aside the feeble attacks thrown against them, would have turned on those Japanese forces that had made it to the airfield and wiped them out. While I do admit things would have been a lot costlier for the Marines, and there might have been a disruption in air operations, neither Vandergrift nor the commander of the Marine and naval aviation units on the island, Brigadier General

Geiger, would have admitted defeat. Somehow they would have managed to pull things together and carry on, just as Marines always have done, and hopefully always will.

BLOOD BOND

HAROLD ROBBINS

HAROLD ROBBINS (1916–1997) was one of America's bestselling authors, selling more than fifty million copies of his novels during his half-century career. His books were notable for their thinly veiled depictions of famous people, including Howard Hughes, Lana Turner, and Jimmy Hoffa. He blended fact, drama, action, and sex into bestselling novel after novel. He used elements of his own life growing up as an orphan on the streets of New York City, and in later books took on Hollywood, the televangelism industry, and unions. Several of his novels were made into films, including *A Stone for Danny Fisher*, which was shot as *Kid Creole* and starred Elvis Presley. His first novel, *Never Love a Stranger*, was filmed in 1958 and featured John Drew Barrymore and Steve McQueen.

ONE

Blut.kitt [German: blood + cement] The Nazi pact that evil acts bind together members of the SS into a brotherhood
— DEUTSCH DICTIONARY

BAVARIA, GERMANY • JUNE 1, 1944

The Luftwaffe flight attendant on the Junkers Ju 86 had frontal artillery that jutted out straighter than the barrel of the 7.92mm machine gun in the bomber's nose. She was peaches and cream with juicy red lips. Just before dawn, ten thousand feet over Munich, she'd cooed over my SS captain's uniform and run her fingers through my golden locks. I had to admit that I looked good in the black uniform of the Master Race. Wouldn't she have been surprised if I'd told her I was Jewish.

I kept asking myself, What's a nice Jewish boy from Jersey doing riding in a Nazi plane? It started

with the Japs bombing Pearl Harbor and just kept
getting worse until finally I was sent to Germany to
kill some Nazi bastard who sorely deserved it. Back
on Saturday, December 6, 1941, the day before the
Japs hit us, I had pitched a two-hitter at a charity
exhibition game at Ebbetts Field beating the Chi-
cago Cubs, three to one. I was the best left-handed
power pitcher on the Dodger roster. Arnold Berkowitz is my real name, Arnie the Barber is what the
boys in the press box called me because of my reputation for shaving the chins of batters who leaned
in too close on my inside fastballs.

That Saturday night I'd gone out to celebrate the
win with my teammates. I awoke the next morning
with a hangover, a naked redhead, her naked bru-
nette sister, and news that the Japs had pulled some
real shit in Honolulu harbor.

Everybody ran down on Monday morning and enlisted. Except me. I figured the war could wait until
I got another season or two under my belt, but Wild
Bill Donovan started a superspy outfit called the
OSS and jerked me in. He said it was because I
was raised in Germany by American parents until
I was thirteen and spoke the vernacular. That's what
he said, but I think the guy just liked to talk baseball, and I was a captive audience. I hated like hell
exchanging a baseball uniform that paid me twenty
thousand a year to an army one that paid about
twenty bucks a month. It wasn't that I was unpa-
triotic. I'm as rah-rah as the next guy. But a guy
could get his nuts shot off throwing pineapples at
the krauts or Tojo. Wasn't that what happened to
one of those guys Hemingway wrote about?

Not that there wasn't one good aspect of living in
wartime Washington. The town had mushroomed
with the war boom, and the gold to be mined was

women. All kinds of women, ready to wave the flag for the country. There was so much action, I'd heard Goodyear was running short on rubber for jeep tires. I was batting a thousand until my foot landed in my big mouth.

After a few too many one night in a DC bar, during an argument about whether the Georgia Peach was a greater player than the Babe, I told Wild Bill that Cobb couldn't carry the Babe's jockstrap. I bumped up my expert opinion a notch by letting Wild Bill know in front of a senator that he didn't know shit from shinola about baseball.

Next thing I knew, a tailor was measuring me for a storm trooper uniform. Actually, it was a black SS uniform, which strictly speaking wasn't a storm trooper outfit—that was the old brown shirt SA designation—but that's what we called all those goose-stepping bastards.

Oh, yeah, it was also my perfect German. That was the important part, Wild Bill said. That and some bullshit about my blood type. The assignment had nothing to do with an argument over baseball. *Jawohl, Herr General!*

TWO

Looking out the window as we began the descent for the airfield outside Berchtesgaden, I could see the Obersalzberg, the sixteen-hundred-foot-high mountaintop above the town. The terrain below was all peaks and valleys, crowned by the Walzmann, the country's second highest mountain, and the Königssee, a dark, deep, and mysterious alpine lake that had an almost mythical essence to me as a child. In the distance off to the left, were the spires of Salzburg, Austria.

The Obersalzberg, which literally translated meant "top of the salt mountain," was just about the most important chunk of real estate in the Third Reich, the Nazi empire that had most of Europe under its goose steps. Back in medieval times, they called salt taken out of the mines "white gold" and fought wars over it. Now the Berghof, Adolf's favorite residence, was up there, along with his Eagle's Nest retreat and the summer houses of Goering, Bormann, Speer, and other Nazi bigwigs. So was an operations center for the OKW, the Oberkommando der Wehrmacht, the German High Command. Along with ten miles of fence and more SS Leibstandarte—der Führer's personal bodyguard—than you could shake a stick at.

I wasn't overly confident about keeping up the pretense of being an SS captain. I was relying on other people and didn't know how well they'd done their part. The real SS Captain-Doctor Erich Wolfhardt had been kidnapped and murdered when he left his parents' house in Hamburg around midnight to go to the airport. I was smuggled into Hamburg and boarded the plane in his stead without ever seeing him—dead or alive. But, if the German underground agents carrying out that part of the mission had failed to make Wolfhardt disappear, or any number of other things had gone south, I would be exposed as a fraud as soon as we landed.

My destination was to a hospital tucked up in the mountains near Lake Königssee. The OSS agents who briefed me on the mission told me the hospital was in a picture-pretty setting. That was great, but I wasn't there for the flora and fauna. My big mouth had gotten me into what could only be described as a suicide mission. I was going to kill Adolf, you see.

The plane began its descent, and the Fräulein with blower's lips and tits that stood at attention said farewell.

"Lebewohl, Herr Hauptmann."

"Hauptsturmfuhrer," I corrected her. A captain in the regular army was called a Hauptmann. We storm troopers were a private club with our own unique ranks. Translated in a straight line, my SS rank meant captain-storm-leader.

"Sorry, Herr Hauptsturmfuhrer." She touched the two lightning-strike SS-runes on my right collar.

"You must be on a very important mission. The plane was diverted from a general's use to fly you. The rumor is that you are to see der Führer himself."

Her blue eyes were wide with admiration and her red lips moist and swollen. What do they say about lips? That they're a sex symbol because they resemble the lips between a woman's legs?

"I serve der Führer," I said. "Obedience unto death." That last bit was the initiation pledge of new SS members. I thought it was a nice touch, a little humility while facing death.

I squeezed her fleshy, succulent tush. There's something about a woman in uniform—it makes them horny for a man in uniform. I found that out in DC before I rerouted my fate by pissing off General Donovan. He *was* wrong. Cobb was a prick who didn't do a fraction for the game of baseball that Ruth did. Wasn't Yankee Stadium the House That Ruth Built? What fucking luck, to be hit by a beanball—and not even in a ballpark.

"Perhaps on your return trip . . ." Her fingers brushed my crotch.

At which moment the navigator yelled back for us to strap in, we were coming in for a landing.

I'd have given anything to stay on board and hit one out of the park with the Fräulein: The plane was perfect for it. The Junkers was comfortable, a light bomber that looked tough on the outside with its three 7.92mm MG15 gun mounts—nose, dorsal, and a drop-down belly gun called a "dustbin turret." But the Ju 86 was a notoriously poor combat performer, and this one had been turned into a luxury suite inside for Nazi brass.

It would have been nice to have stayed aboard, sipped champagne, and given her a thorough examination, relying on my medical training. Did I mention that I was a gynecologist? A *Frauenarst,* as the krauts put it. I had a day's training for the rank of an SS captain and five hours of gynecological training, all by the OSS. That left me with the ability to tell a private from a general and know where to put the clamp when a woman was on the stirrups.

"Auf Wiedersehen, Liebchen." I gave her plush tush another squeeze before I went through the hatch. I knew exactly what I would ask for as my last meal if there was a firing squad waiting for me as I stepped out.

I climbed down the ladder to the tarmac as a staff car drove up and parked nearby. I pulled up the collar of my trench coat and headed for the car, my knees going soft as I got closer. A Standartenfuhrer, SS colonel, stepped out of the back door and waited for me. His Walther P38 was holstered on his hip. He had one hand on it while he used his other hand to bang his swagger stick against the side of his leg. He looked like a man waiting for a dog to kick.

This was going to be my first test. The only person I'd had to fool up to now was the flight attendant.

"Hauptsturmfuhrer Wolfhardt, reporting, sir." I gave him my best German, a stiff-arm salute, a *Heil Hitler!* and clicked my heels. Then I waited for him to take out his Pistole and shoot me between the eyes. I expected him to see through my act on sight.

The colonel, whose name was Vogler, returned my salute, didn't shoot me, and we climbed into the backseat of the staff car.

"What have you been told about your assignment?" Colonel Vogler asked. He had a Swabian peasant's square face, paunchy, unhealthy skin pallor with pox facial pits, fat purple lips, and teeth so yellow it looked like he brushed his teeth with a plug of tobacco. He stared at me with small restless eyes, the eyes of a nervous Doberman.

I would have guessed that all SS officers were spit-and-polish nuts, but Vogler wasn't. His black SS uniform was just a bit off kilter. Not wrinkled, not sloppy, just not perfect. It needed to be let out a little to reduce the stretch at the belly, the collar points on his shirt were browning from too much hot iron-on starch, his boots were highly polished but showed old scuffs at the toes. But maybe it was the shape of his body that made him look less than snappy. He bulged in the middle from wide hips, the look some older women get. Decked out in the all-black uniform with a red-and-white Nazi armband, he looked like an eight ball that had been knocked around too many pool tables.

I wasn't sure what military unit he belonged to. The designation on his uniform was the Totenkopf, the skull and crossbones of the Death's Head detachments. All us SS wore the Totenkopf on our caps, but Vogler also had it as a unit designation. During my OSS briefing I was told that the Totenkopf unit insignia was worn by panzer combat divisions and "special" units behind the lines that guarded prison camps, but I didn't see how that would fit into a hospital environment, which was, I was told by the OSS briefers, my destination.

I wasn't impressed with either his SS colonel's uniform or the threatening implications of a special Death's Head unit. Watching the American military establishment burst at the seams during the early part of the war, with unqualified officers skyrocketing in rank, I'd learned that when a tide comes in it carries a lot of garbage with it. Vogler struck me as someone who flowed in the current when der Führer and his Beer Hall Putsch pals got the keys to the Reichstag. I figured he was a waiter at some Nazi social club before the war, and was standing in the right line when SS officer uniforms were passed out.

"I was merely told to report to the airfield. What my destination was, what my duties were to be—"

"And you weren't even curious." It wasn't a question.

"Curious? Of course I was curious. But I obey orders."

"Why do you think you're here?"

"To serve der Führer," I said with conviction.

"Nonsense, that's not an answer, we all serve der Führer every moment of every day, that is a duty imposed by the uniform we wear. Why do you think you were suddenly ordered to report to this particular area?"

I hesitated. Sounding too stupid would raise as much suspicion as being too knowledgeable.

"I'm a medical doctor—"

"Newly licensed, and a Frau's Doktor at that." He waved aside my medical qualifications. "No one would let you operate on a *Schweinhund*."

"Then there is another matter—"

"Yes?" He leaned toward me. His eyes had the preternatural gaze of a Doberman with a smaller dog in its mouth. His uniform had a musty smell of beer yeast, an unpleasant accompaniment to a peppermint scent on his breath. The combination meant he was a drinker trying to cover his tracks.

"But I'm not permitted to disclose it."

"Ja!" He slapped my leg with the swagger stick. "Very good, Hauptsturmfuhrer, that is exactly the correct answer. Had you given any other, I would have my driver turn around and take you back to the plane, with orders for the Eastern Front."

Now that was a chilling thought. The Russians had been pushing the krauts back since they knocked out Hitler's Sixth Army at Stalingrad last year, taking revenge all along the way for the butchering of their people. The krauts had shot Russian prisoners of war rather than feed them. The Russians shot the krauts rather than feed them. And everybody was freezing his ass off. Wouldn't it be ironic if I fucked up and found myself shipped out to the Russian front, a place colder than polar bear shit and hotter than the hinges of hell.

"You are one of a select group wearing the uniform of the Schutzstaffel who have been chosen to give a blood transfusion to der Führer should it become necessary. You must suspect that your sudden reassignment had something to do with that."

"Herr Colonel, I've dreaded the thought that my service might be needed because it would mean something is wrong with der Führer—"

"No, no, der Führer will have a minor operation, nothing more. You will be told the details when we reach the hospital. But that is why you are here."

I leaned closer to give the colonel a confidential look. "You understand, Colonel, that should der Führer need my blood, I would gladly give every drop." I touched my arm where my "A" blood type had been tattooed in the SS manner. "Bearing the same blood type as our leader is a matter of honor for me, not a sacrifice."

"Hauptsturmfuhrer Wolfhardt, if der Führer needed *all* your blood, I personally would cut your throat, hang you by your heels, and bleed you white. But that's not the case. This time."

"I can't tell you how happy I am to hear that der Führer's condition is not serious." Jesus H. Christ, what if the man's a bleeder?

"Listen carefully, Hauptsturmfuhrer. Prior to being honored as a potential donor for der Führer, you passed the investigation of those charged with checking your background. You have the correct blood type, you have no current diseases or history of hereditary diseases, you are considered to possess some intelligence, your blond hair, blue eyes, and pale skin are Aryan traits, and genealogists have confirmed no Jewish ancestors going back at least two hundred years." He tapped my leg with his swagger stick. "But you have not passed my investigation yet."

"Which is?"

"I am in charge of security at the hospital. It is my duty to ensure that der Führer's stay will be a safe one. That means anyone who is at the facility must be checked and double-checked by me. I will be observing you, Wolfhardt. When you look over your back you will see me. I'll be under your bed when you rest your head at night. Raise my suspicions and . . ." He made a cutting motion across his throat with the swagger stick, then tapped me again on the leg with it. "Is that understood?"

"I am here to serve mein Führer, Colonel. Like you, I will do whatever is necessary to achieve that goal. If it means laying down my life, I will do so."

"Since your selection you have been ordered to maintain a strict vegetarian diet. Have you followed that mandate?"

"Of course."

"You have never seen combat, have you, Herr Hauptsturmfuhrer?" As Vogler spoke, his chest expanded, pushing the combat medals on his chest out a bit farther.

I recognized an Iron Cross, second class, a silver wound badge—indicating he'd been wounded more than twice—and an infantry assault badge.

There were a couple others, but I couldn't remember what they stood for. I had to admit that the combat medals belied the impression he gave as a putz, but from everything I'd heard about the SS, these guys awarded each other medals faster than Girl Scouts handed out cookies.

"I understand that before your training to look between a Frau's legs, you worked as a *librarian* at the Wewelsburg. Personally, I find the smell of a battlefield much more invigorating than that of a library. Or what you find between a woman's legs."

I got it. The colonel thought of himself as a grizzled combat veteran and me as a milquetoast. I murmured something inconsequential. I hadn't been told about Wolfhardt's librarian stint—like what I was told about the SS, all I got about Wolfhardt was a thumbnail sketch. But I had been briefed about Wewelsburg. It was Himmler's fantasy castle, a fairy-tale place like Mad Ludwig's Neuschwanstein, but one created by a darker vision.

Himmler thought of his black corps as a mystic order of knighthood, like the Teutonic legends of the past. To serve as the spiritual center of his knightly brotherhood, he chose Wewelsburg, a castle in Westphalia, and spent a bundle of marks making it into his own Neuschwanstein. I was told that the library at the castle was a center for "racial research," with twelve thousand volumes of Aryan lore and anti-Semitic propaganda. The genealogical tables of SS members were kept in the library, and Himmler pored over them like a horse breeder examining studbooks.

The OSS briefers told me there was even an Arthurian "Round Table" for Himmler and twelve of his closest hangers-on, commanders he'd awarded SS "knighthoods" and chivalric coats of arms.

Adolf and Himmler carried the knighthood crap
into the whole SS, from the mystic lightning-strike
runes that symbolized the SS, to the daggers with
"My Honor Is Loyalty" inscribed on the blades and
swords handed out by Himmler to new officers. The
silver SS ring I wore not only had the Totenkopf
skull and crossbones, but mystic runes around it and
Himmler's signature on the inner side. To keep up
the pagan image, they even created their own mystic
"religion," with marriage, christening, and death
rites different from the Christian traditions.

It was all designed to create a fighting force that
was not just a brotherhood, but one totally dedi-
cated to Adolf and his pets. The strutting, goose-
stepping bastards looked comical to the rest of us—
until they started spilling blood. The SS isn't just
Adolf's personal bodyguard, it's also his personal
murder squad. The world's known since the Night
of the Long Knives in '34 that Adolf had hundreds
of political opponents murdered in cold blood.
There'd been stories coming out of Europe about
the SS rough treatment of the Jews and Slavs, people
rounded up, sent off to prison camps, or working
as slave laborers in factories. At OSS headquarters,
General Donovan hinted that there might even be
worse things going on, but he hadn't elaborated.

I would have liked to have asked Herr Colonel
Combat Veteran what he was going to do after we
finished kicking his and Adolf's asses and took away
their fancy uniform and toys. Tough guys when
they're ganging up on some shopkeeper with his
wife and kids looking on, but how do they stack up
man to man?

The staff car turned off the main road and began
winding up a narrow, one-lane graveled passage that

carried us from the valley floor. Not in the direction of Obersalzberg.

"I had expected to go directly to the Obersalzberg and der Führer's headquarters," I said.

"We're not going to the Obersalzberg, though we won't be far away. There is a medical infirmary there, but it is inadequate for der Führer's current needs. The procedure will be done at another medical facility, the one I am attached to. It's called Grunberg. You've heard of it?"

It wasn't just a question—there was something in his voice that said it was another trap. Was I supposed to have heard of it? Was the "green mountain" hospital so famous any German doctor would know about it? I decided there was no reason for him to be suspicious of me. That meant there must be something secret about Grunberg, something I wasn't supposed to know about. "No, I haven't," I said.

He grunted. "I'm not surprised. Prior to the war, it was a small sanitarium, for wealthy patients with tuberculosis or some like condition. It is now an SS facility. You would not have heard about it because its existence is on a need-to-know basis." He leaned toward me again to speak confidentially. "What you learn at Grunberg must stay there. Like me, you wear the uniform of the Schutzstaffel. You know that the SS has duties that the ordinary German citizen would not understand the necessity of, duties specified by der Führer himself and delegated to Reichsfuhrer-SS Himmler to carry out. Those duties must be kept confidential until they are completed. Ja?"

"Of course, Herr Standartenfuhrer." Sure, I got the message. There was something weird going up at the green mountain sanitarium that der Führer and his Dobermans didn't want anyone to know about. But what the hell was it? And why was a Death's Head combat colonel attached to a medical facility? The OSS briefers hadn't told me anything about the hospital, it hadn't even got mentioned in the briefing. They had assumed the surgery would be done at the Obersalzberg medical clinic. Was there something going on at the hospital that's going to get me in deeper shit than I was already in?

At times like this, I wished they'd shipped Wild Bill out to the Pacific Theater before he got around to punishing me, shipped him out to someplace like the beach at Guadalcanal at the time the Nips were defending it.

"What exactly is the nature of the medical work done at Grunberg?" I asked.

"Experimental."

"Ah, yes, of course. What kind of experiments?"

He tapped my leg with the stick. I really hated that tapping bit. I had a coach once who walked around with a bat in hand all the time and would nudge players with it to get their attention. I let the coach know where I was going to stick it if he continued to nudge me, but I didn't think that was a good approach with an SS colonel.

"Important experiments," he said, "perhaps the most important medical procedures ever attempted. It makes me proud to be a part of it." Another tap. "It is inevitable that you will learn a great deal during your short stay at the facility. You understand the consequences if you engage in loose talk once you leave."

"Loose lips sink ships," I chirped.

He stared at me, and I froze in place, too terrified to even wet my pants. I realized immediately I had made a mistake. The expression, a War Department message to soldiers and sailors to button up their lips, was on posters from Jersey to Frisco. It was hardly something a German would know.

"Loose . . . lips . . . sink . . . ships." He screwed his lips about and repeated the words again. "Where did you hear that expression?"

"Nowhere, Herr Standartenfuhrer, it just came to mind."

He went back into a brown study for a moment, frowning at the back of the driver's head. I wondered if I should leap out of the car and throw myself off the mountainside, or stay in the car and wait to get shot.

"Interesting," he said. "As a high-ranking security officer, I know only too well how many of our troop movements end up in enemy hands because of loose talk by our soldiers in beer halls and the bedroom." He nudged me in the ribs with the butt end of his swagger stick. "You know what I mean, pillow talk sinks ships, ja?"

"Correct, Herr Standartenfuhrer, that is exactly right."

Vogler gave me an appraising look. "You know, Wolfhardt, this phrase about pillow talk sinking ships, it is exactly the sort of thing that Reich Minister of Propaganda Goebbels needs to educate our troops about the dangers of loose talk. The person who provides the phrase to Herr Goebbels will be on the receiving end of some considerable credit if the minister finds merit in the suggestion."

"The phrase belongs to you," I said. "After all, you were the one who saw the merit in it. Please leave my name entirely out of any communications with Reich Minister Goebbels."

"Ja, Hauptsturmfuhrer,"—the swagger stick banged my leg—"from the moment you stepped off the plane, I recognized you as an officer whom I could have confidence in." He leaned over and blew beer and peppermint in my face. "Too many of you young Schutzstaffel are sheep in wolves' clothing, ja!" He poked my stomach with the stick. "No guts. They wear the black shirt because of family connections. Not like us, eh, Wolfhardt. We know why we are Schutzstaffel. We are the broom carriers, and the Jews are the vermin we sweep away."

THREE

Grunberg was tucked away in a meadow above Lake Königssee. The main building had the look of a mountain chalet, and perhaps it was the hunting lodge of a nobleman of an era past. The outer buildings were of more recent vintage, military-looking Quonset-type huts. A guard shack and barbed-wire fencing gave it the look of a prison camp. Despite its picturesque setting in a stand of subalpine spruce, the place gave me the cold chills after Vogler's cryptic hints about things going bump in the night at the place.

I was staring at the limestone-and-dolomite cliffs that plunged into the dark waters of the lake when Vogler asked, "Have you seen Königssee before?"

"When I was a twelve," I said, truthfully. "I came with a youth group that took a boat ride on the lake." The ride took place in 1926, a year before we left Germany. Adolf had been at his Jew-baiting for years before the trip, and I ended up in a fistfight with older boys after they made remarks about the Jude kid. I

got my ass whipped, but I had long arms and big fists
for my age and got in some good punches before I
went down with three of them on me.

As we pulled up to the entrance to the main
building, a man wearing a white smock and carrying
a clipboard was returning from an outer building.
He greeted us after we got out of the car.

"Sieg Heil."

Vogler introduced me to the man, Dr. Dorsch,
director of the hospital. Dorsch was tall and slender,
with a long, thin nose he could have batted three
hundred with. He was dressed as the well-groomed
SS officer should be—you could slice cake with the
creases of his trousers, his white smock was starched
to the point of standing at attention if he took it off
and set it on the ground. His SS rank, Obersturm-
bannfuhrer, lieutenant colonel, was sewn on his
medical smock.

Doctors, especially psychiatrists, have always struck
me as people with deep patience and listening ability. Dorsch broke that mold. He was a machine, in
his walk and talk. Leaving Vogler somewhere along
the way, he took charge of me to show me the facility. He almost goose-stepped me down the polished wood floor of the hospital as he briefed me
about the place.

"I cannot tell you how honored we are that der
Führer will be treated here. It will give me the
opportunity to instruct him upon the important research that is being conducted. Frankly, Dr. Wolfhardt, we work in absolute secrecy and without the
honors showered upon us that would come if the
world knew what we were discovering within these
walls."

"What is the nature of your work, Herr Direktor?"

Dorsch stopped and pulled me aside, out of the mainstream of people using the corridor. He spoke in a low, confidential voice, which struck me as odd because I assumed people walking by would be staff members who knew what was going on at the hospital.

"The work of Grunberg is authorized by Reichsfuhrer-SS Himmler himself. It is an important step in the final solution of racial purity."

There was that expression again, the *final solution.* As far as I was concerned, the final solution would happen when we finished mopping up the krauts and started looking under garbage can lids in Berlin and Hamburg for hiding Nazis.

Dorsch went on in a confidential tone. "I know that as an SS officer, you will appreciate our work more than the ordinary person. Even more important, as a doctor, perhaps you will even be motivated to join us. You will find the work more vital to the future of the Fatherland than serving at the front."

"It sounds interesting, but I really don't know exactly—"

"It is the most exciting and satisfying work I have been involved with in my twenty years of psychiatric work. You understand, of course, that everything you see and hear must be kept in absolute secrecy."

"Of course."

"One can understand der Führer's disappointment and impatience with our regular armed forces, the Wehrmacht. It has had great success in conquering territories, but has no ability to implement Lebensraum, ja? As der Führer has said many times, eighty million Germans being crowded into a small territory is ridiculous, of course. The lands to the east must be cleared to make room for our expansion, for the Germanic people to occupy the soil

and territory to which we are entitled on this earth.
The final solution to the Jews and dealing with the
Slavs have become the prime duties of the SS. I am
proud to say that we are making a major contribution here at Grunberg."

I smiled and nodded and tried to look intelligent,
but I didn't know what he was talking about. Everyone knew the Nazis were anti-Semitic and had been
abusing the Jews, confiscating property, and throwing them into prison camps by the thousands—and
weren't treating the Slavs and other ethnic groups
much better, but what did he mean by *the final solution?* Lebensraum, that was Adolf's dream that the
Germans live like colonial masters over millions of
people. I remember my father telling me about
Adolf's crazy dream—people the Germans lorded
over would live in pigpens while the goose-steppers
would live in palaces and manor houses.

But I guess someone forgot to tell Stalin he'd
have to move out of the Kremlin and live in a pig-
pen. Adolf said Stalin's boys fought like "swamp
rats" at Stalingrad. Those same swamp rats and
"General Winter" had kicked der Führer's ass up
and down several thousand miles of Russian front.
Don't these guys read the papers? Hadn't anyone
told them they were losing this war? If they would
just face reality, I could pack up and go back to
Brooklyn.

"Before Reichsfuhrer-SS Himmler assigned me to
head this project, I was attached to an Einsatzgruppen in Poland," Dr. Dorsch said. "Before that I had
been attached to a Totenkopf unit that specialized
in confining undesirables. Colonel Vogler was with
the same unit."

He spoke proudly, like a kid bragging about a Boy
Scout merit badge. The OSS officers were supposed

to have briefed me on everything they knew about the SS, but they'd left out die Einsatzgruppen. Another item on the laundry list the OSS had ignored.

The SS, officially the Schutzstaffel, originally were Adolf's Praetorian Guard and, after the war commenced, encompassed entire divisions called Waffen-SS. Suffice it to say, the SS did not play by German law or Wehrmacht regulations. I knew the Totenkopf, Death's Head units, were special SS prison and combat units. Dorsch and Vogler appeared to be in some sort of prison unit; "die Einsatzgruppen," which meant something like "task force," was new to me.

Dr. Dorsch was brimming with excitement. "I cannot tell you what total research freedom has, meant to me. Sometimes I feel like Galileo, peering into his telescope, seeing new worlds for the first time. That I am performing a great duty for mein Führer and the Party, gives me endless joy."

A door flew open down the hall and a soldier wearing an SS sergeant's uniform burst into the hallway.

"I can't!" he screamed. "I can't do it anymore! They're staring at me, I see them at night staring at me!"

Two orderlies grabbed him and pulled him back through the door and closed it behind them.

Dr. Dorsch grabbed my arm and pointed at the closed door. "You see, you see, weaklings, incompetents, this is exactly the defeatism that we must deal with. Our Führer says we can win the war and accomplish our mission only if we have a positive attitude.

Do you understand the necessity for the program now?"

"Ja," I said.

What the hell was he talking about? I was curious, but decided that whatever it was, I wanted no part of it. Things were already too complicated as it was.

He gave me an appraising look. "I like your attitude, Wolfhardt. You must consider requesting a transfer into our program. I have a bit of influence at headquarters and would be able to implement such a request."

"Thank you, I am privileged and delighted at the suggestion. Unfortunately, my expertise is that of Frauenarst. I'm sure a Frau Doktor will not—"

"Nein, nein, a Frau Doktor would—ah, here is Dr. Dietrich."

A woman wearing a white smock with medical insignia approached.

"Dr. Hildegarde Dietrich, this is Hauptsturmfuhrer Wolfhardt." Dorsch lowered his voice. "Wolfhardt will be providing blood for the procedure that will be taking place here in a few days."

Dietrich's eyes widened. "What an honor for you! To know that your blood will be in the veins, in the brain, of our Führer." She clasped her fists to her chest. "You will be immortalized!"

Yeah, if I wasn't hung by my heels first.

Hildegarde meant "battle maiden," and the phrase fit Dr. Dietrich perfectly. She was a big blond Mädchen, a Brunhild, the warrior queen from the *Nibelungenlied,* with wide shoulders, strong arms, and powerful legs, the kind of legs that could wrap around a man and squeeze tight when she's getting laid. With her high heels, she was as tall as my five-foot-ten. I weighed in at one-sixty, and I'm sure she tipped the scale at not much less than one-fifty. She looked more like material for the Deutsch shot-putting team than a doctor.

"Dr. Dietrich will be your guide for the rest of the

tour of the facility," Dorsch said. "Don't let her lure you on one of her climbs unless you are accustomed to bouncing up mountains like a mountain goat."

Dorsch left and I began goose-stepping down the corridor with her. Like Dorsch, she walked like she had a Luger up her ass.

As we went by the closed door, I said, "A sergeant in some mental distress burst out of there a moment ago."

"Yes, that's Dr. Dorsch's program. What did he tell you about *my* program?"

"Nothing."

"You will find my program very interesting, more so than Dr. Dorsch's. I am sure you will be so fascinated by our work, you will want to join the project. The work we do is vital to the mission der Führer has given to the German people."

I shook my head regretfully. "As a Frau Doktor—"

"Perfect. I, too, am a Frauenarst. It is mandatory for our work."

Oh shit. If the woman started talking shop, expecting me to discuss female problems, she'd find that the only thing I knew about a woman's anatomy were the sexual orifices.

"In fact, I am in great need of an assistant," she said. "My last assistant was suddenly transferred to the Eastern Front when reinforcements were needed. I understand that most assignments today are to the east. I knitted a pair of wool socks and sent them to him. He will need them." She gave me a look of pity.

What if I got stuck in this Nazi monkey suit and was sent off to be butchered and eaten or whatever the hell the Russians did to captured SS? When— *if*—I got back, I was going to stick a howitzer right up Wild Bill's ass.

"Your first assignment will be delivering a baby."

"A—a what?" I felt the earth opening up under my feet.

She stopped and faced me. "You know, Herr Hauptsturmfuhrer, a baby, a thing about this size" (she spaced her hands about a loaf of bread apart) "that cries and wets its diapers just like the dolls they sell at Christmas." She laughed at her joke. "We have a woman in heavy labor. Your services will be needed at any moment. From the look on your face, perhaps they forgot to show you how to cut a cord in medical school. Or are you one of these Frau Doktors whose only expertise is sticking his head between a woman's legs while she's riding the stirrups."

She laughed and gave me a good-natured shove that sent me reeling.

Jesus H. Christ. This was not going as planned. I had two doctors competing for my help with whatever weird medical experiments were being conducted in this loony bin, while I was expected to practice medicine. Der Führer better show up before the baby, or my next assignment would be to ship out to the Eastern Front and let a Russian T34 tank run over my frostbitten toes.

"As you well know, Hauptsturmfuhrer, all SS members are commanded by der Führer to have at least four children. By the laws of birth averages, two would be boys. That would guarantee that each man would bequeath two more like himself to serve der Führer. This order is for all SS men to impregnate their wives and to assist unmarried childless women over thirty to conceive. Naturally, only women who qualify racially are to receive SS sperm. That way we can guarantee that we remain an Aryan society with pure Aryan looks."

I almost had the bad manners—*fatally* bad manners—to laugh and ask if those "Aryan looks" were the "blond" hair of der Führer, the tall stature of Little Josef Goebbels, the slender waistline of Goering the Blubber Ball, or that of Himmler, a pathetic putz.

"After I received my medical degree, I was an organizer of Lebensborn facilities, the life fountain maternity homes that care for genetically and racially valuable mothers." Brunhild stopped and faced me with her hands on her hips and a defiant expression on her face. "I hope, Herr Doktor Wolfhardt, you are not one of those who have derided these necessary facilities as little more than brothels for SS members. I can assure you—"

"No, no, Dr. Dietrich, of course not, the Lebensborn are a valuable weapon in der Führer's arsenal."

I followed her outside to one of the large military huts that looked newly constructed. At the hut, she pushed open swinging doors, walked past a seated guard, and stopped at a department store–size window.

Half a dozen women and half that number of men were in a room. They were dressed in comfortable, lightweight clothing, the sort of thing one wore around the house to relax. All were young. I'm sure the women were all under twenty and the men not much older. They were socializing with each other, laughing and talking, sitting together, interaction that struck me as bordering on intimacy. Brunhild's defensive statement that she hadn't run brothels struck me. I noticed the young people didn't have a "street" look about them, they looked more like farm and college kids, but I got a sense of intimacy from the expressions on their faces and their body language.

The next thing that struck me was what incredible physical specimens they were. All of them. They had those classic "Aryan" looks that der Führer, Himmler, Goering, Goebbels and the rest of the Nazi gang fawned upon but lacked.

"Who are these people?" I asked. "Why are they on display?"

"These are my subjects," Dr. Dietrich said. "Come with me."

She took me through a door and into a dark hallway. She stopped suddenly and faced me. "You understand, Herr Hauptsturmfuhrer, that what you are about to see is top secret. Your position as a Frau Doktor and an SS officer gives me trust in sharing with you this monumental program."

"I can assure you, Doktor, there would be no loose pillow talk on my part that would expose the secret."

"Ja, pillow talk, that is exactly what we must avoid." She seemed to find great amusement in the comment. "Pillow talk, so appropriate."

Proceeding down the hallway, we passed curtained windows on the right side. The windows were smaller than the large department store window out front.

She stopped in front of a window and paused to give me another inquiring look before she turned and pulled back a curtain.

I gaped.

A man and woman were engaging in the preliminaries of what my grandfather would have called "coitus."

The naked couple, uninhibited by our presence— or the window was one-way glass—were passionately kissing each other. Their bodies glistened, as if they had been oiled before they started making love. The woman's breasts were full, her erect nipples were dark red. The man cupped one breast with his hand. The hand holding her breast moved down her stomach. She sat up a little, spreading her legs, to let him massage her vulva, all the while gripping his throbbing member.

"Why are they doing it here?" I asked.

"They are participating in my project."

"Just what is the nature of your project?"

She stepped closer to me. I felt her heat and a surge of my own. She ran her finger over my lips and down to the breast of my uniform jacket.

She jerked the curtain shut and led me back out the way we had come.

"Mein Freund, der Führer has invaded east and west, conquering everything for hundreds of miles in each direction. He has ordered that space in these conquered territories be cleared so they can be populated by Germans."

Here we go again. These people had *Lebensraum* on the brain. Adolf must be some orator to have pumped these people up so high that they're still preparing to colonize the world. The last time I heard, the Germans were in retreat on the Eastern Front, the Allies had taken North Africa and were pushing up the Italian boot, and there were more rumors about an impending invasion of France by Eisenhower crossing the Channel than Carter had pills. One thing I was discovering about average Germans was that they had the political IQ of baboons. Sure, they knew how to follow, but they didn't know how to ask questions about *why* they were in line.

"But where are we to get the people to populate these areas?" she said. "Not just ordinary people, of course, but those with the racial and genetic qualities that der Führer decreed have a right to living space? As you have no doubt already guessed, it is the repopulation of these conquered territories that our project is concerned with."

No, I hadn't guessed. I thought she was running some sort of officially sanctioned whorehouse. What she said made me stop in my tracks and stare at her. "Do you mean those people in there are *making babies?*"

Her laughter shook the Alps.

"How do you think babies are made?" she howled. "By planting a pea under a can in the garden?"

"Doktor—"

"No, I am sorry, Wolfhardt, but I wish I had a picture of your face when I told you about our experiments. The project is not making babies, as you put it, but sexual conduct. It has been pointed out that a hundred good German soldiers could easily impregnate a thousand German women and create five hundred future soldiers every nine months. Think of it, Wolfhardt, each German soldier reproducing himself five times over every nine months! Isn't it a marvelous plan? But we need to know what makes a man and a woman unite sexually in a way that furthers the chances of fertilization. This is especially important where a woman is concerned because women are less able to get aroused than men. We are also experimenting with why some children, even with the same biological parents, come out with different-colored hair or even different-colored eyes."

"Marvelous," I muttered. Jesus H. Christ. It was an experimental breeding farm. A sex study to see how fast boys and girls could pump out babies. Along with some junk science about how Aryan types are produced. But the plan was beginning to grow on me. It was a sex study, pure and simple. Hell, it was a big relief that something dark and dangerous wasn't going on at the hospital. Sex was harmless—and a lot of fun. There I was worried about having fallen into some house of horror, and instead I had landed in the Garden of Eden—after the snake wised up Adam and Eve. I thought the math was interesting, too. Assuming that there was usually one man to one woman ratio in this world, SS members would have to use the wives and girlfriends of other men to impregnate women at a ten-to-one rate. Himmler really knew how to take care of his bully-boys.

"A marvelous plan, Doktor. Your project deserves the highest accolades from der Führer. When I see him, I shall heap praise that would please Caesar upon you and your project."

"You do not know how pleased I am to hear that. To be truthful, my project occupies only a small part of the funding and facility here. Dr. Dorsch's project gets the lion's share. Perhaps if der Führer himself was informed—"

The door to the rear of the main building opened, and two aides came out with the agitated sergeant between them. He was foaming at the mouth and muttering something incoherent. The only word I caught was *Mord.*

Hildegarde Dietrich and I stared at each other.

"Dr. Dorsch's program—" I started.

"Is exactly the opposite of mine."

"What do you mean by that?"

"It must be explained to you by Dr. Dorsch." An emotion swept across her face, as if she was struggling to tell me something. But was afraid to. She stepped closer and straightened my collar. "I must go now. Perhaps later, Herr Hauptsturmfuhrer, we will discuss your participation in my project at greater length."

"Whenever you are ready."

She nodded at an orderly approaching. "Scharfuhrer Hans will show you to your quarters."

A Scharfuhrer was a staff sergeant. As I followed the orderly, the word that the distraught soldier kept uttering stayed with me. *Mord* was the German word for "murder."

Hans, the orderly, showed me to a cottage. "It is reserved for visiting party dignitaries who wish to visit the facility and vacation here. You are being given the cottage despite your low rank because of your assignment."

He had one arm and an Iron Cross, first class. I asked him in which battle he had earned the prestigious medal.

"The English took my arm at Ypres. It cost them dearly."

I hadn't heard of the battle and my face showed my ignorance.

"The First World War, not this one," he said.

He was gruff, with a sandpaper personality. He went around opening windows, then stood at attention in front of me. I noticed he wore the insignia of the Leibstandarte, Adolf's personal SS unit.

"I am not attached to the hospital," he said. "I am part of the Obersalzberg SS detail, an orderly in der Führer's quarters. Any commands, Herr Hauptsturmfuhrer?"

"Were there any messages for me?" I regretted the question the moment it slipped out. An "orderly" to der Führer might be a Gestapo agent sent to check me out. Obviously, he had been sent to look me over, not serve me. I asked about a message because I was told that a member of the German underground at the facility would contact me. No clues as to who it might be were given to me for obvious reasons—if I was captured and tortured, I'd reveal the name.

"No messages. Were you expecting a communication?"

"No, not really, I just thought my family may have been told my new assignment." I kicked myself again. I was sinking a whole fleet with my loose lips. Families weren't told about secret military assignments. "You are excused," I told him.

I shut the door behind him, leaned back against it, and sighed. Jesus H. Christ, how had I gotten myself into this damn spy stuff. I promised myself that if I got out of this thing alive, I would get down on my hands and knees and kiss Donovan's ass until the man forgave me for my transgressions—as long as he kept me at a desk in D.C.

I didn't belong in this spy game. I didn't belong in the war. I knew the krauts were pricks and hated Jews, but hey, I'm not David the Giant Killer. As soon as the war was over, it would be business as usual—for everybody but me. I would be too old and too far out of shape to go back to playing major league ball. Most of the players in sports managed to dodge the draft. All except for me, old wrong-place-wrong-time Arnie Berkowitz. The injustice of it all was giving me a headache.

I went into the bathroom to look for an aspirin. I found headache powder in the medicine cabinet, probably something for VIP hangovers. I stuck a glass under the sink faucet and started to turn on the water when I saw the message. It was scribbled in soap on the basin. *PLAY BALL.*

I quickly washed away the message. Those were the code words for the underground contact. But

who the hell had left them? And when would I get
my final instructions?

I was sacked out on the bed late that night, lying
on top the covers, wearing only my pants, when I
heard a discreet tapping on my door. My heart did
a flip-flop. This was it—I was about to meet my underground contact. I swung my feet off the bed and
hurried to the door. Restraining an impulse to jerk
it open, I quietly opened it a crack and peered out.

"Guten Abend, Erich." Dr. Hildegarde Dietrich
grinned lewdly at me. She had two bottles of champagne. "I have a medical problem, a female one, I
need to consult you about. May I come in?"

I cleared my throat. "Of course." Christ, could this
kraut broad be my contact? She didn't act the cloak-
and-dagger type, but I didn't either.

Inside, she sat the champagne bottles on the table.

"What's bothering you, Fräulein?"

"Call me Hildegarde," she purred. She moved
closer to me.

I could feel sexual heat radiating from her body.
Her cheeks were flushed rosy red. She wasn't wearing the starched white uniform I had seen her in
earlier, but had on a soft silk dress, fastened by a
row of small buttons down the front. Her blond hair
lay in long waves.

"I need you to examine me."

She unclasped the top of her dress in one swift
move, exposing her firm breasts, free of a brassiere.
It knocked my breath away. Brunhild was stacked
like a brick shithouse. She had extraordinary
breasts—the pearly round mounds perfect, her
plum-colored nipples erect. Under the clothes she
was a typical kraut Fräulein, robust, well nourished.

"I have a problem here," she said, huskily, touching her nipples.

"I'll check them," I croaked. I put my fingers on her nipples. "These are all right," I whispered.

She slipped her dress off, letting it fall to the floor. No panties. She stepped away from the dress and stood naked in front of me, wearing only her high heels. The bush between her legs was blond.

She ran her fingers down my bare chest, giving me goose bumps. She moved in closer, rubbing her breasts against my chest. I was usually the more aggressive partner with women, but Brunhild had her own agenda, and I let her play it out.

She pulled down both my pants and shorts, pushing her breasts against me again. "And here," she said, touching her mouth. Her full lips closed on mine. Her tongue licked my lips and moved down the side of my face, the side of my neck, down to my chest and suckled a tit. I nearly jumped out of my skin.

"Now you must examine me here," she said, guiding my hand to her bushy mound.

FOUR

I was in a deep sleep early the next morning when my door burst open. I jerked up in bed. It was Hans, the orderly.

"Wake up, Hauptsturmfuhrer, you are going on a hunt."

"A what?"

"A hunt. Colonel Vogler will explain. Get dressed, I will take you to the armory for a weapon. As an officer, you will be expected to be armed with a P38."

What kind of hunting can you do with a semiautomatic pistol?

The armory was an underground bunker away from the main building and huts. There was another building beyond it, in a grove of trees on a hillside. The building hadn't been explained to me during my tour. While the other buildings appeared to be made of inexpensive military materials, this one had a sturdier look to it. And a seven-foot electrified barb-wire fence surrounding it. A kraut guard with a German shepherd on a leash was patrolling inside it. I asked Hans what function the highly guarded building served.

He gave me a moment of silence. "I am just an orderly. I do not know all the tasks for der Führer that are being performed here at Grunberg."

His reply was stiff and formal. I gave the fenced building another glance. It looked more like a prison building than a hospital facility.

The underground armory was much bigger than it appeared on the outside. And filled with large quantities of high explosives. Much of it was canisters with timers. Enough to blow the lid off the mountain.

"For mountain passes and bridges in case of invasion," Hans said. "The Obersalzberg is not far. It's possible the enemy might drop parachute troops into the area. If that happens, we are under orders to destroy bridges and roads."

Hans escorted me to where Dr. Dorsch and Colonel Vogler were selecting high-powered rifles with scopes.

"Did you wish to arm yourself with something that has more firepower than a pistol?" Vogler asked me.

"A pistol will be fine, unless you tell me we are hunting lions or tigers. I wasn't aware that there was big game in these mountains."

Vogler chuckled humorlessly. "This is two-legged game." He exchanged looks with Dorsch. "I believe a pistol will be adequate for your first time out."

Two-legged game. What the hell was going on at this place?

Two half-track troop carriers, each with twelve men aboard, were waiting, along with a four-wheel-drive staff car. I sat in the backseat of the staff car with Dorsch, and Vogler rode up front with the driver. I was curious as hell as to what was coming down, but kept my face blank.

Dorsch said to Vogler, "What do you think, Herr Standartenfuhrer, should we tell our young friend here what we are hunting or surprise him?"

Vogler glanced back with his Doberman eyes. "Tell him."

The doctor leaned closer to me. "You are going to be let in on a secret, Herr Hauptsturmfuhrer. I noticed when I mentioned yesterday that I had been in an Einsatzgruppen unit, you did not appear to know what it was."

"I've heard the name—"

"No, no, it's not necessary for you to apologize for your ignorance. Had you served in the conquered territories, I would have expected you to have some familiarity with the units. All top SS commanders know of the units, but that information is available at lower levels only on a need-to-know basis. There are some people, especially officers of the Wehrmacht, who do not agree with the program and criticize it. There have even been instances in which their failure to cooperate resulted in missed opportunities."

Vogler cut in, "In order for you to understand the Einsatzgruppen mission, you must go back to the premise of der Führer's mission for Germany."

"To give the German people breathing space," I said. "To ensure that the less advanced people of the conquered territories, the Slavs and other non-Germanic races in eastern Europe and the Soviet Republics, are obedient and serve us."

"Exactly. And in terms of our discussion, to cleanse the conquered territory of unfit life."

"Unfit life," I repeated.

"Which, as you well know, are the Jews, Gypsies, Asiatic inferiors, along with useless eaters such as the insane, retarded, and physically deformed, all of whom der Fuhrer has decreed must not be allowed to exist because they take up resources needed for our own people. In the case of the Jews and Gypsies, they are also subversives who must be eliminated to keep them from plotting against the Reich. In addition, it was necessary to wipe out the entire body of Polish intelligentsia, not just its military and political leaders, but the people who could take their place once they were eliminated. With that done, there would be no fear of a Polish leader stirring the people against us."

A cold feeling gripped me. I knew these Nazis were nutcases; hell, you just had to read some of the crap in Adolf's *Mein Kampf* to know that. I hadn't actually read the book. I figured anything that took me away from the pitching mound other than getting my cock lubed was a waste of time. But I had friends who said the guy needed electroconvulsive therapy. But what the hell was Dorsch talking about? It was beginning to sound like something more than harassing Jews or rounding some of them up and sticking them in prison camps was happening.

Dorsch went on. "Der Führer has analogized the Jewish presence in this world to a virus. In fact, I have medical colleagues who suspect there is an actual virus carried in Jewish blood and who are resolved to find it. But even if we think of the infestation as a social one, it must be eliminated because Jewish blood will poison our Aryan blood, weakening us when we fight our enemies. To eliminate the infestation from the conquered areas, der

Führer empowered a special action force, the Einsatzgruppen, to deal with it.

"Himmler assigned the responsibility to General Heydrich, probably the finest SS general who ever lived. That was in 1941, as Russia was being invaded. As you know, General Heydrich was murdered by the Czech underground the following year."

Vogler turned in the front seat. "And we retaliated against the Czechs and the Jews a hundred thousand to one."

I recalled reading about the incident. The entire male population of a Czech town, Lidice, was massacred, the town burned, the ruins dynamited, and the ground leveled. Barbaric punishment worthy of the Khans.

"Anyway," Dorsch said, "four Einsatz units, several thousand strong, were sent in behind the Wehrmacht advancing to the east, into Poland, Czechoslovakia, the Baltic region, the Ukraine, and so forth. I pride myself, as Colonel Vogler also does, on being members of the officer corps of this momentous undertaking. It may surprise you to learn that the people entrusted to lead this historic task were not professional soldiers but doctors, lawyers, accountants, and even a minister of the faith. In fact, Colonel Vogler, prior to the war, was an accountant with Krupp."

The frumpy Doberman glanced back, and I muttered something that made it sound like I was duly impressed.

"Our task was to sanitize the conquered area, to remove the infection," Vogler said. "We were under orders from the Reichsfuhrer-SS to eliminate the unnecessary life as humanely as possible, along with carriers of the virus."

Creeping horror started at the soles of my feet

and worked its way up as I listened to the accountant and doctor use businesslike language to explain how people were murdered.

"You would be amazed at how many of these people went to their deaths," Dorsch said. "Most of the virus carriers lived in urban areas. That made them easier to round up in large numbers. And in those cases where they have lived under the Soviets, they often welcomed us as liberators rather than an enemy. We were also surprised at how cooperative the non-Jews were in turning over their Jewish neighbors to be eliminated. Often we were able to organize extermination units from the local areas to supplement our own work. This was especially effective in Latvia and Lithuania. In the beginning we would round up the Jews and unfits, march them into the woods, have them dig trenches for graves, and shoot them."

"That proved highly inefficient," Vogler said. "Fortunately, we were able to institute what came to be called the 'sardine method.' After a deep trench was dug, the first line of unfits were stood at the edge and shot in the back of the head so they fell forward into the grave. Then the next set of unfits had to lie down on top of the bodies and were then shot. Another layer was ordered to lie on top of those bodies, then the next and so on."

"Sometimes we could get five or six layers," Dorsch said.

I had a blank look frozen on my face. It was all I could do not to scream and jump at their throats. Two men, one of them who had taken the Hippocratic Oath to save lives with his training, were talking about mass murder with far less emotion than they would discuss the last soccer scores. The driver did not even appear interested in the conversation.

"Ja, the sardining helped, but we had other problems," Dorsch said. "The first was that the traditional method of execution was to have three soldiers shoot the victim at the same time. This tradition arose to spare the feelings of the executors. But it was too inefficient, much too slow. As we became overwhelmed with necessary executions, we stopped the practice of having three men fire simultaneously and had a single shooter place a well-placed shot at the back of the head. As a medical man, I can say that one shot usually did the job as well and humanely as three."

"Three was unnecessary," Vogler agreed. "Especially with the women and children."

My hand had found the door handle. I had an urge to leap from the car. I felt suffocated. I was a trapped animal, a mute witness to the indescribable horror of two educated, professional men talking about murdering thousands of helpless people, men, women, children of all ages. All because of a crazed notion that they were superior to their victims.

When Dorsch started explaining how more efficient it was to herd people into a building and set it on fire than shooting, I broke in, and asked, "It's still going on?"

"Going on? You mean the cleansing? Of course, it is. However, a more efficient way has been found to deal with the problem. My understanding is only about a million were eliminated by our Einsatzgruppen units, is that correct, Colonel?"

"I have heard a slightly higher figure."

Over a million people. Human beings. *Shot by hand, individually by individuals.* Not "statistics" killed by bombs or in battles during the blind fury of war, but shot one by one by other human beings. People

simply pulled out of their houses, off the streets, out
of line at the bakery, and murdered. What kind of
animals could do such a thing? I felt as if I had
stepped out of my own world, straying into some
other dimension where everything was backward,
where evil was good. For a moment I wondered if
the two were joking with me, that it was some sort
of SS mind game played on new initiates, something
like a fraternity party snipe hunt. Had either one of
them shown the slightest emotion, I would have figured they were faking it and that it was a joke. But
they discussed the situation with total scientific detachment—the kind of scary bullshit science the Nazis were consumed with.

"What is the more efficient way that was found?"
I asked. I didn't want to know, but I felt drawn by
the sheer horror of what I had heard to hear more.

"The camps, of course. The process was enor-
mously sped up. What is the matter, Wolfhardt, you
look ill?"

"The road, the winding road, I've always gotten
sick on mountain roads. They say it's an inner ear
problem." Something occurred to me, and I used it
to distract them from their focus on me. "But the
Einsatzgruppen troops, there have been problems,
haven't there? The soldier in the hospital corridor
yesterday . . ."

"Yes," Dorsch said, "that soldier is an example of
the problems facing the project. We found an interesting phenomenon occurred among those SS assigned to do the killings. Some men were not able
to continue long term, especially when it came to
eliminating the women and children. Yet others not
only operated efficiently, but seemed to enjoy it.
Some men were able to pull the trigger after simply
being told that it was their duty to der Führer. Oth-

ers needed more persuasion, to be told that it was a moral thing to do, that they were exterminating an enemy, even if the person to be terminated was a small baby. We needed to know why different men had different reactions to the situation. So now, Wolfhardt, you have discovered what our Grunberg project is about."

I nodded. "You're examining men, testing them to see if they can take the killings. More to the point, you're figuring out what the best motivating factors are."

"Excellent, Herr Hauptsturmfuhrer. You see, Vogler, I told you he was a quick study."

"He looks green to me," Vogler said.

"The road," I said. "But if more efficient ways have been found, what is the necessity—oh, I see, someone always has to do it, correct? Even if it's assembly line, like that American, what was his name, Henry Ford, even if it's done efficiently, still someone has to do . . . it."

"Yes, there's always a need for individual action, but also for the individual units," Dorsch said. "It's true that the camps now take care of the mass exterminations, but the final solution still requires that we have SS units who can handle matters on a local level. Someone has to round up these vermin, and sometimes that requires hunting them down. This will become especially true when we occupy Britain and the American continent. Can you imagine how many Einsatzgruppen we will need to ferret out the virus carriers and unfits in an area the size of America? With all its forests and mountains?"

Vogler turned in his seat again to lecture me. "We have developed what we call 'poacher units.' They are the creation of der Führer and Himmler putting their heads together. At first people were simply

rounded up. They were told they were being trans-
ported to another area, to a camp, or were simply
told they would be questioned and released. A different type of unit was needed after word spread
among our targets that everyone being arrested was
being eliminated. Pockets of resistance arose, such
as in Warsaw, and there are many instances of Jews
and Gypsies fleeing into the forests to hide. For
those hiding in the forests, der Führer realized that
there are many men in our jails for poaching game."

"A successful poacher must be a good hunter, a
good shot," Dorsch said. "Why should they be
wasted in jail when they can go into the forests and
hunt down the unfits who are hiding there? So der
Führer ordered that these criminals be put to good
use. But we have found that many of them are unfit
for the task When word got around the prisons what
the task was, there were many volunteers. Those volunteers, many of whom were incarcerated for violent acts, proved much more effective than the
common poachers. We are studying a cross section
of men at the hospital, some who adapted well to
the work, others, like the man you witnessed, who
are too weak to assist in the program."

"Trying to find out why some men enjoy the task
and others feel like murderers," I said.

Something in my tone ticked off Vogler. "Not
murderers," he said, "but executioners. Every society
in history has had a need for executioners to ensure
that the public is safe from antisocial types who
would do harm. Der Führer has instructed us that
the Jew spreads his disease by violating Aryans with
his blood. He is a rapist who hides in the dark to
attack our young girls, to spread his seed and disease. Those of us who have the strength and con-

viction to carry out der Führer's command take up
the slack for the weaklings."

His tone didn't leave any doubt who he thought
of as a weakling. "What's going on now," I said, "is
we're a poaching unit, hunting down Jews?"

"Exactly." Dorsch rubbed his hands together.
"This is an excellent opportunity to have the men
track down and exterminate vermin in the actual
conditions they experience in the field. Having the
men perform under actual conditions is so much
more valuable than what we are able to provide at
the hospital."

I thought about the building surrounded by barb-
wire. Was it sturdier to make it soundproof? Is that
what was going on inside it? Men were committing
murders? Killing people in cold blood so that this
sick bastard of a doctor beside me could see their
reactions?

Now I knew what Hildegarde Dietrich meant
when she said her project was exactly opposite to
Dorsch's. He was studying more efficient ways to
eliminate the populations in the conquered areas.
She was figuring out how to populate them with
people having blond hair, blue eyes, and shit for
brains.

"We're here," Vogler said.

"Here" was a pleasant viewpoint meadow on a
ridge that gave us sweeping views of the areas below.
A gourmet picnic was set out for Dorsch, Vogler,
and me. The men on the half-tracks, the poachers,
spread out to do a sweep down the hillside. A radio
operator stayed with us to relay messages from a reconnaissance plane that was spotting the prey.
Dorsch and Vogler drank wine and ate bread,
cheese, and sausages while they used binoculars to
get close-ups of the action below. They sounded like

two kids arguing over a game of marbles. I realized that there were two different units. Vogler and Dorsch had made opposing bets as to which unit would capture the most undesirables.

I stood around like a mechanized zombie. I smiled when I was supposed to smile, laughed when it was called for, agreed when it was necessary. But my mind had shut down, and I was operating purely off nervous energy. The thought occurred to me that the atrocities taking place, the mass murder apparently of millions, wasn't known to the Allies. If Roosevelt and Churchill knew it, they kept it under their hats. Wild Bill hadn't dropped a hint to me that I might encounter this kind of insanity. The fact that the Jews were brutally treated and imprisoned was common knowledge. And the Russians were always howling about how many of their people—and soldiers—had been killed by the Germans or were working as slave laborers in German war factories.

But it was all thought of as being in a combat context, even the civilian deaths. I didn't know what "efficient" mode of death was being used at the camps, but the concept that thousands of men were being trained to perform cold-blooded murder was enough to fry my brains.

The call came in that captures had been made. We rode part of the way down, then left the car and walked in thick forest. At first I was curious as to why the prisoners weren't just brought out to us, but the reason struck me as we walked—the people were to be killed, buried in the dense forest. I hoped to God it was over before we got there.

We found them in a clearing, a younger and older man, a woman and two children, boys about eight and ten, huddled together and surrounded by SS. From the explanation given to the two officers by the poacher noncom in charge, the older man was the father of the younger one and the woman. The children belonged to the woman. The woman's husband had been eliminated a year earlier in a poacher action.

I stood a little apart from the group. My hand kept going to the Walther P38 on my hip. But there weren't enough bullets in the clip to hit even half the SS present, even if I managed to get off more than two shots before I was mowed down.

I sensed someone beside me and flinched as a little girl came up next to me. She was about five, a pretty little thing with big brown eyes. She looked at me gravely and took my hand. Her mother screamed for her to run. She looked frightened as her mother was silenced by the threat of an SS. She took my hand.

I stared down at her, at the hand in mine. I was petrified. My breathing stopped, my heart stopped, the world stopped spinning.

Vogler was suddenly beside me. "Is your pistol loaded, Herr Hauptsturmfuhrer Wolfhardt?"

I stared at him.

"I asked if your pistol was loaded."

I don't know what I said. I'm not even sure it was German. Something dribbled out of my mouth, some nonsense, maybe they weren't even words.

"Shoot the child!" he snapped to the noncom.

I turned my back on him and walked away. He called after me, and I kept walking. I fought a terrible urge to turn and pull the pistol and fire and fire and—

I heard a shot. My knees gave out on me and I stumbled and dropped to the ground. More shots. Not the blast of machine gun fire, but individual shots. Six people. Six shots. Nothing wasted.

FIVE

I was sitting on the fender of the staff car smoking a cigarette when Dorsch and Vogler came out of the bushes. They were in high spirits, laughing and talking. Their jolly mood disappeared when they saw me.

We got into the car with a cold silence among us. We hadn't gone more than a hundred meters over the rough terrain when Vogler twisted in his seat.

"You know, of course, that your reluctance to do your duty will be reported. I suspect that it will affect your next assignment." He rolled down his window and spit out. "In our group, we had a Dirlewanger box. Men without the stomach to do their duty went into it. They came out of it either as killers . . . or dead."

Dorsch smiled with false sympathy. "I suggest you write home for heavy winter socks. You have not fulfilled your obligation of Blutkitt."

I was no longer mortified or petrified. "Herren, I was selected for the present assignment by

Reichsfuhrer-SS Himmler and der Führer. I will be having private conversations with both of them. I would hope that I will not have to explain that I am not physically up to giving blood because I was diverted from my duty to der Führer by being forced to participate in a mission for which I had received no training."

I couldn't have gotten a better reaction if I'd shoved Herr Colonel's swagger stick up their asses. One thing about bullies—they can always be bullied. By the time we reached the hospital, they had both adopted the intimate *du* in addressing me, as opposed to the formal *zie.*

We all laughed heartily at their jokes and sipped fine brandy from Vogler's silver flask. By the time we got back to the hospital, we were downright jovial.

Parting, I clicked my heels smartly and snapped an enthusiastic *Heil Hitler!* By the time I reached my quarters, I was more relaxed and mellowed out than I'd been since I got word that I was being jerked off the pitcher's mound and into an army uniform.

Isn't life funny? Full of twists and curves. It's like watching a movie—you see someone driving down a road, and something happens that sends them off on another road, one that they never would have driven. I guess that day I slid off the main road and onto a detour. When it happened, so many other things about life, love, and the pursuit of happiness, what make Arnie the Barber tick, all fell into place. I no longer resented being selected for this mission. I was no longer even pissed at Donovan. He was wrong about the Babe—like I said, the Babe did more for baseball than Cobb, and if you counted walks as singles, his on-base percentage dwarfed Cobb's, as did his slugging average.

For the first time in my life I was enveloped in a warm cocoon of peace and tranquillity. At peace with myself, instead of constantly driven, worrying about my next pitch, worrying about how to get out of the war and back onto the pitcher's mound.

Suddenly, like a strike of lightning, when I had gotten onto my feet in the forest and walked to the car and lit up a cigarette from a pack I'd found in the glove compartment, I knew exactly what I was going to do with the rest of my life.

I was going to kill those two mutherfuckers *and* their boss, Adolf. If I got my hands on that prick Himmler, I was going to waste him, too.

Having reached that decision, "the rest of my life" was a contradiction in terms.

SIX

That night, I sat in the cottage, and stared out the window, a bottle of German dark in one hand, a cigarette in the other. I liked cigarettes. Like good beer and good women, they're soothing to the soul. But I gave up weeds because in the days when I smoked regularly, I'd wake up in the mornings feeling like a herd of elephants had trampled my chest. I hated making love to women who smoked, too. It was like kissing an ashtray. But now that I was under a self-imposed death sentence, I figured that smoking—along with all the beer and women I could get—weren't unreasonable goals.

Four beers hadn't drowned out the scene in the forest and the little girl with big eyes. It would haunt me for the—*hey, don't worry about that,* I told myself, *I'm not going to live that long anyway.* When I got back to the cottage earlier, I'd gone in and thrown up, but the bad taste in my mouth wouldn't go away.

"How could they do it?"

"*They're animals.*"

I almost jumped out of my skin. It was Hans the orderly. I'd spoken aloud, thinking I was alone. I hadn't heard him come in.

"What'd you say?"

"I told you they're animals."

It took a moment for the fact that we were speaking English to sink in. His was heavily accented with German.

"I spent some time in the States after the last war," he said, "staying with my daughter in Cleveland. I used to watch the Indians play, I was a big fan of amerikanisches Schlagballspiel."

"That's a mouthful just to say baseball."

"We Germans never make anything simple."

"I played for Brooklyn."

"I never saw you play, I left before your time, but I read about you. For years after I left, my daughter occasionally mailed me the sports page from the *Cleveland Plain Dealer.*" He nodded at the gun. "Put it away. *I play ball.*"

I had the automatic pistol, pointed at his gut, without even realizing it.

"Do you know what I saw today?" I asked.

"Everybody at the hospital knows what happened today. To you, it was a life-shattering moment. To me, it is just another day in hell."

"How could they? What sort of human beings—no, don't tell me they're animals, I don't want to hear that. They're not animals, they're human beings raised in a civilized society. I don't have any problem with Hitler being a nutcase, it happens sometimes, a guy gets a fixation on something like Jews or Negroes or paying taxes and goes off the deep end. But what Dorsch and Vogler described today was something beyond individual insanity, something that the whole nation has to be involved

in. Hans, I was raised in Germany until I was thirteen years old. The people I knew weren't any different than the ones I've known in America."

Hans shrugged. "I've thought about it, a thousand
times, a thousand nights in which I wake up, trying
to understand how a man can shoot a child in the
head. And then another. And another."

"Stop it!" I opened another beer and took a long
swig. I had a buzz in my head but I still felt numb.

Hans said, "I heard that there were problems between you and the two senior officers, but the three
of you appeared to be comrades when I saw you
earlier."

"They got on my ass because I wouldn't kill a
child in cold blood, but I threw them a knuckleball,
one that wobbled at their heads all the way to the
plate. I told them I'd tell der Führer I wouldn't be
able to give blood."

Hans chuckled. "Very good. That will hold them
for a while. But the word is that you have violated
the Bluttkitt. They will smile to your face, but will
be making plans behind your back. There will be
repercussions, but let's hope not until after the
transfusion."

"What is this Bluttkitt thing? I'm not familiar with
the word."

"The blood bond wasn't around when you lived
in Germany, it came in with the Nazis, and it is only
used among the SS. I've heard der Führer got the
concept from a history of Genghis Khan that Himmler sent as a Christmas present. The concept is that
blood spilled binds together all those involved. It
started with the Night of the Long Knives, in which
Himmler and others proved their loyalty by murdering Nazis who opposed Hitler, men with whom
they had laughed and drunk and fought together.

When the war started and Hitler began what he calls
his 'cleansing' of bloodlines, it was no longer a small
cadre of SS who were involved in murder, but many
thousands. They began a crime of unprecedented
scope in the history of the world, something that
will haunt the world when its ugliness is revealed.
To ensure that all are implicated in the mass murders, they demand that other SS participate in the
crimes."

"They're scared, that's why they want others to
participate."

"Yes, exactly, together they are a gang of violent
bullies, but separate them from the pack, and they
become rabbits."

"But how? How? How do normal people—"

"Normal? I don't know what that word means anymore. If you mean that before they put on uniforms
and began murdering people, they were not insti-
tutionalized as criminally insane, yes, they were like
the rest of us. Perhaps it is just a matter of statistics."

"What do you mean?"

"In a city of a hundred thousand people, do you
think it's possible that there are a hundred bad people? I mean, really bad, people who kill, rape, rob,
or commit other violent crimes?"

"A hundred violent criminals in a city of hundred
thousand? Probably."

"There you have it. One out of a thousand has
the potential to be a homicidal maniac. There are
eighty million Germans. Statistically, that means
there are eighty thousand potential murders in the
country."

I shook my head. "No, it's not a matter of statistics, that's too easy to account for what's going on
here. You don't kill on the scale they were talking
about, millions of deaths, without millions of people

being involved directly or indirectly and tens of millions more knowing about it and telling more tens of millions. That means most of the country has bloody hands. No, what happened here isn't about statistics, it's about evil. Your pal Adolf opened the Hell Gates, and demons flew out, like one of those viruses he's so frightened of, taking over the minds of all eighty million Germans. That means I should shoot you right now, because it doesn't look like any of you missed getting infected."

Hans sat down and took the cigarette and beer I offered. He said, "It fascinates you, doesn't it? Your rational mind rejects what you saw today. But you know your eyes didn't lie."

"It fascinates me only in the sense of standing at the reptile cage in a zoo and wondering what it would be like to stick my hand in. What I saw today, what you described as happening on a mass scale, is such an extreme side of human nature that it defies rational explanation. I can understand mob mentality, the lynch mobs of the American South, Kristallnacht when mobs all over Germany went after Jews. Mob chemistry creates in people the same sort of mindless violence that coon dogs experience when they're ripping apart a cornered raccoon. But that's not what's happening here; these aren't crimes of the moment, done during an adrenaline high. Cold-blooded mass exterminations are being performed on the same sort of systematic basis that they produce airplane engines. *By ordinary people.*

"There are two types, as Dorsch told me, the ones who enjoy it and the ones who have to be convinced that it's their duty and morally correct. I can see that they're afraid of the ones that enjoy it because they can't be controlled. They might turn on them next. It's the 'normal' ones that can be convinced to do evil that they want. That's what the program is all about, discovering what would make an otherwise ordinary person commit a heinous crime. I need to know that, too. Before I die, I need to know how you krauts get ordinary human beings to commit mass murder of innocent people. I need to know that. I can't go to my grave without knowing how an ordinary Joe can put a gun to a child's head and pull the trigger."

"You're drunk."

"I've only had a couple beers."

He nudged an empty schnapps bottle on the floor with his foot. It rolled toward four empty beer bottles.

"Yeah, those too."

"You have to keep yourself together. The Führer arrives tomorrow."

"Tomorrow? Dorsch said it might not be for a week."

"Dorsch doesn't know; probably even Vogler won't know until minutes before it happens. Even I can't tell you the exact time. The Führer's security people find that surprise is a good method of protection."

"How do you know he's arriving tomorrow?"

"One of my contacts pumps gas for the Obersalzberg vehicles. He heard two of the Führer's radio operators talking about having to get a relay antenna into place on the mountain above the hospital tonight. The Führer keeps in continuous radio contact with his generals. The radio operators are always one step ahead, getting the equipment set up."

"Okay, what's the plan? I was told that you people needed a type A, Aryan type, for your plan to kill the Führer."

"Did they tell you how it would be done?"

"No, but I can guess. You stick a bomb in a briefcase, I put it down near the Führer when I go in for the transfusion, I give blood, walk away, and Adolf gets blown to pieces."

"Your chances of getting near the Führer with a bomb in a briefcase are about as good as Brooklyn beating the Yankees in the next World Series. That's why your superiors were told that we would use polio."

"Polio? How am I to get polio into the—wait a minute, *you're going to infect me with polio so I can transmit it to Adolf*? Are you people fuckin' nuts? You know what that would do to me?"

"No immediate harm would come to you, that was understood. It takes a while for the disease to take effect. The moment the Führer showed any symptoms of disease, you would be taken prisoner by the Gestapo. It is assumed that before you permitted yourself to be taken by the Gestapo or experienced painful symptoms, you would have, ah, completed the last part of the mission—"

"This is a suicide mission? I infect Adolf and kill myself?"

"Of course, that has been understood from the beginning."

Boy, I must have really pissed off Wild Bill. Yesterday, had I known this, I would have packed my bags, hopped on my horse, and headed into the sunset. Even now, the idea of affecting myself with a loathsome disease sent quivers through my crotch. But as long as I can kill myself . . .

I waved my beer bottle at him. "You know what they say, Scharfuhrer—in for a penny, in for a pound."

"The polio plan has been terminated. Our con-

tact was to steal it from an experimental medical
laboratory where he worked. Allied bombers recently destroyed the lab—and our man."

"Okay, so what's the backup plan?"

"I am in the process of finalizing it. It is better
that you be told exactly when you need to. That
way . . ."

"Yeah, if the Gestapo cuts off my balls and sticks
them in my mouth, I won't give it away."

"In the meantime, you need to get psychologically
prepared to meet the Führer."

"Tell me about your leader. What makes the bastard tick?"

"Like all of us, he has his likes and dislikes, his prej-
udices and his real or imagined view of the world and
how he fits into it. But to understand the man, you
have to realize that the Führer's thinking is dominated by the concept of *blood*. He is obsessed with
the notion of purity of blood, even his own blood.
He has his blood drawn by leeches because he be-
lieves it helps keep it pure. And he has Dr. Morell
store vials of his blood. He won't eat meat because
it contains animal blood. He's a vegetarian, with
contempt for meat eaters. He says the strongest animal in the world, the elephant, is also a vegetarian."
Hans laughed. "Sometimes at the dinner table when
his staff is eating wurst, he threatens to have blood
sausage made from his blood for them to eat."

"Did they—"

"Not yet, but who knows when dealing with the
Führer."

"That's his thing about the Jews, the blood thing?"

"He considers Jews a race, not a religion. The
blood sin is a mixing of bloods between races, regardless of whether it's Jewish blood, Negroid, or

any other type, but those mixtures get his biggest tirades. In his mind, the infection of German soldiers by syphilis in their blood during the prior Great War, and a conspiracy by Jews, defeated the old Reich."

"Syphilis? Was it that epidemic?"

"In his mind it was." Hans gave me a strange look, as if he suddenly wondered if he could trust me. "I have been in the Führer's confidence for over twenty years, at his side, opening his mail, seeing his most personal communicates, eavesdropping on the most secret conversations. Do you know why he's so obsessed with purity of blood?"

"Because he's a Jew?" It was a wild-ass guess.

Hans shook his head. "There is a fear in all Germans that Jewish blood may be found in our backgrounds. In Hitler's case, his father was born out of wedlock, the son of a housekeeper or maid in a wealthy household. There have been rumors that the man who impregnated her, the head of the household, was Jewish. Although there is no real proof, because of the Führer's position, even the whispers are dangerous. Rumors have flown since he had the village where the supposed union between his grandmother and the Jew took place destroyed." Hans shook his head. "He is concerned about the possibility of Jewish blood in his veins, but of even more significant import is that the Führer is probably syphilitic."

My jaw dropped.

Hans lowered his voice, as if he feared someone was listening at the keyhole.

"The source," Hans laughed, "of the accusation has become known as 'the blue manuscript.' It is the least talked about—and most feared—secret in the Third Reich. When he came to power, the Führer ordered the Gestapo to seize his medical records from every doctor and hospital he'd been treated by in his entire life. The files came to Himmler, including one from the hospital at Pasewalk where he was treated during the prior war. The blue manuscript is made up of medical records stating that soldier Adolf Hitler has syphilis, the type that affects the nervous system and slowly causes a degeneration of the body. When you see him, you will notice that his left hand shakes. And his walk—he no longer has the forceful strut of the old days. He has started to walk like an old man. And he is only fifty-five years old."

"My God, if that ever came out—"

"No one would believe it. But it is the source of his preoccupation with infection, syphilis, and blood taint in general, what the Jewish-Austrian physician Freud would perhaps have called a pathological obsession. The Führer even devoted a large section in his book, *Mein Kampf,* to the subject of syphilis, ranting about it over and over. One of his favorite tirades about your President Roosevelt is his claim that the man's confined to a wheelchair not by polio but syphilis."

"That's ridiculous. Does Hitler think the Jews gave him syphilis?"

Hans shrugged. "Who knows? If you make the suggestion, he will probably adopt it.'

"The guy needs a head doctor."

"Jewish astrology, that's what the Führer calls psychiatry. He rejects all theories based upon Jewish authorities. I ask you, my friend, when you take all the meat off of science and leave only the bones, what are you left with? If you told him Columbus was Jewish, German geography books would be changed to show the earth as flat. He is so pathological about blood and infection; he will speak one moment of Jewish blood tainting the lifeblood of the nation and the next of a 'Jewish virus' that pollutes the blood of Aryans—as if Jewish blood is an actual virus."

I shook my head. It was mind-boggling. This fruitcake had been halfway to being Master of the World.

"How does syphilis affect his sex life? Doesn't he pass it on to his women friends?"

Hans gave me another strange look.

"He doesn't have sex," I offered. "Or he's queer."

"No, he's not homosexual. But he has . . . unusual sexual needs."

"What do you mean?"

Hans got up. "Enough talk for tonight."

"Sit down, it's not enough. If I'm going to die because of this bastard, I want to know everything there is about him. Put it out on the table, pal."

Hans lit a cigarette and took in a deep drag, slowly letting it out through his nose. "The Führer sometimes says that he fears intimate relationships with a woman because he fears infection. He has said so many times around the lunch table. In truth, I believe he fears infecting the women, perhaps out of respect for them, perhaps out of fear that his syphilis will be disclosed. But there is another twist to the story of the Führer's sex life. It comes from a man who was once very close to the Führer—Otto Strasser. Do you know who he is?"

"Not really. The name sounds familiar," I added, to temper my ignorance.

"Strasser and his brother Gregor were early leaders in the Nazi party, becoming members in 1920. Gregor became, in fact, the second most popular and powerful member of the party, after the Führer himself. The brothers opposed Hitler's domination of the party and were marked for termination in the Blood Purge of 1934. Gregor was murdered in the purge, but Otto fled, finally settling in Canada, I believe. I knew them both, of course, and while my feelings for them were tempered by my loyalty to the Führer, I found them both to be men of high principle, at least in the political realm. They were leftist and opposed the Führer's alliance with big business and his anti-Semitism. However, Otto Strasser naturally hates the Führer.

"Last year Strasser made an accusation to your OSS about the Führer's sex life that was so bizarre, an OSS agent was sent over to ask me if I could verify it. The accusation was about Geli Raubal, Hitler's niece, who was twenty years old when she and her mother moved in with Hitler to keep house for him in 1929. At that time, as head of the party, he was a leading political force in the country but would not be chancellor for another four years. Two years after they moved in, Geli killed herself with Hitler's pistol. Shot herself in the chest. That Hitler was madly in love with her despite the age difference—he was twenty years older—is not disputed. He often has said that she was the only woman he would have ever considered marrying."

"Hitler killed her," I said. "He fucked his niece, incest, then murdered her when he found out she was fucking someone else."

Hans frowned at me. "You Americans have too much of a fondness for motion pictures. They infect your brains like the Führer's viruses. It's true, Hitler found out the niece was having an affair with his chauffeur and broke it up. However, the scenario is even worse than you imagine. Strasser told OSS agents that he had grown close to Geli because he felt sorry for the young woman. Perhaps his real motive was to find some scandal about the relationship between Geli and her uncle. What he learned was so bizarre, that he was never able to use it because he didn't think anyone would believe it.

"Geli told him that rather than having normal sex with her, her uncle would make her undress until she stood before him naked. He would then lie on his back on the floor and have her squat over him. He would examine her female parts at close range, getting excited as he did. When his excitement was reaching its peak, he insisted that she urinate on him."

"Excuse me?"

"Piss, Herr Hauptsturmfuhrer, he had the young girl piss in his face. While he masturbated."

Jesus H. Christ. And I remembered something else weird about the guy. The OSS psychologist who was part of the team that briefed me said they had information about a kinky night Adolf had with a German actress. The woman, Rene Mueller, spent an evening with the Führer. They both undressed and she expected to get into bed and have sex—instead, Adolf got down on the floor and begged her to kick him. She refused, and he pleaded with her for the punishment, groveling and condemning himself as unworthy to touch her. She finally kicked him.

Rene Mueller told her director about the incident. And committed suicide.

Adolf had an interesting track record with kinky sex and suicidal women. A cynic like me might suspect he was smothering potential scandal by having the witnesses to his perversions killed.

"I'm right," I told Hans.

Hans frowned at me. "Right about what?"

"He killed his niece. Or had her killed to shut her up."

"How do you conclude that from the situation?"

I leaned forward and locked eyes with him. "Hans, not many people commit suicide—*by shooting themselves in the chest.*"

SEVEN

June 3

The hospital's air raid siren whined and we all turned out with brass shined and collars starched. As I waited for der Führer's motorcade, I had to admit the guy traveled in style. The road leading into the hospital was lined with flowers and Nazi flags. We stood like schoolchildren waiting for him. Every woman had a bouquet of flowers to shower on him. The first vehicles to arrive were four truckloads of SS. They poured out of the back of the trucks and spread out. There were a hundred machine guns at the ready before motorcycles and smaller vehicles loaded with SS came into view. When der Führer's open Mercedes rolled down the reception line, cheering broke out, and women rushed the car to throw flowers.

The thing that would stay with me for the rest of my life—that phrase that kept jumping off my tongue—was the expression on the faces of the women. You would have thought Jesus H. Christ had just arrived, walking on water. These women were having a religious experience. From the looks of pure ecstasy, some of them were creaming their pants.

What caliber of man could cause this response? The guy who climbed out of the Mercedes, wearing rather ridiculous horse-riding pants, didn't look like a god or even Charles Atlas material. He was more the stuff of Charlie Chaplin. Frankly, der Führer could have starred in silent movies. Funny ones. He would have made a great waiter in a long white apron who trips and dumps a tray of food in a diner's lap.

About five-eight or -nine and maybe one-fifty or one-sixty, he had dark hair parted on the right with a forelock thrown over to his left temple, that funny little sawed-off Charlie Chaplin paintbrush mustache above thin lips, a weak chin, narrow shoulders, a sunken chest, and long feet paddling on the end of short legs.

He looked more like an officious clerk in a government office than the man who wanted to be Master of the World.

What made this guy special? Okay, he sent his goose-steppers all over Europe. But Germany had a population much larger than any other European country. He whipped France because his army was bigger, better equipped, and better led—not to mention the krauts didn't play by the rules, invading neutral Belgium to make an end run around the Maginot Line. Except for Russia, all the other countries he invaded from Norway to Greece were a fraction the size of Germany. And he jumped on the Russians with a surprise attack after signing a peace treaty.

The guy loses the air and sea war with the British to the west, so he turns around and invades the Russkies? Opening a second front before he wins the first? When his boys grind to a halt on the Eastern Front, bogged down in subzero temperatures, he declares war on us, the mightiest industrial nation on earth, after his Nip pals hit us at Pearl? This is the work of a military genius? Stalin has been kicking his ass, Allied bombers have been turning his cities into rubble, we took North Africa and are coming up the Italian boot, and there's talk about *when*—not if—we'll wade ashore on the French coast.

So what makes this guy special? How come grown men weep with joy when they see him? Why do women cream their pants at the sight of him?

And what makes ordinary people put a gun to the head of a small child and pull the trigger for him? Maybe I'll find out before I kill him.

Dr. Dorsch and Colonel Vogler were at the front of the reception line, with the entire staff lined up behind them. Hans was in the group escorting der Führer as soon as Adolf climbed out of the Mercedes. I placed myself near the end of the line so I could get a good look at the man. When Adolf was almost abreast with me, Hans whispered something to an SS officer, who in turn whispered to der Führer.

Suddenly I was facing the man who had conquered Europe. He stepped up to me and locked eyes. I was so startled I nearly stumbled backward. His eyes were shocking. Milky blue, the color of a late-summer sky, they were intense, burning. Curious and probing to the point of being impolite. His face was very pale, and that made his eyes even more startling.

"Mein Führer," I said. I was shaken so bad, it was

the only thing that came out, and it sounded false to my ear. I raised my hand in a *Heil Hitler*. It seemed to break the spell. He took those invasive orbs off my face and stared curiously at my hands.

"Let me see your hands."

I was startled again. And confused.

"My hands?"

"Your hands," an adjutant snapped. "Show der Führer your hands."

I held out my hands. Adolf Hitler, chancellor of Germany, godhead of the Third Reich, stared at them.

Now I have to tell you that I have very special hands. They're big, with long fingers and baskets for palms, but my hands aren't bear paws. They're world-class, elegant hands, the kind a concert pianist would make a deal with the devil to get. My hands are what got me into the majors. I have power in my shoulders, but it's my hand and wrist that control the ball, that send it where it needs to go.

Der Führer smiled at me. Yeah, really smiled. And nodded. "Very good," he said, "very good."

What the fuck was very good? This guy have some sort of fetish about hands? Christ, is he going to make me take off my shoes to examine my feet next?

He moved on, Hans and his personal cadre moving with him.

EIGHT

I was in my room, smoking another coffin nail, a Turkish cigarette that tasted like dog shit, when Hans came in. As soon as he closed the door, he grinned and rubbed his hands together.

"Very good, very good."

"Why don't you clue me in on what's so good?"

He lit one of my cigarettes and sat down, stretching out his legs.

"The Führer has some personality quirks—"

"Yeah, he likes to kill people, mostly Jews."

"Besides that. One of his traits is that he makes up his mind instantly about a person. He either likes or dislikes the person on sight. And once he makes up his mind, he rarely changes it. When I lived in Cleveland, there was an expression about a 'steel-trap mind.' It seemed to imply that once the person made up his mind about something, he locked on it like the jaws of a trap on an animal's leg. The Führer has exactly that type of mind. If there is anything that frustrates those around him, especially the generals conducting his war, it's the fact it's so difficult, or impossible, to get him to change his mind once he decides upon a course of action."

"So I passed the on-sight test?"

"Yes, it's your hands. I hoped it would be your eyes; I never thought about your hands."

"Hands? Eyes?"

"His mother's eyes. He was very close to her. She's been dead for a long time, but he still worships at her shrine, you might say. Sometimes he meets a person with the same shade of eyes. It always affects him."

"Did she have big hands, too?"

"Some people judge others by the bumps on their head. The Fuhrer looks at their hands. His own hands are quite graceful, the hands of an artist, which he is. They say that what most impressed him about Albert Speer, the Minister of Armaments, is his hands. Speer was just an architect, but one whose hands greatly impressed the Fuhrer."

"Hey, no shit, that's great. Maybe instead of killing this asshole, I'll just hang around, flick my fingers, and get a big job. Maybe he'll put me in charge of making bullets to kill little kids with." I got up and walked around to bleed off some of my anger. I was crying in my beer and I knew it. "Sorry," I said, sitting back down. "I just dropped in on this nightmare; you must have been living it for a long time. How did you get involved with the OSS?"

"My son married a Jewess. I got them out of the country in '39, convincing them to move to Cleveland where my daughter had immigrated. But my grandson, a boy of twenty, slipped back into Germany because he was in love with a girl he had gone to university with. She was also Jewish. By then, it was not easy to come and go. The boy and his girl had false papers and were arrested trying to cross the border into Switzerland. I didn't learn about it for months because he was using a false name. By the time I was able to trace what happened to him, he was dead."

"Killed by the SS? Einsatzgruppen?"

"Gestapo. They believed he was a member of an underground group helping Jews escape. They killed him slowly to find out who his contacts were. Had he actually known any, he could have given up the names and died quickly. Unfortunately, he was telling the truth when he said that he knew nothing."

Hans was made of iron. He spoke as neutrally as if he was reading a report about the incident. But there was emotion in his eyes. Not hurt, the years had washed away the pain of loss. What I saw was anger. I changed the subject. "What's the plan, Hans? Do I use my lovely hands to strangle Adolf?"

"He's to be killed with a bomb."

"How?"

"The Führer's room is directly above a waiting room on the first floor of the hospital. That entire wing of the hospital has been evacuated to ensure the Führer's privacy. The waiting room isn't being used. There's a small washroom that's entered from the waiting room. The bomb will go in the washroom."

"How do we get a bomb? Steal it from the armory?"

"I already have it. New weapons are frequently sent to Obersalzberg to be demonstrated for the Führer and the military chiefs. I diverted one months ago while others like it were being demonstrated. I've had it hidden, waiting for an opportunity. I am attached to Berghof security, but the opportunity hasn't arisen to use the bomb because I'm not a member of his inner circle."

"Won't the Führer's guards find it in their search?"

"It isn't there yet. We have to hide it. It's an underwater charge, relatively small and with a simple timer. The toilet reservoir is high on the wall, nearly to the ceiling. The other side of the ceiling is the floor of the Führer's bedroom. We'll put the bomb in the reservoir, set it to go off at a time we know the Fuhrer will be sleeping. When it goes off . . . the chancellor of the Third Reich will be dead."

"What do we do after that?"

"There is little chance we will escape, if that is your question. Suspicion will focus on everyone at the hospital, even me. Every person will be arrested and questioned. It won't be long before they figure out you are not Hauptsturmfuhrer Wolfhardt. My advice to you is to shoot yourself immediately after the bomb goes off."

"Thanks, pal, but how about a dash for the Swiss border? It's probably no more than two or three hours by car."

"Do you think that you can simply drive away from here? You couldn't do it before the explosion, less so afterward, not with the security that surrounds the Führer. And you don't want to let yourself be captured. Grand Inquisitor Torquemada himself could have learned lessons in torture from the Gestapo. I will quickly be in the same situation you are. Once they learn from the residue that it was a specialized marine bomb, everyone who had any access at all to the bomb at Obersalzberg will be arrested and tortured. Unlike you, I would be forced to give up the identities of other members of the underground—and I don't fool myself into believing I would withstand their methods of persuasion. It will be our duty to kill ourselves before we are captured."

I had resolved in my own mind that I would die on this mission, but I assumed that I would go down fighting. But Hans was right—if I was wounded instead of being killed, *I'd regret it the rest of my life.*

Strange, but rather than being uptight about the prospect of dying, killing myself at that, I only had a funny feeling in my dick. Like it was telling me something.

"We can't plant the bomb tonight," Hans said. "Security is too alert the first night in a new location. The operation is set for the day after tomorrow. We will play it by ear, as you Americans say. Our best chance will probably be tomorrow night, or in the morning after the operation."

A knock on the door caused both of us to freeze. It came again, not really a knock, but pounding by a fist. "Hauptsturmfuhrer Wolfhardt, open the door!"

Hans turned ashen. "Colonel Keitel, the Führer's security chief."

I opened the door and found a short, studious-appearing man with thick glasses. Like his bosses Himmler and Hitler, he looked more like a clerk than a colonel.

"Guten Abend, Herr Standartenfuhrer."

"Der Führer commands your presence."

NINE

My goddammn dick was pounding as I marched
with the colonel to the the hospital. It itched like
hell. And burned. What the hell? I wondered. Was
this some sort of nervous reaction to the murder-
suicide plot?

Keitel suddenly stopped and whipped around to
face me. "There is a matter that disturbs me,
Hauptsturmfuhrer. The fact that you have lied."

I nearly pissed my pants. "Ja?"

"About the woman."

"The woman?"

"We are aware of what took place."

"Ja." What the hell?

"Such actions do not please der Führer. You are
on a special duty list for der Führer. You know the
prohibitions, do you not?"

"Yes, of course, Herr Colonel. Ah, which one did
I violate?"

He reddened with anger. "Do you play games with
me, Wolfhardt? You know that you are not allowed

to have sex while you are on der Führer's blood list."

Hildegarde, they knew about me screwing her.

"I can explain—"

"*You cannot explain.* Marriage was expressly forbidden. Having intimate activities with any woman is expressly forbidden because of the possibility of contamination. Der Führer has been told. There was another blood donor on his way to act as backup should you be disqualified, but the man was severely injured in an accident. If der Führer decides not to go through with the operation for fear of contamination, you will be severely punished."

I was speechless. I didn't know what to say. Marriage? My confusion must have helped because Keitel's voice lost some of its lashing tone when he spoke again.

"You must understand, Herr Hauptsturmfuhrer, that it was your duty not to marry while you were on the donor list." He lowered his voice. "Der Führer has a terrible fear of contamination. He saw how his fellow soldiers were struck down by venereal disease in the previous Great War. He carries the entire Fatherland on his back. Without him, the war would be lost, the Reich would fall." Keitel tapped my on the chest with his finger. "You will not be the cause of our thousand-year Reich's fall."

"There was a blood test taken on my arrival. I am not contaminated—"

"If it were not for the results of that blood test, I can assure you, Herr Hauptsturmfuhrer, you would be a guest of the Gestapo already."

On the second floor of the hospital, Colonel Keitel knocked quietly on a door. It was answered by an orderly, who told me to enter. Adolf was sitting in a great armchair overlooking the only window in the room. He was reading papers by the light of a floor lamp standing next to the chair. He didn't look up from his reading to acknowledge my entrance. Standing with the orderly at my side, I had a peaceful moment to study Hitler. His short, brown hair, cut military fashion, fell sideways over his face. His eyebrows and trim-cut mustache were of a shade darker than the hair on his head. What most struck me about the man was a certain quality of sincerity . . . or perhaps one would call it sincerity and resolution. There was a certain air of firmness about his thin lips, and his indomitable chin exuded a convincing air of strength.

It struck me suddenly why the German people followed him, why so many had voted for his party that he was appointed chancellor. *Hitler cared.* He cared about the unfairness of the Versailles Treaty, the punishment that plunged Germany into a state of economic depression. He cared about Germany being treated as a second-rate nation when it was the greatest industrial power in Europe. He told the German people that they were great. Hell, that they deserved to be masters of the world. He told them they had a destiny to fulfill. He told them they were *winners.*

I realized that *Adolf was a great coach.* He gave his people the same kind of inspirational spiel that coaches like Connie Mack gave the Philly players that led them to nine pennants and five World Series. *Get out there and fight fight fight you can do it boys you can do it you're the best.*

Thinking about it, baseball teams aren't run much differently from how the krauts ran their country. Everything was organized, everyone followed orders, it was all a united team effort, there were no individuals—just team members, and there sure as hell wasn't any democratic action. And there

was another thing that made great coaches like
Mack and Little Napoleon McGraw—they were self-
made martyrs. They let everyone around them know
that they were sacrificing their lives for the sake of
the players and the fans.

Adolf gave the papers to the orderly. He indicated
a chair facing him, and said, "Please sit down, Herr
Hauptsturmfuhrer."

I took a seat facing der Führer. The orderly disappeared into the shadows in a corner of the room
while Adolf studied me again with those probing,
watchful eyes.

"Tell me about your wife," he said. He spoke
gravely.

What did I know about my wife? I couldn't make
it up as I went along, either. This guy had secret
police on every corner of the country. I wasn't going
to be able to fake it. I had to try another tactic. Hans
said the guy was real puritanical, like a priest, that
sort of thing. Didn't tell dirty jokes, didn't like them
told in his presence, wasn't the kind of guy to whom
you pointed out the size of a woman's knockers. He
came across as a prudish bastard—even if he did
like having women piss in his face.

"I married her because she's a good woman. Un-
spoiled. I wanted to make sure she wasn't spoiled
after I went off to war. I also wanted to remain pure
for her. And for Mein Führer."

His face lit up and he clapped his hands together.
"Jawohl, that's what I thought. I knew the moment
I saw you that you were not the type to marry anyone
but a good girl. There were reports about her, of
course, but what can you tell from a report? When
I found out she had my mother's name, I was very
pleased."

"That's one of the reasons I was attracted to her."
What the hell was his mother's name?

"I have to tell you, Herr Hauptsturmfuhrer, there
are many things about you that please me. I find it
amusing that I am to be given blood from a wolf."

"A wolf? Oh, Wolfhardt. Hard wolf."

"As you must know, Adolf is derived from the old
German word for noble wolf."

"Of course."

"I will tell you a secret, Herr Wolfhardt. I have
many times used the name 'Wolf' as a pseudonym.
And do you know what I call you SS?"

"A wolf pack?"

"Excellent." He stood up. "Come, it's time for my
evening walk. We can talk as we get exercise."

There was silence between us until we left the hospital, trailed by two SS, with two more in front. We
walked along a path where the lawn reached the
forest. I made out guards among the trees. Hans was
right about me killing der Führer and making a
break—it looked like there were more guards than
trees.

"I cannot tell you how I envy you, Herr Hauptsturmfuhrer. As a young man, I fought on the battlefield for my country, willing to give my life for the
Fatherland, but now destiny has given me another
role, a mission I must live to fulfill. I wish I was a
young man like you, able to serve the Reich on the
front lines. Or perform the special duties that our
country's destiny requires."

"Ja." It was the best I could muster as the face of
a little girl flashed in my mind.

"You probably believe that I do not have fears like
other people, but you are wrong. I have a great fear,
one that dominates my entire life. It is the fear that
I will die before I have left the Reich strong enough

to resist its enemies. The fear that the blood sin that engulfs much of the world will not be eradicated before I take my last breath. You realize, do you not, how important the matter of blood is to me? That blood is the foundation of civilization? That it is the cement that binds the brotherhood of the Schutz-staffel?"

"Of course, mein Führer," I murmured. He was the kind of guy who talked a lot but never listened to others, the kind I'd like to tie to a railroad track to get his full attention. When the tracks started vi-brating because a train was on its way, and he swore he was listening, I'd bend down and say, "About this blood thing, Adolf, you're no Thoroughbred—if you were a stallion, they'd put you to sleep rather than spending the money to feed you. You're life unfit to live."

"One creature drinks the blood of another."

We had been walking quietly, each captured by his own thoughts, when he suddenly uttered this odd statement.

"Mein Führer?"

"It is the way of the world. The Jew knows it well, he's a spider that sucked the people's blood out of its pores. But there is a way to cleanse blood. You kill the carrier of contaminated blood. War, that is what cleans blood. We lost the last war because we did not know our true enemy and let our blood be-come contaminated. The Kaiser did not understand that the war was lost because of the dilution of blood by intermarriage with non-Aryans. When the Aryan gave up his blood purity, he lost his power to win wars, to dominate, he lost his place in paradise."

He was silent for a moment. I realized he was not talking to me but to the world. Hans was right about the steel-trap mind. My presence had gotten him onto the subject of blood. Once he clamped his jaws on, it dominated his thoughts completely.

"If I save Germany, I have performed a great deed. And I can only save the Fatherland if I keep the bloodlines pure."

He stopped walking and faced me.

"Fire, that is the solution, a fire that consumes them all. Let them call us inhuman. Our duty is clear. We must build fires that destroy the two-legged animals that carry the virus."

His eyes were wide—on *fire*. His gaze was mesmerizing. His voice had lost its soft quality. It was powerful, a sound that came from deep within him and exploded out his mouth like a shot from a cannon.

He spun on his heel and went back toward the hospital, leaving me standing by myself as his personal escort rushed by.

I felt the chill of the night and pulled my coat collar up higher. I stuck a cigarette in my mouth but quickly removed it, wondering if it was on the list of prohibitions.

Hans was right—the man had magnetism. He was totally consumed with his passions. And his passions were loony tunes. In the horror of what this nutcase was doing to the rest of the world, I saw a kind of ironic pathos for the German people. They got screwed over after WWI, and things really went to hell when inflation got so insane, a loaf of bread cost a billion marks. Then along came the stock market crash in America and a worldwide depression. One thing about Adolf and his goose-steppers, they had something going for them that none of the politicians in power did—they really cared. The man and his wolf pack really cared about Germany and wanted to see the country great again. The only problem was they had a twisted vision of what made the country great. If someone had assassinated der Führer in '39, he would have gone down in history books as Adolf the Great.

Someplace along the line of life, he got his head screwed on backward. Obsessive-compulsive, like someone washing his hands all day long. Only his obsession was blood. I heard that there are people who are fascinated with their own shit, you know, like to feel it, smell it. And about a guy who drank his own piss. But what made Adolf so weird about blood?

Maybe the blue manuscript was the key. He got a dose of syphilis in the army. A guy like him would lie awake nights, imagining millions of infectious microbes marching in his veins, being carried around by his rivers of blood. And he'd look for a scapegoat for the infection. He couldn't hate himself, he was too narcissistic to blame himself. There had to be a defect in the world that caused German soldiers to get a dose of the big S. The Jews, that was it, they polluted the blood of good German soldiers, made them susceptible to VD. Caused them to lose the war. And created an economy where it took a wheelbarrow full of marks for a loaf of bread.

It was all quite logical. All you had to do with start off with a bizarre premise and keep building on it. Adolf has such a fanatical belief in his crazy ideas, he convinced millions of Germans who didn't bother to think for themselves.

Good work, Adolf. It's thinking like that that's turning your cities into rubble and will someday see guys like Ike and Monty turn Germany into one big grave. You've got the fucking virus, Adolf, and it's between your ears.

I was stomping so intensely to my cottage I almost

ran into Hildegarde without seeing her as she stepped out of the bushes near the cottage.

"Guten Abend, Herr Hauptsturmfuhrer."

"No fucking tonight," I told her. "Orders from headquarters."

"Ja, ja. Ah, are you, uh, well. Have you been experiencing any difficulty?"

"What kind of difficulty do you mean?"

"Nothing, nothing. I just, well, I know you are a donor for der Führer. Out of my love for him, I just want to make sure that you are quite well. In my role as a doctor, of course."

"Hildegarde, I am as healthy as a horse. Is that satisfactory?"

Relief washed across her face. "Ja, ja, that is perfect. Well, you have a good night, Erich. You must get your rest so your blood is strong for der Führer."

I went inside the cottage and lit my cigarette. The ambush by Brunhild and the burning in my pants had settled one thing in my mind—the bitch had given me a dose of clap. She probably sat on every Aryan-looking cock that reported to her program and saluted her. It was inevitable that she'd get nailed with something. If her Führer found out she'd passed on clap to his blood donor, we'd both be guests at the nearest Gestapo hotel.

I hit the sack, my head buzzing from my conversation with Hitler. A pack of wolves, that's what I was surrounded by. And I'd have to get by their snarling teeth to kill White Fang.

TEN

JUNE 4

Hans was standing over my bed when I awoke.

"It's time," he said.

"Time?"

"You have to report to the hospital to be examined by the Führer's physicians prior to the operation. You have already had your blood test, so it will be a visual examination. This gives us the opportunity to deliver the bomb."

I dressed and found him in the living room, smoking one of my Turkish cigarettes.

"How do we get the bomb into the hospital?" I asked.

"It's already there. I hid it in the basement the day I arrived. The operation is set for this afternoon, but you are going in early for the examination. If we hurry, we can catch the Führer in bed."

"It's almost nine. Won't the Führer be up and out of bed?"

"He's rarely up before ten. He stays up late at night, sometimes all night, talking to his cronies or having Waeger, his half-witted aide, sit and listen to him drone on endlessly about the old days."

"Okay, let's play ball."

He looked me over. "Where's your pistol?"

"What do I need that for? There are fifty SS with machine guns hanging around that place. I wouldn't stand a chance in a shoot-out."

"You need it to kill yourself with after the bomb goes off."

"Oh."

"Give me the gun, it will be easier for me to carry it in. The guards are used to me and will not look twice." He tucked the gun in his waistband under his coat. He hesitated at the door and turned to me. "Are you prepared to die today?"

"Fuck no. When that bomb goes off, I'm going to grab a machine gun from one of your Führer's wolves and shoot my way out. I don't mind dying, but I hate the preliminaries."

Approaching the guards at the hospital entrance, I tried not to look like a man who's already had his last meal. It was hard not to look grim. I felt numb inside. And distant, as if my mind and body were separate entities, with my mind about to fly away at any time. I wasn't thinking about the fact I was going to die. What struck me was that I was going to kill a man who was no ordinary mortal—he was someone children prayed to.

I thought about the children he had killed, and it steadied my resolve.

Hans identified me, and we entered. There were more guards in the reception area inside. We went through swinging doors on our right and down an empty corridor.

"The whole hospital's been evacuated," Hans said.

We paused at an open entryway three-quarters of the way down the corridor. "The waiting room," he whispered. He indicated a door across the room. "The toilet room." He pointed at the ceiling above the waiting room.

I got the idea. Adolf's bedroom.

"Stay here." He turned from the door and went down a nearby stairway that led to the basement. He came back a moment later with a sack that hung across his chest from a strap around his neck. It said "Marine Bomb" on it and must have been heavy—Hans was sweaty and out of breath. For the first time he looked rattled.

"Am I doing the right thing?" he asked me.

"What?"

He grabbed my arm. "The right thing, Wolfhardt, tell me, is this the right thing?"

"A child held my hand yesterday, a little girl. Then they shot her in the head. These are animals, not people. Think about your grandson."

He took a deep breath and wiped his forehead. "You are right, I don't know what came over me. He—you understand, I have known him and served him. Personally, he is a good man, a good man."

"Yeah, that's why he lets everyone else do his killing. Let's get this over with."

I followed him across the waiting area and was behind him as he opened the door to the toilet room. He came to an abrupt halt with an exclamation.

Colonel Keitel was seated on the toilet—reading a copy of *The Black Corps.*

We froze and stared at each other. The colonel's pants were down below his knees. His small eyes darted to the right—his pistol belt was hanging from a hook. He went for the pistol as Hans fumbled with getting out the one he'd tucked under his coat.

I shot by Hans and body-blocked Keitel, sending him into the wall. It was like hitting a cannonball. I was several inches taller, but the colonel was built broad and solid. He banged against the wall and bounced back at me, hitting me with his shoulder, ramming my solar plexus. Stunned, I swung feebly at his head with my right, hitting air. He pounded me in the stomach with piston blows, burying his fists in my stomach. I hit the wall behind me, and my knees folded. I scooted down to the floor on my ass, the wind knocked out of me.

Blurry motion off to my left told me that Hans was getting knocked around by the colonel. I saw the pistol go flying. The colonel went for the gun, and Hans ran out of the room. The colonel grabbed the gun and raced after him.

By sheer willpower, I dragged myself through the toilet room door. I got myself half-standing as Hans disappeared down the basement stairwell. The colonel pointed the gun down the stairwell. I tried to tell him not to shoot, that Hans had a bomb strapped to him, but it came out as a gasp. Then an explosion blew me to hell.

ELEVEN

Darkness and shadows, murmurs of ghost voices. I was dead. It wasn't the sort of feeling that I expected from being dead. I thought heaven and hell were both brighter. Dark shades of light slowly brightened, growing until it hurt my eyes. The light at the end of the tunnel.

But the light at the end of the tunnel became a lamp over an operating table. A face came into focus. Dr. Dorsch stared down at me.

"I'm in hell," I croaked.

"Just Bavaria," Dorsch said.

The next face was that of Colonel Vogler. He stared down at me. I flinched. For sure, he was going to shoot me between the eyes.

"Let's get him into the operating room," Dorsch said.

Jesus H. Christ. I'm not dead. Hans had warned me not to let them take me alive. They're going to

operate on me, take slices off until I told them
everything I knew. I really fucked up. I wished I *was*
dead.

I gurgled something about kill me quickly.

Vogler's face appeared over me again. Peppermint breath blew in my face. "You're a hero, Wolfhardt."

I must be in hell, I thought. How could I be a hero
of the Third Reich? I and one-armed Hans just tried
to blow der Führer to pieces.

I started moving. At least, the cart under me did.
Dorsch talked as the cart rolled into and down a
corridor.

"You've been unconscious for hours. You only got
minor injuries from the explosion, but it gave you
a concussion. Really nothing to worry about."

"Hans—"

"Yes, we know, he's a traitor, tried to kill der Führer. Your bravery in killing Hans is realized. Colonel
Keitel was killed, too."

How the hell could they figure I killed Hans? It
didn't make any sense.

"Where am I?"

"You're on your way into the operating room. The
surgical procedure on der Führer is about to be
done. He decided to go through with it despite the
attempt. It's a very minor procedure, and he needs
to get it out of the way."

The cart I was on was brought into the surgery
and docked next to another cart on which Adolf lay
on his back. He turned his head and smiled at me.

"I knew my wolf would protect me. You will not
find me or your country ungrateful. You are a hero
of the Third Reich."

Jesus H. Christ.

TWELVE

Albert Speer, Minister of Armaments and Munitions, stepped out of a staff car in front of the Berghof on the Obersalzberg. It was five minutes to ten in the morning. He was there to attend a strategy meeting.

A tall, slender man who was once der Führer's personal architect, at thirty-nine years old, he was the youngest of Hitler's top echelon. Some people believed that Speer, more than any other single person, kept the German war machine operating. He was also sometimes described as the closest thing that Hitler had to a friend. Der Führer loved to talk to Speer about architecture, about the grand monuments in the capital city called Germania he would someday build.

Officers representing the army, navy, air force, joint command, and SS were waiting in an anteroom where tea and pastries had been set out. General

Merker, representing the OHK, the high command
of the army, rushed to Speer as soon as the minister
entered the room.

"Have you heard? The invasion has begun. The
Allies have made a landing along the Normandy
coast."

"When?"

"It began around midnight. Full-scale at dawn."

"What does der Führer say? What is our response?"

Merker avoided Speer's eyes for a moment, then
pulled the armaments minister into a corner.

"Der Führer has not been notified."

"What?"

"His orderlies refuse to notify him until he awak-
ens and has his breakfast."

"That's insane."

Merker did not reply, and Speer knew why. An
Allied invasion of France was expected as inevitable.
Rumors daily flew in and out the window about
when and where it would occur. Der Führer was
convinced that Eisenhower would first feign a landing to draw the German response, then make an
actual landing at another location. No one wanted
to give der Führer bad news if he believed an actual
attack had occurred. Or be subjected to his anger if
he believed the attack was a false report.

"What does the army think?" Speer asked.

"Rommel is convinced that it is a major offensive
and not a diversionary action. He has begged der
Führer for weeks to give him authority over armored
divisions held in reserve to drive the enemy back
into the sea. But der Führer has refused the request
and insists that he alone will give the order for the
tanks to advance and only when he is convinced that
it is not a ploy. The field marshal has been calling

all morning, trying to talk to der Führer. Rundstedt can't get through, either. No calls until he rises."

"He should be advised of the matter immediately," Speer said.

"Perhaps, Herr Minister, *you* would like to be the one who enters der Führer's private quarters to tell him to come to the strategy meeting."

Speer had not become possibly the second most important man in Germany by being a fool. Der Führer would have a mind-set about the situation when the briefing began. To get him to change his mind would be as hard as talking a dog off a meat wagon.

Speer was not a military man. He was a designer with a good sense of organization. But even he realized that Rommel should not be left dangling when it was possible there was an actual Allied invasion. He found Waeger, der Führer's chief orderly, in the kitchen inspecting the preparations for his master's breakfast.

"When will der Führer be notified of the *potential* for invasion." Speer carefully chose his words.

"Soon," the orderly said, "very soon."

Waeger brushed by Speer and returned to Hitler's private area, posting himself outside der Führer's bedroom door. He had served Adolf Hitler for twelve years, but he was not allowed to enter without knocking and actually hearing der Führer's voice approving the entry. Adolf Hitler was a very private person. He had seen the man with his shirt off only once and had never seen him with his pants off. To his knowledge, his master did not undress completely even for medical doctors. His obsession with privacy started many rumors, including one that der Führer had only one testicle, but Waeger did not gossip or listen to rumors. His only life was serving

der Führer, and he did that as a faithful dog. He
was told not to disturb his master, and he would not
disobey the order.

That was true in any case, but was especially true
this morning. Several times Waeger had heard dis-
turbing noises coming out of der Führer's bedroom.
An hour earlier der Führer had opened the door a
crack to tell him to get his doctor, Morell, on the
telephone. He had made the connection to Dr. Morell, who was several hours away in Berlin, before
passing the call to der Führer.

Dr. Morell was in Berlin, and it would be hours
before he would arrive by plane. There was another
doctor on call, Brandt, but der Führer refused to let
him see him. Waeger knew that when it came to
anything der Führer considered personal, he con-
sulted only Morell. Frequently, der Führer's problems had to do with stomach pain and stomach
gases. This morning, Waeger had heard der Führer
go into his private bathroom several times.

Even stranger, before getting off the telephone,
he had heard der Führer say something about his
penis being swollen.

THIRTEEN

The strategy conference did not begin until early
afternoon. Speer noted that his prediction was correct—Hitler resisted the idea that an actual Allied
landing was taking place on the Normandy coast.
He was convinced that the necessary size of an invading force meant that the Allies had to strike at a
major port. Based upon that presumption, the
larger ports had reinforced with heavy fortifica-
tions—bunkers and pillboxes. If the landing took
place at a beach rather than a fortified port, the
Germans would have fallen into the same Maginot
Line mentality that cost the French the war.

Speer noticed that Hitler seemed more distracted
than usual, sometimes unable to focus on the problem, even when confronted with patent evidence
that an actual invasion had taken place. He fidgeted
in his chair as if he was in pain and abruptly left the
room several times. Speer wondered if der Führer
was having a medical problem that was causing him
discomfort.

Hours into the discussion, der Führer finally ca-
pitulated after descriptions of the Allied landings at
Arromanches and Omaha Beach brought home an
undeniable fact: The Allies had brought their own
"ports" with them.

General Merker was red in the face and sweating
profusely by the time the meeting ended. Speer
walked out with him to where their chauffeurs and
staff cars were waiting.

"Congratulations," he told Merker. "You won der
Führer over."

"We have lost the war."

"What?"

"We have lost the war."

"Lower your voice," Speer said. They continued
to walk. "Why do you say we've lost the war? Der
Führer released the armored divisions Rommel
asked for."

"It's too late."

"Why? The reports are that the invasion forces are
still securing the beach area. They can still be driven
into the sea."

Merker whipped around, still red in the face.
"You're not a military man, Herr Speer, and neither
is der Führer. It's too late, not because of men on
the beaches, *but those in the sky.* Because of the delay,
by the time the armored units are ready to move
out, they will still be on the road when daylight
comes. They will have lost the protection of darkness. The American and British air forces will
butcher them."

He stomped off to his car, but swung around before he reached it. He shouted back to Speer, "Do
you remember the story about the horseshoe nail?"

Speer mulled over the comment as he got into
his own car. He recalled something about a

horseshoe nail, a poem or proverb from his boyhood. He didn't remember the exact words, but recalled that the loss of a nail in a horseshoe set off a chain reaction—the shoe was lost, the horse went down, the battle and the kingdom lost.

"All for the want of a horseshoe nail," he said, aloud.

"Herr Minister?" his driver asked.

"Nothing. Take me back to my house."

Dr. Morell arrived as Speer's car was pulling out. Speer saw Morell exit his car and hurry into the Berghof as if the hounds of hell were at his heels. Speer wondered again if der Führer was having a medical problem.

Der Führer had been later than usual for the strategy meeting and had been more than ordinarily preoccupied. At times he appeared to be in pain. Speer wondered what it was that caused his distress. He hoped the illness didn't turn out to be the horseshoe nail that loses the kingdom.

FOURTEEN

My dick still hurt like crazy from the clap as I sat in the back of the Mercedes with Dr. Dorsch and Vogler. I asked Dorsch for the German version of penicillin, telling him I was afraid of infection from the minor shrapnel wounds I got from the blast. He gave me enough to cure all the whores in Hanover. I could have asked to fuck his wife, and he would have spread her legs for me.

You don't say no to the guy who saved der Führer's ass.

It was the two dirtbag black shirts, Dr. Dumb Nuts and Colonel Blimp, whom I had to thank for making me a hero. It was Dorsch who noticed the bullet wound in the top of Hans's bald head after Vogler had body parts collected on a hospital cart. Colonel Keitel hadn't stopped when he was ahead—after shooting Hans in the head, his next shot hit the bomb.

Dorsch removed the slug and Vogler compared the rifling on it to the only pistol around—mine. And presto! I was a hero, the guy who shot one-armed Hans after he tried to blow up der Führer with a stolen bomb. Colonel Keitel was also getting honorable mention and an Iron Cross, after I described his heroic—but fruitless—attempt to subdue the assassin.

Both men were in a jolly mood as we drove toward the airfield. Vogler whistled an SS marching song through his teeth, and Dorsch beamed like the midday sun. Life was good. Adolf had been in a jolly mood following the attempt on his life. A firm believer in his own destiny, he had taken it as part of the Universal Plan that the assassination attempt had failed. He had complimented both Dorsch on his hospital and Vogler on his security measures.

Was I devastated because I didn't kill Adolf? That I didn't die trying? Yeah, I felt real bad about it.

Okay, that's not exactly the truth. Like der Führer, I also believed in what's meant to be is meant to be. I was willing to go the whole nine yards—Adolf's ass was grass and I was a lawn mower. But it wasn't my fault that Colonel Keitel decided to take a crap at that precise time and place—it was divine intervention for all I knew. At least until I could get away from these Nazi bastards for five minutes and do some thinking. Ever since I received hero status, Dorsch and Vogler had been sticking to me like shit on a stick.

Vogler stopped whistling through his teeth long enough to ask, "You understand, Herr Sturmbann-fuhrer, no mention of this attempt on der Führer's life must ever be made."

"Absolutely. My lips are sealed." Oh, that "Herr

Sturmbannfuhrer" bit—did I mention I was now a major?

"Pillow talk sinks ships!" Vogler said.

"What's that you say?" Dorsch asked.

Vogler smirked and winked at me. "Top secret, Doktor, not for your ears." He checked out the window. "We are getting close to the airport. I can tell you now that der Führer has arranged a surprise for you."

"Yes, I know. I am very appreciative. I will wear the medal with honor." I was getting an Iron Cross, First Class. I just couldn't tell anyone how I earned it.

Both men laughed.

Dorsch shook his finger at me. "Ha, nein, nein, you cannot wear this surprise. Although it will no doubt bring you some comfort."

Vogler giggled like a girl. "And it will keep you warm in the winter, eh Doktor?"

"Ja! Ja! You can even pet its fur."

The two howled with laughter again.

My good feelings about the world were quickly evaporating. The last thing I wanted was a surprise. But it sounded harmless enough. "Der Führer's giving me a dog?"

Dorsch laughed so hard he lost his breath.

"Nein! Nein! Not a dog," Vogler said. "A pussy, you are getting, a pussy!"

A coldness had started in my feet, worked up the back of my legs, into the small of my back, and was crawling up my spine, fanning the hair on the back of my neck. I couldn't imagine what sort of surprise Adolf had planned for me. But I began to suspect that I would regret it *for the rest of my life.*

Yeah, that phrase had worked itself back into my head. *They're going to kill me. That's the surprise.* The realization flashed in my mind like those neon signs in Times Square. Der Führer wanted to keep the assassination attempt on his life secret. I was an eyewitness. But why bring me to the airport? Why not kill me back at the hospital? Maybe they were going to take me a couple miles and toss me out without a parachute.

The car pulled to a stop near a plane that was putting down its boarding ladder.

"Get out, Wolfhardt, get out, your surprise is waiting."

I got out with a dry mouth and the hair on the back of my neck standing straighter than a *Heil Hitler.* Both men got out and stood by me. A woman stepped out of the plane and started climbing down the ladder.

Vogler slapped me on the back.

"You see! You see! Isn't der Führer wonderful?"

What the shit?

"He had Frau Wolfhardt brought to you. *Your bride is here!*"

Jesus H. Christ.

THE EAGLE
AND THE CROSS

R. J. PINEIRO

R. J. PINEIRO is the author of several techno-thrillers, including *Ultimatum, Retribution, Breakthrough, Exposure, Shutdown,* and the millennium thrillers *01-01-00* and *Y2K.* He is a seventeen-year veteran of the computer industry and is currently at work on leading-edge microprocessors, the heart of the personal computer. He was born in Havana, Cuba, and grew up in El Salvador before coming to the United States to pursue a higher education. He holds a degree in electrical engineering from Louisiana State University, a second-degree black belt in martial arts, and is a licensed private pilot and a firearms enthusiast. He has traveled extensively through Central America, Europe, and Asia, both for his computer business as well as to research for his novels. He lives in Texas with his wife, Lory, and his son, Cameron.

LVOV, THE UKRAINE • JUNE 22, 1941

The thundering sound of heavy artillery ringing in his ears, Colonel Aleksandrovich Nikolai Krasilov bolted out of bed and stormed out of his tent, racing across the dusty airfield toward the communications building on the other side of the short runway. To his surprise he was the first one outside. Other pilots began to emerge from their tents just as he tugged on the door and stepped inside.

The base's primitive communications room consisted of two ten-year-old two-way radios and three operators, who were currently pacing in front of their equipment. The trio turned in his direction, fear widening their stares.

"What is going on? The artillery rounds are coming from the west!"

"Ye . . . yes, comrade Colonel," responded the youngest of the operators. "We're under attack . . . by the Germans."

Krasilov, a twenty-year veteran of the Red Air Force, knew better than to jump to conclusions based on a comment from a young enlisted man, but the fact still remained that someone had ordered the artillery to fire, and its reverberating rumble was definitely coming from the border. "How do you know this?" he demanded.

"The radio, sir. Our bases by the border ... the screams, sir ... the planes at Novovolynsk are being strafed on the ground ... their radio just went dead!"

Krasilov inhaled deeply. "That's impossible! We have a nonaggression pact with the—"

"*This is Colonel Vasili Petrosky, anyone come in, come in!*"

Krasilov raced for the microphone on the table. Colonel Petrosky was in charge of the defense for the border town of Rava-Russkaja, fifty miles northwest of Lvov.

"This is Aleksandrovich, Vasili. What is your situation?"

"*Flames, Aleksandr! There are flames everywhere. Our fighters are burning! Our tanks are burning! We need help immediately, or we'll be forced to retreat. The German panzers are just a few hills away! Their planes fill the sky!*"

"Hold in place, Vasili. We'll contact Kiev!"

"*Na pomosh, Aleksandr. Na po—*"

"Vasili? Vasili?"

No response.

Krasilov pounded a fist on the table. Petrosky's cry for help was all the convincing Krasilov needed. "Get me Kiev Military District headquarters immediately!"

"Yes, sir!"

The young radio operator jumped on a chair and dialed a new frequency while Krasilov went back outside. His pilots' gaze was on him. They looked as confused as he felt. He saw fear in their eyes, but none said a word. They waited for Krasilov to speak.

After months of warnings, the inevitable—at least in Krasilov's mind—had happened. The undeniable signs that something significant was about to happen were everywhere: German planes flying reconnaissance missions over Russia for months; German ships pulling out of Soviet ports in a hurry; German embassy officials in Leningrad, Stalingrad, and Moscow burning documents and getting ready to depart. Yes, the signs were all there, but what was more incredible than the reports themselves was the Kremlin's refusal to publicly acknowledge them.

"All I know is that we're under attack," he said. "Get to your planes and wait for my order. Move!"

The pilots looked at one another. Krasilov understood their hesitancy. TASS—the official Soviet news agency—communiqués over the previous two weeks had indicated that the two nations were at peace and that war was not a possibility. In fact, many Red Air Force pilots of the Baltic, Minsk, and Kiev Military Districts had been allowed to go on leave by Moscow Military District headquarters after a recently completed night training exercise that not only left them short on fuel, but also short of sleep.

The pilots continued staring at Krasilov.

"Are you deaf? Move it! Now!"

The pilots ran to their planes.

"Sir?"

Krasilov turned. The young operator stood by the doorway.

"Yes?"

"The rifle division at Mostiska briefly came in. They were also pleading for help, sir. Then communications ceased."

"Damn! Where is Kiev?"

"I've just got them on the line, sir."

Krasilov rushed past him and snagged the microphone. "Kiev Military District, this is Colonel Aleksandrovich Krasilov of the Red Air Force in Lvov. We're under attack by German forces. Repeat. We're under attack by the Germans. Request instructions."

"You must be insane, Colonel Krasilov! Why is your message not in code?"

Krasilov narrowed his eyes at the odd response. He pressed on. "Did you hear me? I said we're under attack! German forces are wiping out our border defenses this minute! Where is General Kirponos?"

Another voice came through on the radio. *"Colonel Krasilov, this is Colonel Timoshenko. General Kirponos received orders yesterday to move his headquarters to Tarponol. They are en route. His orders were that no action must be taken against the Germans without Moscow's consent. Comrade Stalin has forbidden our artillery to open fire and our planes to fly."*

Hearing the sound of his own planes revving up, Krasilov's grip tightened around the microphone. The response was unsound. Was Stalin that far out of touch with reality? He pressed further. "It's not possible! Reports are flowing in. Our troops are being killed. Towns are in flames!"

"The order stands, Colonel! No attack must take place against the people of—" The line went dead just as a powerful explosion shook the base.

Krasilov dropped the microphone and ran outside, his stomach knotting when he spotted what must have been a hundred planes across the sky. He turned and saw the cause of the explosion. Three craft were burning at the edge of the runway from a direct hit by a German Messerschmitt fighter, which was now rolling its wings and disappearing behind the trees that bordered the airfield.

Enraged, Krasilov raced for his old Polikarpov I-16. His ground crew stood by the short, stubby plane as he climbed into the open-canopy cockpit, ignored the preflight check, flipped the master switch, set the air/fuel mixture to full rich, and threw the engine starter. The propeller turned a few times before the engine engaged with a cloud of smoke that was quickly blown away by the slipstream.

Another explosion.

As he advanced the throttle, Krasilov spotted a German plane pulling up. Four I-16s were in flames less than a hundred yards away as two other Messerschmitts entered a dive. Krasilov could see their muzzle flashes and the resulting lines of dust peppering toward three stationary Polikarpovs on the other side of the base. The planes exploded a moment later in a sheet of fire that reached up to the sky. One of the German planes flew through it before lurching skyward.

Krasilov reached the end of the runway. One plane was in flames halfway down the runway, blocking it. Krasilov pressed the top of the rudder pedals, applied full power, and lowered flaps. The forty-five-hundred-pound plane trembled under the conflicting commands. Rpm increased to twenty-seven hundred. The tail rose, and the nose dropped to the horizon under the powerful pull. He eased back the stick, used the elevators to control the nose's attitude, and waited. Three thousand rpm. He could hear the rivets squeaking as the stress on the monocoque structure reached the outer edges of its design. Krasilov held out for a few more seconds while firmly clutching the control stick. The craft began to slide over the ground.

He lifted his feet off the pedals, and the I-16 snapped forward, pressing him against his seat. His eyes shifted back and forth between the burning craft and the airspeed indicator:

"Speed, speed!" he hissed.

Eighty knots . . . ninety.

The flames rapidly accelerated toward him.

One hundred knots.

He shifted his gaze up once more and spotted a German plane breaking through the heavy smoke rising over the burning I-16. The wing-mounted guns came alive with muzzle flashes.

Krasilov pulled back on the stick and squeezed the trigger. The slow Polikarpov left the ground. Krasilov pointed the nose directly toward the incoming German craft flying at fifty feet above ground.

Krasilov stopped firing the moment the fighter, which he now recognized as an Me 109F Franz, broke its run and pulled up. He cleared the downed craft, broke through the dark smoke, and also pulled up, but could not even attempt to catch up with the departing Me 109F. The German craft outperformed him by over a hundred knots.

It didn't matter. He was airborne with full tanks and a full load of ammunition. Besides, the Franz was not what he was interested in stopping. Krasilov's eyes were fixed on the large bombers that the German fighters were trying to protect. He pushed full power and set his craft in a fast climb.

The bombers almost within reach, Krasilov cut right to fly past them, turned again, and faced them head-on to avoid the deadly guns on top and aft of the craft. As he made his turn he noticed something behind him.

An Me 109F.

Krasilov watched his airspeed alarmingly increase past three hundred knots, almost fifteen knots above his maximum rated speed, and he was feeling it in the powerful windblast that the short windshield barely deflected, and in the savage vibrations and rocking wings. He had to slow down fast or face midair disintegration. But slowing down meant giving the Messerschmitt glued to his tail an even better chance to score.

The thundering cannons, followed by several bullets ripping through the wooden skin of his right wing, made him cut back the throttle, lower flaps, and pull up the nose. A few more rounds blasted through the left wing, and a moment later smoke and oil began to spew from the engine, but the maneuver worked. He watched in satisfaction as the German flew past him at great speed but quickly turned away from the range of Krasilov's guns.

The dense haze blinding him, Krasilov lost track of the fighter. He wasn't sure what section of the engine the German had hit, but it had at least left him with enough power to remain airborne. He pushed full throttle, and the engine responded, but only at the cost of belching even more smoke and oil.

The Russian's eyes burned not just from the smoke, but also from the anger gripping him. The Germans were just picking their targets at will and blowing them up. There was no defense. He was the only fighter that had gotten airborne. Five planes burned on the runway, and dozens were in flames on the side of the airfield. The communications building was also burning. From this high up he could see the Junkers dropping load after load of bombs on Lvov! The city was quickly being engulfed by flames.

"Not on the city, you bastards! Only civilians live in the city!" he screamed at the top of his lungs. Krasilov's wife and two daughters lived on the outskirts of Lvov.

Through tears of rage, Krasilov spotted a pair of Messerschmitt Me 110s, the heavy twin-engine fighters. They were flying in formation a thousand feet below him. Krasilov pointed his craft in that direction and idled the engine to reduce smoke and improve visibility. It worked. In a dive, his I-16 gained airspeed, but without engine power. The Me 110s were five hundred feet below and closing awfully fast. He lined up the rightmost craft in his sights and squeezed the trigger.

Nothing.

Startled, he squeezed it again.

Nothing.

The Franz must have damaged something vital to the I-16's weapons system. The Me 110s were two hundred feet away. Krasilov could see the large white-on-black cross painted over each wing. He briefly looked into another possibility for attacking the bombers and made his decision.

Perspiration and hot engine oil rolling down his creased forehead, Krasilov aimed for the right wingtip. He had to get the entire aileron, or the bomber might survive the attack.

One of the Me 110's cannons began to move up. Someone on the plane had spotted him.

Airspeed quickly rushed above three hundred knots. The craft quavered from the windblast on all leading edges. The attitude indicator told him he had achieved an eighty-degree-angle dive, way beyond the Polikarpov's specifications. Muzzle flashes broke out of the single cannon now pointed directly at him. Sparks flew out in all directions as the Me 110's rounds struck the massive radial engine, but it was to no consequence. Krasilov maintained his dive. The wing loomed closer.

Three hundred twenty knots.

Both hands firmly gripping the control column, Krasilov saw the white-on-black cross grow larger until it filled his entire windshield. He lowered his head below the glass at the very last moment.

The impact was soul-numbing. The vibrations felt as if they were going to shake the life out of him as a hasty vision of fire engulfed him. Krasilov let go of the stick and put both hands over his face as the heat intensified. The back of his shirt was on fire, but he was still alive. He pressed his back against the flight seat to put out the flames. It worked. His back stung on contact, but it was tolerable.

The propeller was bent back over the fuselage. The nose was still in one piece, and so were the wings and tail, but the rear of his craft was ablaze. He had to land fast to avoid an explosion.

Tongues of fire pulsated from the engine. Krasilov turned it off to prevent more fuel from reaching the front and pulled on the fuel-dump lever on the side of the seat to minimize the chance of an explosion during his emergency landing.

The smoke and fire subsided, enabling him to pick a spot to land, but before he could do that, Krasilov lifted his head and searched the skies for his victim.

A smile flickered on his face when he spotted the Me 110 with a missing wing gyrating in a fatal spin several hundred feet away.

He focused back to his own problem. He still had to find a place to land. The wind intensified the flames behind him. He slowly eased back on the stick and held his breath. The craft's nose rose a few degrees. Airspeed decreased below three hundred knots. He tried to lower flaps, but they didn't work. He briefly tested the rudder and ailerons. They were operational. Krasilov pulled up the nose several more degrees.

Altitude two hundred feet. Speed two hundred knots. A field of sunflowers extended from where he was all the way to Lvov. Krasilov glided down.

One hundred feet; one hundred fifty knots.

Still too fast for a controlled landing, but he didn't have a choice. He was approaching Lvov at great speed. He had to slow down, but without flaps he was forced to set the craft down at that speed or risk running out of room or stalling. The burning buildings rapidly grew in size.

Krasilov breathed deeply, held it, and lowered the nose. The landing gear hit hard, instantly shaking the craft. Krasilov didn't mind the vibrations as long as he could keep the craft in control.

The gear hit a ditch. In a flash, the nose dove into the thick field and the tail went up in the air. The craft flipped once before landing on its side.

Krasilov smashed his head against the windshield, bounced, and crashed his back against the flight seat. He was disoriented from the blow. Half his body lay outside the cockpit. He opened his eyes, and through blood he saw . . . sunflowers. The airplane lay on its side. The left wing was gone. The right stuck straight up in the air. He kicked his legs and pushed himself away from the wreckage. His back burned, and so did his forehead. He felt the torn flesh above his eyebrows. It was in shreds, but he had survived.

Krasilov staggered away from the wreck, tearing

off a sleeve of his shirt to bandage his forehead as best he could to stop the bleeding.

Breathing deeply, he walked toward the city. The sounds of German fighters mixed with explosions. Cries hung in the air like the smell of gunpowder filling his nostrils.

Krasilov picked up his pace as he reached the rubble of the buildings on the outskirts of town.

The dive-bombers had temporarily stopped, although Krasilov didn't think they could destroy much more with another run. He couldn't see a single building intact. Most had collapsed over the streets or were about to from the intense fire.

He turned into his street minutes later, spotted a woman in the middle of the road with . . . two kids!

Krasilov's heart jumped, and he ran, desperately hoping they were his wife and daughters . . . "Zoya! Zoya!"

"Please help us, sir. Please!" Two small boys screamed as they ran up to him and hung on to his pants while the woman pulled on his hand.

"The people in this building, woman," Krasilov asked, as he pointed to a three-story building that had collapsed on itself. "Did you see anyone coming out?"

"Please, sir. Please. Help us. Help us!"

Krasilov pulled out two small dark chocolate bars from his pocket. "Here. Take this and run out of the city with your children. The Germans are coming. You must leave! Tell everyone you see to head east. You got that? Head east!"

The woman snagged the chocolate and ran away with her two kids.

Krasilov faced the ruins that had been his building. His family lived on the third floor. Krasilov walked on the sidewalk, climbed on top of the mound of rubble, and began to paw through the debris while praying that he would not find them. Perhaps they heard the noise and fled. Perhaps they managed to leave the building in time.

Time.

Tears rolled down his blackened face as he moved rock, brick, and wood aside. His muscles burned, and his head throbbed, but it did not matter. He had to know. He needed to know.

An overwhelming sense of despair suddenly filled him the moment he spotted his wife's body under a wooden panel. His two daughters were next to her. They wore their sleeping garments. Still hopeful, he knelt next to his wife, but froze when something didn't look right. His wife lay on her stomach, but her eyes stared up to the sky. Her head had been twisted at a repulsive angle.

"Zoya, no . . . no!"

Mustering savage control, Krasilov walked over to his twin daughters, Marissa and Larissa. Their bodies also faced down, but appeared intact. He turned the first one over . . . her face and chest were gone! Krasilov let her go and leaned to the side. He controlled the first convulsion, but the second reached his gorge. He couldn't even tell which of his daughters that was!

His body tensed and he purged. A third convulsion came and went, quickly followed by a fourth, this time only a dry heave.

Krasilov straightened up, breathed deeply, and walked over to his second daughter. He turned her over. It was Larissa. Her body was not maimed, but the purple hue of the flesh around her neck told Krasilov everything he needed to know.

He dropped to his knees and bellowed a scream of anger, frustration, and pain, before he burst into tears again, before he cried the desperate cry of a desperate man.

Later that morning, as German planes flew overhead and panzer divisions streaked across the Ukrainian planes, Krasilov headed east.

Hordes of Russians civilians ran past him as they fled the advancing German army. Krasilov didn't run. He wasn't afraid of the Germans. There was nothing else they could take away from him besides his life.

And that would be a blessing, he reflected.

There were dozens of airstrips between Lvov and Kiev. Krasilov headed toward them. War had come to his home. To his country.

War had taken his loved ones.

As his *Rodina* burned under Germany's crushing attack, Aleksandrovich Nikolai Krasilov concluded there was nothing left for him to do but fight.

Fight back with uncompromising resolve.

He had sworn that over three lonely graves in a sunflower field outside Lvov.

BAHRAIN, SAUDI ARABIA • NOVEMBER 25, 1942

U.S. Army Air Corps Captain Jack Towers zippered up his leather jacket and took a last, long draw from his cigarette while staring at the large merchant ships quietly steaming north, toward the port of Abadan, Iran. He slowly exhaled through his nostrils and stepped away from the edge of the hill, returning to the dirt runway, where he had landed the night before. His back still ached from sleeping on the floor, but as Jack saw it, at least he'd had a relatively quiet place where he could get a few unin-

terrupted hours of sleep without being disturbed by
gunfire. That alone was a luxury these days.

On the way to the mess tent, Jack walked next to
his plane, a Bell P-39D Aircobra he had baptized *The
Impatient Virgin* after one of his wilder girlfriends
during his short but busy stay at Cochran Field,
Georgia, where Jack had trained side by side with
Royal Air Force pilots on advanced dogfighting
techniques with the Aircobras. From there Jack was
transferred to Dale Mabry in Florida for additional
dogfighting training. Eight months later, Jack, along
with two dozen other pilots who had logged over
one thousand hours, spent a week in Camp Kilmer,
New Jersey, where they boarded a ship loaded with
four hundred P-39Ds destined for the Red Air Force
as part of President Roosevelt's Soviet-American
lend-lease program.

He sighed. Little did Jack know during his year
and a half of training that his first official overseas
post would be teaching Soviet pilots to use their new
equipment, but as it turned out, the aircraft that he
had learned to master ended up being pushed aside
by both the U.S. Army Air Corps and the RAF in
favor of the faster and much more agile P-40 Kitti-
hawk. The surplus P-39Ds were shipped to the Soviet
Union, where their fighter aircraft technology
lagged the West by a few years.

But there was another reason why Jack had been
selected for this not-so-glorious duty. Jack was born
under the name Jackovich Filipp Towers. His
mother was a Soviet nurse his father had fallen in
love with during World War I, and whom he subsequently married and brought home to Indiana.

Raised mostly by his mother, Jack spoke perfect
Russian by the time he was four years old, and his
mother saw to it that Jack didn't forget it by refusing

to speak to him in English—something his mother did to this day.

Jack smiled as he rubbed a hand over his jacket and felt the letter—written in Russian—he'd received a few days before from his mother. He always got letters from his mother, never from his father. Jack's father was always too busy selling used cars at his used car lot—or so he claimed.

That's just as well, reflected Jack. All his old man wanted to talk about was used cars anyway. He couldn't care less about Jack's aviation career.

There had been a time, Jack remembered as he walked around two parked jeeps in front of the mess tent, when his father had had a chance to pull him closer. It was when he was about to turn seventeen. Jack had commented several times how much he would love to own a car, and in his mind he'd hoped his father would get him one. So much did Jack expect the car, that he had told his friends he was getting one. That proved to be a grave mistake, because to Jack's surprise, the old man forgot to show up for his birthday party. *I had a last-minute customer,* Jack recalled him saying when he arrived empty-handed two hours late. The carless son of the car salesman. His friends gave him a hard time about that for weeks.

Jack shrugged and exhaled as he reached the front of the tent. Maybe that experience was the reason Jack felt as if he always got the short end of the stick in life.

He pushed the canvas flap and stepped inside the mess tent. On one side was the cafeteria line—if one could call two Arab cooks with a pot filled with eggs and another with a white soggy substance they called grits—a cafeteria line. On the opposite side were two midsize tables with six chairs each. Jack grabbed a metal plate, got some eggs and ... grits, and walked next to one of the tables, where a pilot was already going through seconds.

"This is a warm meal, Jack. Might as well enjoy it while it lasts," said Major Kenneth Chapman, Jack's commanding officer. Chapman was also fluent in Russian. "Heard up north the Russkies are undergoing food rations."

"That's just great, sir. I can't wait." Jack sat down and filled his mouth with two spoonfuls of eggs.

Chapman pushed his plate to the side and downed a glass of water. "The latest news from the Eastern Front's that shit's just about to hit the fan in good ol' Stalingrad, pal. Better enjoy the powdered eggs while you can eat them. Most Russians are on a bread and butter diet, but heck, at least that's better than the Germans. Last I heard, those Nazi bastards are eating their own horses. Guess that's good for the assholes."

Chapman grinned, exposing the gold caps on his two front teeth.

Jack couldn't help a frown. War wasn't going exactly as he had planned it. He had visualized himself fighting Messerschmitts over the English Channel and across the French and German countryside, not in below-zero-weather eastern Russia, but orders were orders. He had to go where the Air Corps told him to. He did get to participate briefly in the battle of North Africa. Flying his *Impatient Virgin,* Jack had distinguished himself by shooting down three Italian Macchi Mc.202 single-engine fighters over Libya in the week he'd spent there.

Chapman checked his watch. "We're leaving in an hour, Jack. Our red buddies got a couple of hundred planes just sitting around waiting for us to show them how to use them. No sense in making them wait, right?"

"I guess so, sir."

"Good. Don't forget to pick up a set of long johns from the supply tent. It's gonna be one motherfucker of a winter." Chapman got up and left.

Jack slowly shook his head. His mother had told him stories of people freezing in minutes at forty below zero, and because in her days as a nurse she had seen more than her share of amputations due to frostbite, Jack received lecture after lecture on how to dress not just warm, but dress warm for a Russian winter.

There is a difference, my dear Jackovich Filipp. The Russian winter will rob you of your heat, freeze you to the bone, then cover you with so many inches of snow that your stiff body won't surface until the following spring.

The grits tasted terrible and stuck to the roof of his mouth. Jack ate them anyway and went back to the line for seconds.

STALINGRAD FRONT • DECEMBER 13, 1942

Colonel Krasilov allowed his Lavochkin La-3 fighter to reach ten thousand feet before easing the control column forward. He glanced to his right and left and nodded approvingly when spotting his seven-plane squadron adopting an arrowhead formation.

A soldier from the Soviet Fifth Armored Division had spotted a formation of German bombers possibly carrying supplies for the trapped German Sixth Army of General Paulus in the Stalingrad pocket. Krasilov's mission was simple: Search and destroy all enemy craft in the region with priority to bombers.

Upset at his government's lack of better intelligence reports, Krasilov scanned the skies and saw nothing but blue. A rare day in the Soviet winter, but Krasilov didn't mind. Hopefully temperatures would warm up to ten below so that his men could get some relief from what had been a bitter winter. On the other hand, the cold winter at that moment affected the Germans more than the Soviets. Krasilov had grown up in these regions and was used to the long, cold months—and was also well dressed for them. The Germans, on the other hand, were still wearing their summer uniforms. Paulus's army had taken Stalingrad in early September just to find that all that remained from the once-picturesque city were the charred facades of the buildings that still stood. The Soviet people, by order of the Soviet High Command in Moscow, set fire to all buildings, equipment, and anything else that could be of any use to the Germans that couldn't be hauled east in time. The Russian winter caught General Paulus and his glorious but exhausted Sixth Army hundreds of miles from home in a ghost city with fresh Soviet troops attacking from all flanks. Hitler had ordered the Sixth Army to adopt a hedgehog, or all-round, defensive position and to wait for relief. That created the Stalingrad pocket, where the Germans now slowly starved to death by an ever-decreasing channel of supplies.

Good for them, Krasilov decided. After all the atrocities that the invading troops had committed in Krasilov's motherland, he had not one ounce of pity for them. On the contrary, the Soviet pilot firmly believed that the Hitlerites had not only needed to be repelled from Russia, but also followed all the way to the heart of Berlin and exterminated.

"Germans! Three o'clock high!" came the voice from Krasilov's right wingman, Lieutenant Andrei Nikolajev.

Krasilov snapped his head to the left and spotted the formation.

"Scramble, comrades! Scramble! The Hitlerites shall not get their supplies today!"

The craft broke formation in pairs. Krasilov pushed full power. The Shvestov fourteen-cylinder radial engine puffed two clouds of black smoke before pulling the craft with monumental force. Even at a twenty-degree angle of climb Krasilov watched the airspeed indicator rush past 350 knots and climb as fast as the altimeter. He closed the gap in under a minute. Andrei remained glued to his side.

The bombers, which Krasilov now recognized as the large Heinkel He 177, opened fire from all angles, but after a few encounters with the He 177, Krasilov had learned that the Heinkels were most vulnerable underneath, where there was only one machine-gun pod. The other five were scattered on the top, front, and rear, but were ineffective against an attack from underneath.

To protect themselves from such attack, the German bombers had opted to fly in a combat-box formation. The combat box resembled a slanted flying wedge with the lead squadron in the middle. Other squadrons were stacked three hundred feet from the lead squadron's left and right. This arrangement enabled the bombers a clear field of fire for the bomber's front gunners and also allowed for coordinated cross fire of the attacking fighters. Each bomber covered the other one's bottom. The planes on each end of the formation were the most exposed, but those were usually protected by escort fighters.

Krasilov saw no escorts in sight and exhaled in relief as he approached the leftmost Heinkel. Although his La-3 plane was a remarkable improvement over the old I-16s, the craft was still not as fast and maneuverable as the Messerschmitt Me 109F or the even faster Me 109G.

The Heinkel's underside dual machine-gun pod located between the wings in the forward fuselage swung in his direction and opened fire. Krasilov broke left, away from the formation. The gun followed him.

"It's all yours, Andrei!"

Krasilov saw a few rounds exploding through his Lavochkin's wooden skin as he diverted the gunner's attention away from his wingman. The craft shuddered but remained airborne. A backward glance, and Krasilov watched Andrei unload round after round on the Heinkel's underfuselage.

The gun-pod emplacement exploded.

Andrei broke its run while Krasilov made a 360-degree turn and came back around for his pass. This time there was nothing defending the bomber. Krasilov made the turn wide enough to allow him ample time to fire. He completed the turn and aligned the Heinkel's center fuselage, using rudders and ailerons.

He squeezed the trigger. The dual cowl-mounted 20mm cannons came to life and fired at the rate of two hundred rounds per minute in synchronized fashion, through the propeller. One in every ten rounds had a phosphorus head that burned bright yellow the moment it left the muzzle. Krasilov used the tracers to guide his fire.

Pieces began to come off the middle of the bomber. Krasilov pulled back throttle to allow himself an extra second or two of firing time before he had to pull—

A bright explosion and the tail separated from the front, catching Krasilov entirely by surprise. The tail section flew down while the front fuselage shot up and to the left, blocking Krasilov's planned tight left turn.

Breaking right was out of the question. Dozens of Heinkel guns would be waiting for him in a deadly cross fire. Krasilov continued to fire and held his run.

Another explosion. The left engine went up in flames, tearing the Heinkel's wing along with it.

Krasilov rolled the wings ninety degrees and flew through the debris, fire engulfing him for a second, before turning to thick smoke followed by blue skies.

He watched in satisfaction as the wounded bomber's right engine continued to run, pulling the remnants of the Heinkel against an adjacent bomber. The two went up in a huge fireball that engulfed a third bomber.

The remaining bombers, which Krasilov had estimated at thirty, continued their trajectory toward the Stalingrad pocket.

"Messerschmitts! Five and ten o'clock!"

"Got them! Break left, Andrei! I'll handle the right!"

Krasilov swung the stick right and saw an Me 109G "Gustav" coming straight ahead. He leveled off and approached it head-on. The German opened fire. Krasilov's index finger reached the trigger and pressed it, but the game didn't last long. With a combined speed of over eight hundred knots, the two planes closed in awfully fast. A bullet crashed against Krasilov's propeller hub and bounced away. There was no smoke.

Krasilov waited until the very last second before breaking left. The German broke right and tried to execute a tight 360. Krasilov was about to do a left but instead he swung the stick back to the right, instantly pulling a few negative Gs. The restraining harness kept him from crashing against the canopy, and he completed the maneuver while the German pilot was still halfway through the turn. The Hitlerite had apparently failed to consider Krasilov's change of strategy, and was caught with his entire flank exposed. The Gustav's pilot had made a basic but fatal aerial combat mistake. Krasilov was surprised. German pilots were much more disciplined than that.

Krasilov smiled as his finger squeezed the trigger. At such close range the Messerschmitt broke apart after a three-second burst from the 20mm cannons.

As debris slowly fell from the sky, Krasilov broke left and raced after the bombers, most of which already had their payload doors fully open. The German Stalingrad pocket was less than a minute away.

The Heinkels went for a dive to increase the gap between them and the pursuing La-3s. Krasilov wished someone had informed them earlier about the incoming bombers. Maybe they could have intercepted sooner and taken out more bombers, but just like a dozen times before, all his squadron had was a ten-minute warning from field spotters.

Krasilov watched in utter disappointment as packages dropped from the bomb bays. Bright white parachutes opened a few seconds later. Krasilov pressed on. There was still a chance to prevent some of the droppings.

He approached a Heinkel from the rear at full speed and with the cannons firing. He adjusted to take out the rear gun emplacement of the closest bomber. The guns swung in his direction, but before a single round left them the tail section blew into three large pieces just as the packages began to drop. Krasilov did not let up. He maintained his run while keeping the pressure on the trigger. *C'mon, blow, dammit. Blow!*

Like a heavenly chastisement, the sixty-six-hundred-pound bomber went up into a fiery ball that also engulfed Krasilov's plane. This time, however, the fire lasted several seconds, enough to ignite the waterproof lacquer protecting the La-3's wooden skin.

He left the burning debris behind and immediately cut back power and pushed the stick forward. He had to reach land before the craft exploded, but at an altitude of over five thousand feet, he doubted he'd make it. Most of the wings and rear fuselage were already covered by flames. It was just a matter of time before the heat caused the gas tank to blow.

Krasilov leveled off the plane, turned it upside down, and pushed the nose just a dash below the horizon to get the tail out of the way. He slid the canopy open and pulled on the release mechanism of his restraining harness.

He free-fell through the open canopy and cleared the vertical fin by a couple of feet. The windblast was much more powerful than he had been told. It kept him from breathing for a few seconds. The earth, burning craft, and blue skies changed positions over and over as a peaceful feeling of isolation suddenly overtook him. Although it felt as if he was just standing still in midair, Krasilov knew he was plummeting to earth at over 150 miles per hour.

He reached for the rip cord and pulled it hard. The pilot chute came up and dragged the main canopy, which blossomed bright red, giving Krasilov the tug of a lifetime. Fortunately for him, he had managed to fly far away enough from the German pocket before bailing out. Krasilov didn't think the starving Hitlerites in Stalingrad would treat well a downed Soviet pilot who had just been shooting down supply craft—not that the Germans treated Soviet prisoners of war with any decency anyway.

He watched most bombers in the distance drop their payloads before turning back, while the remaining Messerschmitts kept the rest of his squadron busy.

Krasilov shook his head in disappointment. They needed more time to intercept, and better planes.

He silently glided over the River Volga.

KALACH AIRFIELD, TWENTY MILES WEST OF THE STALINGRAD POCKET • DECEMBER 13, 1942

For Krasilov the nightmare had returned. His wounded I-16 plummeted to earth in flames. He had no control of the air surfaces or engine. Through the flames coming from the exhausts he could see the bent propeller. His face began to burn from the intense heat.

He looked behind him and saw the Messerschmitt. The pilot was waving at him while his cannons took out the I-16's tail. Chunks of wood blew in all directions, some striking Krasilov in the back as the craft went into a reverse spin with the nose pointed at the heavens. Krasilov saw the blue sky while desperately reaching for the release handle of his restraining harness, but he could not find it. He looked to his left and watched the German pilot salute him and laugh. The bastard was laughing as Krasilov hopelessly struggled with his harness. The Messerschmitt remained there, as if hovering next to him. The pilot continued to smile. Krasilov could not unstrap his harness. The heat intensified. The heat...

"Colonel Krasilov? Colonel Krasilov! Wake up, sir. Wake up!"

Krasilov opened his eyes and saw Andrei's round face. He inhaled, sat up, and rubbed his eyes. He had nearly frozen from his five-mile walk in thirty below following his landing until a T-34 tank from the Second Mechanized Division picked him up and brought him to the air base, where it took him an hour to thaw and less than a minute to fall asleep.

Krasilov ran his tongue inside his mouth, which felt dry and pasty. He reached for the bottle of vodka next to the bed and took a swig. He inhaled as his throat and chest warmed up, and stared at Andrei's clean-shaven face once more.

His subordinate, a recently graduated pilot from the Red Air Force, had joined Krasilov's fighter wing six months ago and had since worked his way to the top, taking second to no one but Krasilov. In fact, Andrei had already shot down over sixty enemy fighters with a loss of only three planes, a record that only Krasilov, with over a hundred air victories, could surpass. Krasilov liked the young pilot from the Ukraine, who enjoyed women and dancing as much as he loved flying.

"What is it?" Krasilov asked, taking another sip, letting the alcohol do its magical work.

"We've got company, sir. Americans."

Krasilov bolted to his feet. *"What?"*

"Americans, sir. Actually only *one* American, but over three dozen American fighters. Three dozen, sir!"

"So soon? They weren't supposed to be here until..."

"They're here, sir, and the fighters are being unloaded from the cargo planes as we speak."

Krasilov put on his skin boots and heavy coat and followed Andrei outside, where five huge American cargo planes were parked on the far left side of the snow-covered runway.

As a true Bolshevik, Krasilov did not care for the Americans and their flying machines. He wanted more Lavochkin La-3s and perhaps a squadron of the newer but still scarce La-5s, but given the large need for fighters to support the Russian defense and new winter counteroffensive, Stalin had agreed to the American lend-lease program. This was one of the first shipments.

He spotted a dark-haired man wearing a black leather jacket, matching boots and gloves, and dark sunglasses. *So it is true then,* Krasilov reflected as he walked away from his bunker. *American pilots do wear sunglasses, even on an overcast day.*

Krasilov approached him, flanked by Andrei and two other pilots. The American smiled and extended his hand. Krasilov didn't take it. The smile on the American's face vanished. He removed his sunglasses and stared back at Krasilov with indifference.

"You were not supposed to have been here for another week. What gives you the right to barge into my airfield with little warning?" Krasilov asked in Russian, not expecting a response from the American.

"Is that how you welcome your allies, Colonel?" responded the American in flawless Russian. "I would hate to see what you would do to a German."

Krasilov was impressed, although he did not show it externally. The young man knew the language well.

"I shall consider you my ally when my men have

been trained and your planes prove themselves in my eyes . . ."

"Captain Towers, Colonel. Jack Towers." He put the sunglasses back on.

Krasilov didn't respond right away. He simply stared at his own reflection on the American's glasses and pointed toward a single tent on the other side of the runway. "You will sleep and eat there, when there is food. When there is none, you will starve with the rest of us. There will be no special privileges for you. You will answer to me while training my men, and the moment the training is complete, you shall leave my base at once. Is that understood, Captain?"

"I will only answer to my superior officer, Major Kenneth Chapman, sir."

"Is that so, Captain. And where is this Major Chapman right now, may I ask?"

"He's training another fighter wing a hundred miles north of here."

"Like I said, Captain. You will report directly to me while on my base!" Krasilov turned and headed back for his tent. "Andrei, show him what he needs to know!"

"Yes, comrade Colonel!"

Jack frowned. This wasn't exactly the type of reception he'd had in mind, but then again, nothing had gone his way since he'd joined the damned Air Corps. Why would this be any different?

"Charming fellow, your colonel," he said to Andrei.

Andrei smiled and extended his hand. Jack shook it.

"I'm Lieutenant Andrei Nikolajev. Please forgive him, Captain Towers—"

"Jack."

"Jackovich?"

Jack laughed. "Sure, Jackovich is fine, too."

Andrei smiled, nodded, then frowned. "Don't take Colonel Krasilov too seriously today. He's pretty upset. He got shot down early this morning and spent the last seven hours getting back to the base through the snow. He's not in the best of moods."

"Well, neither am I. I've just spent the last three days traveling halfway across the world to get here."

"I understand. How long before the planes are ready?"

Jack shifted his gaze to the transports and the army of Russians dressed in white camouflage jackets unloading the P-39Ds wingless fuselages down the rear ramps. "I'll say another day at the most. Maybe less. How many pilots are available?"

"Plenty. We just need a more competitive machine than the La-3. We lose too many of them in every battle."

Jack exhaled. The P-39D Aircobras were relatively faster than the La-3s, but not as fast and maneuverable as the Messerschmitts. "How good are they?"

"Excuse me?"

"Your pilots, Andrei. How good are they?"

"We have the will to learn and the will to fight, comrade Jackovich. We are all prepared to die for the *Rodina*."

"Well, let's hope it doesn't come to that. The best pilot, in my opinion, is a live one."

The Russian gave him a puzzled look that didn't surprise Jack one bit. Chapman had warned him about the courageous—and at times suicidal—Soviet pilots. Jack wondered if perhaps that kind of spirit was what was really necessary to win a war. Maybe his cool American attitude was not what got things done, but the boldness, take-no-prisoners approach that the Russians were so famous for.

"This is a war, comrade Jackovich. Our lives are expendable. We all must fight to defend the *Rodina.*"

Sure, Andrei, Jack thought as he stared into the Soviet's ice-blue eyes crowning the remnants of what appeared to have once been a boyish face. The fine lines on Andrei's forehead and around his eyes told Jack that the young Soviet pilot must have already seen more than his share of battle—probably more than Jack would ever get to see.

"Would you die for your country, Jackovich?"

Jack considered that for a moment before replying, "That's why we're here, right? Why do you ask?"

"Our perception of the American pilot is one of more show than actual fight. That's what we get told anyway. I think that's part of the reason the colonel reacted—"

Andrei's words were cut short by the high-pitched sound of an engine in full throttle very close to ground.

"Shit. I hope that's one of yours," Jack said as he scanned the skies.

"I . . . I'm not that . . . damn! It's a Gustav!"

They ran for the shelter on the far right side of the concrete runway. Jack crouched next to Andrei as the Messerschmitt zoomed over the runway.

"Damn! The Aircobras!" Jack shouted, glancing at the wingless fuselages wrapped in thick green plastic stacked next to the cargo planes.

Without firing a single round, the Messerschmitt pulled up and rolled its wing while maintaining a vertical climb. Jack saw the craft execute the corkscrew until nearly reaching a low layer of cumulus clouds some five thousand feet high.

"What's he doing?" asked Jack.

"Challenging."

"What?"

"He's challenging the best of our pilots for a one-on-one duel."

"Are you shitting me?"

Before Jack got an answer, Andrei leaped forward and raced toward Krasilov and the other pilots already gathered next to the La-3s.

"Please. Let me handle it, Colonel," Andrei said, as Jack finally reached the group.

Krasilov looked around as the Messerschmitt continued to circle overhead. "Any other volunteers?"

The rest of the pilots raised their hands. Krasilov fixed his gaze on Jack, who remained a few feet behind the group. "How about you, Captain? Would you like to show us the real capability of your craft? Up there is a good opportunity to do so."

All the eyes were on him. Jack inhaled deeply and scanned the curious looks on the Soviet faces.

"I can't, Colonel. My orders are very strict. I'm only supposed to train . . ."

Krasilov raised his right palm and waved him off. "Andrei, the German's all yours!"

Andrei raced for his craft. Krasilov stared at Jack long and hard. Jack thought he saw a smile briefly flickering across the Russian's face.

"There is an old saying in my hometown of Lvov, Captain Towers," Krasilov finally said. "Knowing and not doing are the same as not knowing at all. This is a war. Up there is the enemy. You are a pilot. It is all very plain and simple." Krasilov turned and joined the other pilots, who had circled Andrei's craft to wish him good luck.

Jack closed his eyes and frowned.

————

Andrei pushed the throttle handle forward and tax-ied the craft onto the wide concrete runway. He thought about taxiing to one end, but decided he had more than enough runway to either side of him for a short takeoff. He turned his craft into the wind, pressed the brakes, lowered flaps, and applied full throttle. The liquid-cooled Klimov bellowed dark smoke for a few seconds before slowly begin-ning to drag the seven-thousand-pound craft over the slippery surface.

Andrei let go of the brakes, and the La-3 shot forward at great speed. He pulled the stick when the indicated airspeed read 120 knots, and the Lavo-chkin fighter left the ground.

Andrei raised flaps and gear, trimmed the eleva-tors, and turned off the auxiliary fuel pump. The La-3 cleared the trees and sprinted upward. The moment he reached the Messerschmitt, the German plane flew next to his right wing. Both pilots looked at one another for a few seconds before breaking in opposite directions.

Andrei went for another climb and reached a cu-mulus cloud ten seconds later. The German was no-where in sight. The cloud engulfed him. Andrei leveled off, pulled back the throttle, lowered flaps, and began a slow and tight 360-degree turn.

Next to the runway, Jack squinted as he lost Andrei in the clouds. He anxiously waited for him to reap-pear at the other end, but the Lavochkin remained hidden. He spotted the German fighter circling the area, looking for the Soviet.

Andrei inverted his craft and continued his turn while slowly descending. He did six more revolu-tions before the canopy broke through the clouds.

His head felt about to burst from the blood pressure of being upside down. He remained like that for a few more seconds as he looked up toward the ground . . . *there!* He smiled when the German fighter came into plain view a thousand feet below him.

The Soviet pulled the stick back, and the machine adopted an inverted dive profile. Airspeed quickly began to gather. The German kept the shallow turn. Three hundred knots. The German was no more than five hundred feet away, and still did not see Andrei . . . now he did! The Gustav also inverted and started a dive, but Andrei already had more speed than necessary to close the gap in five more seconds.

The Gustav's tail filled his windshield. Andrei squeezed the trigger, and the single, nose-mounted 20mm cannon began to fire. Dozens of rounds ripped through the German's rear fuselage. Three more seconds was all Andrei had before he had to pull up to avoid ramming the German, but that was all he needed. The empennage broke off from the fiery punishment.

"Left, left!" He told himself aloud as he changed his evasive at the very last second, opting for a hard left instead of a pull-up to avoid flying into the tail. A mild two Gs pressed him against his seat as he continued the turn at the same altitude while looking backward and down at the falling craft.

Without a tail section, the Messerschmitt, whose engine was still running, spun out of control along all axes for another minute before crashing next to a stream a mile east of the runway. Andrei saw no parachute.

———

Jack watched the La-3 rock its wings and make two full-speed low passes over the airfield as the pilots broke into a loud cheer. The Lavochkin came back around, dropped its landing gear, softly touched down, and taxied back to the side of the runway. The pilots gathered around the craft. Jack saw Krasilov staring at him as Andrei jumped out of the plane and climbed down the wingroot. The Soviet colonel shook his head, smiled, and turned around.

Jack silently cursed the Air Corps for sending him here.

KALACH AIRFIELD, TWENTY MILES WEST OF THE STALINGRAD POCKET • DECEMBER 14, 1942

Jack Towers had an audience of seven pilots, including Andrei and Krasilov. The grumpy Soviet colonel with the scarred forehead had already told Jack that he had no interest in participating in the class, but since his new La-3 would not arrive for another two weeks, he had no other choice in order to remain airborne.

Temperatures had increased to ten degrees below, creating what most Russians considered a warm winter day. The sky, however, remained heavily overcast, and a light breeze swept over the clearing.

Andrei and Jack had dragged the heavy P-39D simulator outside so that he could explain more easily to the men the basics of the Aircobra's cockpit before each test-flew his "lend-leased" craft.

There had been an instant chemistry between Jack and Andrei. The young Soviet pilot's openness and friendliness had made up for Krasilov's querulous behavior. From Andrei, Jack had learned that he was the younger of two brothers. His older brother, Boris Ivanovich, had been reported missing during the Battle of Moscow several months back. Jack saw pain in the Slav's blue eyes as he related the incident to him. Andrei's only hope was that his brother had been taken prisoner, but that hope was also a curse. Death was sometimes preferable to a German prison camp for what the Nazis considered a lower race.

Jack knew he was dealing with professional fighter pilots, most of whom had seen more aerial combat than Jack ever saw during his short posting in North Africa, and probably more than he would ever expect to encounter during the entire war.

Next to the runway, all the P-39Ds had already been assembled and their engines tested by Krasilov's mechanics, some of whom, to Jack's surprise, had been women. The craft were parked in a three-sided earth-and-wood shelter, and were spaced roughly 150 feet from each other. These precautions were to protect the aircraft from indirect hits of enemy fragmentation bombs, and also to minimize the chance of one plane's explosion igniting the craft on either side.

"All right, listen up," he began, as all eyes focused on him. "As most of you probably realize by now, the Aircobra is different from all other fighters in that it uses a tricycle-style landing gear instead of the traditional three-wheel rear landing gear scheme that all of you are used to working with. This will make your landing a bit different because right before touchdown you will have to pull the nose up and let the main gear touch down first. After that, don't force the nose gear down, simply cut back power and let it fall by itself. Everyone with me?"

Jack noticed a few of the pilots barely nodding. "All right. Next thing that is nonconventional is the engine location. As most of you have probably heard from your mechanics, the Aircobra's engine is located directly behind the pilot. That has both advantages and disadvantages. On the positive side, in addition to providing better overall balance because of its proximity to the plane's center of gravity, if the engine catches fire, the flames will be directed away from you. That's good. Also, for the most part, unless you make a basic dogfighting mistake and get caught broadside, the enemy will try to shoot you down from the rear . . . well, with the Aircobra you don't have to worry about getting your head blown off. There is a ton of aluminum and steel behind you to absorb the bullets. That is also good.

"Now, on the negative side, since the engine is on back, most of the ammo is carried in the nose. That has the effect of changing the weight ratio of the plane as the ammunition is consumed. The more you fire, the lighter the nose will get, and the more you will have to trim the elevons. It will be awkward at first, but with time it'll become second nature.

"Something that will feel strange in the beginning is the use of the 37mm nose-mounted cannon. From what Andrei has told me, the highest caliber that most of you have in your La-3s is 20mm. Well, 37mm is an entirely different beast. It will take some time to get used to its recoil, so go easy on it at first. Any questions so far?"

He got no response. Jack took it as a no and continued for another thirty minutes, covering everything from the locations of the instruments, weapon systems, radios, and throttle controls, to critical airspeeds, maximum speed, and G forces.

When he finished, he stepped away from the simulator and looked at the Soviets. "Any questions?"

All of the pilots glanced at Krasilov, who simply

nodded and headed for his Aircobra. The other pilots did the same.

"Wait, Andrei. What in the hell is going on?"

"No man will dare ask a question unless Krasilov asks it first, Jackovich."

"Are you serious? You mean to tell me that those pilots would rather risk their lives and try out something they're not sure about rather than just ask?"

Andrei raised his eyebrows. "We are all professional pilots, Jackovich. To us a plane is just a plane." The Soviet pilot walked away and joined the others.

"Crazy bastards," he murmured in disbelief as he headed for the nearest burning barrel in the base. Almost an hour outside in ten below had stiffened Jack's muscles.

As he reached the barrel, Jack pulled out his gloved hands from inside his leather coat's side pockets and extended them in front of the fire. The P-39Ds' engines came alive one after the other.

· Jack turned his head and watched the pilots play with the throttle controls, elevons, rudder, and ailerons, before taxiing away single file behind Krasilov.

"Crazy bastards," he murmured again, as Krasilov and the other pilots reached the runway and positioned themselves in pairs. A green rocket was fired, and the first pair rolled down the concrete runway, which was roughly two thousand yards long by about five hundred wide, and ran east–west to go along the region's prevailing wind direction. The surface was made up of octagonal concrete paving slabs about two yards across. As Andrei had explained to him earlier that morning while they dragged the simulator, hundreds of civilians had laid this surface in a vast interlocking honeycomb pattern soon after the ground had been leveled by Red Army engineers. Jack saw the advantage of such a runway when it came time to repair it by simply replacing individual slabs.

In all, the base was built with safety and practicality in mind. All ammunition and fuel was stored in underground dugouts, and all the buildings and hangars had camouflaged roofs.

"Are you going to join the crazy bastards, Captain Towers?" said a low and deep female voice behind him.

Startled, Jack spun around and stared at a tall woman dressed in an old-fashioned aviator suit—the type he'd seen in World War I pictures, with the high sheepskin boots, heavy leather helmet, scarf, and thick jacket. A pistol leaned into her slender waist as she bent to pick up another log and throw it into the barrel.

"Fire's dying out," the woman said while she pulled up her leather cap. She wore an elegant pure silk helmet underneath, which she carefully removed, folded, and tucked away in a coat pocket. She let her blond hair fall down to her shoulders, tousled it up, then regarded Jack with a mix of curiosity and amusement.

"Anything wrong, Captain?"

Jack was shocked to see an attractive Slavic women in such a harsh place. Her inquisitive hazel eyes were fixed on him.

"Ah . . . no. I'm not allowed to go along with the pilots. I'm just here to train them, Miss . . . ?"

"I'm pilot Natalya Makarova, Captain," she responded with an air of confidence that Jack was not used to seeing in a woman. Much less a woman pilot.

"You're a pilot?"

Natalya tilted her head. "Does that surprise you, Captain?" she asked with humor. The hazel eyes crinkled slightly as she grinned.

"I never thought that—"

"A woman could actually fly a fighter plane? Well, welcome to the twentieth century, Captain Towers."

Jack couldn't help but smile.

"You think it's funny I'm a pilot, Captain?" This time her tone of voice became a bit more serious.

"Oh, no, no. It's nothing like that. You'll have to forgive me, Natalya, but this is the first time that—"

"It's all right. I've seen that reaction plenty of times before. I'm used to it."

Jack extended his hand, deciding that his stay at this base might not be as bad as he had first imagined. He wondered if all of the other women pilots were this beautiful. "Well, it's a pleasure to meet you, Natalya Makarova."

Natalya pumped his hand firmly. "The pleasure is mine, Jack Towers."

"Call me Jack."

"All right."

"So, what kind of planes do you fly, Natalya?"

Natalya frowned. "What plane I would *like* to fly? Or what plane Colonel Krasilov *makes* me and the other women pilots fly?"

Before he could say a word, Natalya added, "I fly something you would never dare set a finger on, Jack." She gave him a final smile and started to walk away.

"You never told me how you knew my name."

She turned briefly. "News travel fast."

"Natalya, I . . . where are you staying . . . I'd like to get to know you better."

The smile disappeared from her face. The look

in her eyes was now as cold as the Russian winter. "This is war, Jack. There isn't time for anything else. I'm having a hard time proving myself to these bunch of chauvinist pilots as it is. I don't need . . . complications, especially with an American. It was nice meeting you."

Jack exhaled in disappointment, watching her walk away and disappear behind some tents on the other side of the airstrip. Resigned to the fact that his stay here would be as bad as it had first appeared, he turned to the fire and extended his hands against it once more. These Russians were certainly different from the jovial crowd he knew from his mother's family.

He raised his gaze and saw the formation of P-39Ds in the distance.

Crazy bastards.

Kalach Airfield, Twenty Miles West of the Stalingrad Pocket • December 15, 1942

REF: CX/MSS/T347/67   HP3434

ZZZZZ

((HP 3434 & 3434 CR ONA GT OX YKE GU 7 & 7))

ORDERS AT ONE TWO ZERO ZERO HOURS TWELFTH FOR THIRTEENTH. FIRSTLY, JAGDGESCHWADER 52, GRUPPE I TO ATTACK TEN MILES NORTH OF AKSAI RIVER IN SUPPORT OF GERMAN TANK ATTACK IN THE KOTELNIKOVO AREA. SECOND ALTERNATIVE EIGHTY MILES SOUTHWEST OF STALINGRAD. GENERALLEUTNANT VON HOTHZZZZZ

AM

CR   150700/12/42

Holding the piece of paper that a Soviet radio operator had just passed to him, Jack Towers quickly jotted the Russian equivalent at the bottom, and a minute later, he entered the briefing bunker where Krasilov and his pilots had gathered to go over the day's next mission. Krasilov's mood seemed to have improved from the day before. The Soviet colonel was laughing loudly as he and Andrei slammed two empty vodka glasses on a wooden table.

Krasilov's face was streaked with oil from a heavy leak in one of the last few La-3s on the base. Krasilov, as Andrei had told him earlier that chilly morning, had gone on a two-plane hunting trip looking for Germans, but instead of taking one of the new Aircobras, the stubborn colonel had opted for a weathered La-3 instead. As it turned out, the engine began to leak oil shortly after takeoff, and Krasilov had to make an emergency landing.

As Jack got closer to the table, he could see the imprints of Krasilov's oily fingers on the empty glass. His flying helmet, also stained with oil, lay on the table next to a thick belt with a holstered pistol. The Russian colonel lifted his head.

"Ah, comrades, look. It's the impatient virgin!"

Some of the men roared with laughter. Two fell to the floor and slapped the top of their legs with mirth. Andrei slowly shook his head.

Jack reddened for a moment before sitting across from a snickering Krasilov. The smile froze on the Russian's face as Jack stared at him and slid the piece of paper across the table. The Russian's scarred forehead wrinkled as he narrowed his eyes.

"This just came in for me, Colonel."

Krasilov read on for a minute, then his face turned red. He abruptly got up, tipping his chair and stomping his large fists on the table.

"It's too late to intercept! What took this message so long to get here?"

"It went through a lot of hands to reach this side of the world, Colonel."

"Well, it's useless! The fighting starts in a half hour and it's over seventy-five miles away. We won't get there in time!"

Krasilov picked up his chair and sat back down. His face showed obvious frustration. This time it was Jack's turn to smile.

"You're overlooking one important fact, Colonel."

Krasilov briefly studied Jack. The ends of the Russian's thick eyebrows dropped a bit. "What's on your mind?"

Jack reached for the bottle of vodka, which also had Krasilov's oily imprints, took a sip, and set it down in front of him. "Even if your fighters don't get there in time to help the ground troops, you can still get there after the German planes have exhausted their fuel and ammunition . . . and simply shoot them down."

Krasilov remained silent. Everyone else in the room quieted down. For a few seconds, the only sound inside the bunker was the crack and fizzle of the stove and the constant wail of the wind outside. Then Krasilov got up slowly, glanced down at Jack once more, and scanned the room.

"Everyone to his plane! Now!"

The men rushed outside the bunker. Jack remained seated. He felt Krasilov's eyes on him. "Are you coming, Captain?"

"I'm not allowed to engage in battle, sir. My orders are strictly to—"

"You mean to tell me you get information like this and come up with this clever idea, and then you, a pilot with a plane ready to fly outside, are just going to sit and listen to the radio?"

"Colonel, I've been ordered not to—"

Krasilov exhaled. "You are a virgin after all."

Jack clenched his teeth as Krasilov walked outside. The Russian stopped by the doorway and turned around. "You wouldn't mind if I take your *Impatient Virgin*, ah, Captain? A plane without a pilot is like a woman without a husband. Perhaps she will grow to like me better than you."

Jack tried to control his anger but failed. Krasilov had crossed the line. He could take the colonel's bad attitude toward him, a sarcastic remark here and there, but not that. It was bad enough he had been sent to this godforsaken place to freeze to death, but he was not going to put up with the colonel's harassment any longer.

"The fuck I do mind, you hardheaded, egotistical bastard! You keep your damn hands off my plane! I'll fly it myself!" Jack stormed past Krasilov and headed for his plane.

Krasilov went after him. Jack picked up his pace and got to his Aircobra before Krasilov got a chance to catch up. As Jack stepped up to his plane, Krasilov extended his arms in the air.

"Listen, everyone! Listen!"

All the other pilots, including Natalya and three other women working on the engine of the La-3 Krasilov had flown earlier that morning, turned their heads.

"Today," Krasilov said in a sarcastic, half-humorous tone, "we'll be honored by having Captain Jack Towers from the United States Army Air Corps come along with us!"

"Who's gonna be his wingman, Colonel?"

screamed Andrei from the cockpit of his Aircobra. "We're already teamed up in pairs."

Krasilov's smile grew wide. Jack didn't like the looks of it. "We're gonna let one of our own virgins fly with the American virgin. Natalya! You will be Captain Tower's wingman today!"

The pilots burst into a loud laugh along with Krasilov. Jack grinned and glanced at Natalya. Their gaze met. Jack winked. Natalya threw down the rag in her hands and headed over to an La-3 parked next to the one she was working on.

Jack shrugged, donned a parachute, and crawled inside the Aircobra's cockpit. He was airborne five minutes later. "Stay on my tail no matter what, Natalya," he said over the radio.

"You worry about the Germans in front of you, Jack," Natalya replied as she kept her fighter plane slightly behind and to his right. "I'll handle the rear."

TEN MILES NORTH OF THE AKSAI RIVER •
DECEMBER 15, 1942

Jack Towers watched Krasilov take the lead with his wingman, Andrei. He cut back the throttle and let Krasilov get a thousand feet in front of him. Airspeed was three hundred knots, and the plane felt just right. The trimming on both throttle and elevons was as it should be, reducing to a minimum the effort Jack had to exert on the stick to maintain a level flight. He glanced backward and saw Natalya glued to his left.

"Up above, Jack!" he heard her voice crackling through his headset.

"What? Where?"

"Germans. Nine o'clock. About three thousand feet up."

Jack squinted. Even though he wore sunglasses, the glare from the early-morning sun filtering through the curved canopy glass stung his eyes. A few more seconds, and he spotted them.

"Damn! Look at them! It must be at least ..."

"I'm counting over thirty planes, free hunters," Krasilov shouted. "Scramble! Work in pairs! Dive-bombers are the highest priority!"

Jack slammed full throttle, jammed the stick back, and lifted the trigger-guard case. The Gs piled up on him as his craft roared higher at great speed. The altimeter dashed above nine thousand feet ... ninety-five hundred ... ten thousand. Airspeed quickly began to decrease. Jack lowered the nose by a few degrees and pointed it toward the rightmost Stuka formation, but he didn't get much farther in his pursuit. The escorting Gustavs broke flight in all directions. One of them made an inverted dive right turn and threatened to come around on Jack's tail. Jack broke left, rolled the plane on its side, and faced the incoming Gustav head-on while quickly verifying that Natalya was still with him. She was.

The Gustav was less than a thousand feet away and closing at great speed. Jack squeezed the trigger as he coordinated the rudder, ailerons, and elevons to keep the German aligned in his sights. The 37mm blasts started, two per second. The mighty recoil pounded against the entire fuselage, giving Jack the impression of having a second heartbeat in his chest. He noticed the airspeed indicator needle quivering with every burst. For a second he wasn't sure if it was just the vibrations from the recoil, or if the powerful guns actually had enough energy to slow down the plane momentarily. It didn't matter.

His airspeed had already gone through the roof at 410 knots, way beyond the safe envelope.

The Gustav grew larger. Jack could now see the muzzle flashes from the nose-mounted cannon. There were no hits. Jack waited until the last minute before pulling up . . . and the German also pulled up!

"Jack!" he heard Natalya scream.

Instinctively, Jack swung the stick right and forward. For a brief second his entire field of view was nothing but the large cross painted on the underside of the Messerschmitt's left wing. Jack thought he was going to collide. In a blur, the Gustav's gray underside grazed his canopy as he heard the loud thump from the tail wheel striking his rudder. It was over before his mind got a chance to register it all. He had come within inches of disaster.

Jack snapped his head back as he applied both left and right rudder. The tail was not damaged, and the Messerschmitt had gone for a steep dive

"Stay with me, Natalya!"

Without giving any further thought to his near destruction, Jack pressed full power and hauled the stick back. His body was slammed down as the Gs tore at him. His vision became a narrow tunnel, but it didn't last long. The moment he reached the top of the loop, blood rushed back to his head. He continued the rear pressure until he was pointing straight down, and centered the stick. Airspeed went above 420 knots again. The craft trembled. The vibrations on the stick were getting out of control.

"Jack! We're going too fast!"

"Slow down now, Natalya, and he'll get away," he said in the most confident voice he could fake.

The Gustav continued its dive, and Jack, topping nearly 450 knots, caught up fast, but at the same time, he was dropping at a staggering rate. With sweat rolling into the corners of his eyes, Jack saw the altimeter dip below five thousand feet. The Aircobra plunged into a cloud. Jack lost the German for a second, acquiring again as he left the cloud behind.

Five hundred feet. The gap between the planes was being closed too fast. Three hundred feet . . . two hundred . . . The Gustav remained on his dive. Jack cut back power and squeezed the trigger.

The Gustav pulled up while breaking hard left. The sun flashed off the Gustav's wings as Jack tried to follow it; but outspeeding the German by a hundred knots, Jack found his craft making a wider turn than he liked. Instead of cutting back power to get some relief from the titanic centrifugal force that made his limbs feel five times his weight, Jack added throttle and instantly saw his vision reduced to a small dot—his body's warning that he was pushing maximum G. Anything more and he would either pass out . . . or the wings of the Aircobra would fold. Neither happened. Jack's gamble worked. He kept on pursuing, and as he completed the turn and leveled off, he was only three hundred feet from the German at roughly the same airspeed.

The Gustav pulled up in full throttle. Jack saw condensation pour off the wingtips as the Gs blasted over the Messerschmitt struggling for altitude. He stayed with it.

Another two turns, a throttle adjustment, and a final turn, and Jack opened fire. This time it was easier. A few short bursts, and the Gustav arched down toward the ground, leaving a trail of smoke on its path. Jack saw no parachute, and glanced back and noticed that Natalya was still with him.

"Good flying, Natalya!" he said in a more naturally confident voice.

"Good shooting, Jack."

Jack pointed his craft back toward the Stukas, who continued to fly in formation toward the Soviet tanks north of the Aksai River. He approached a Stuka from its most vulnerable spot: the rear underside. It was the rightmost plane of the rightmost formation. As two small clouds of black smoke bellowed from the exhausts and wafted away in the slipstream, Jack let go several rounds. A river of holes exploded across the Stuka's right wing before it broke apart from the fuselage. Jack cut left, dove to three thousand feet, made a 360, and as the Stuka spun down to earth, he advanced the throttle, tugged back the control stick, and aligned the next dive-bomber.

"Left, Jack. Break left!" Natalya screamed as she broke right.

Jack automatically responded to Natalya's shouts while moving his head in all directions to find . . . there! Another Gustav diving toward him. The craft caught him broadside. Natalya was trying a 360 to get the German fighter before it got Jack.

The muzzle flashes started. Jack had to figure a way to get out of the German's line of fire before he got closer. He briefly glanced at Natalya coming to his rescue at full speed, but she would be several seconds too late.

Instincts took over. As the rapidly approaching dark green Messerschmitt became hazy behind the bright flashes of its cannon's guns, Jack idled the throttle, added flaps, and dropped the gear. Airspeed quickly plummeted to two hundred knots, and two seconds later the Gustav zoomed past Jack's field of view at great speed, too fast for Jack to fire,

but close enough for him to go in pursuit. The
German went into a steep climb.

Gear and flaps up, full throttle, stick back, and
the sun bathed his canopy as he pointed his nose at
the heavens. The Gustav was pushing for altitude
five hundred feet above him. Jack squinted at the
glare, but it was not the sun. There was something
else reflecting the bright light. Something flying
very high.

Jack applied full power and slammed the stick to
the right to close the gap on the departing Messerschmitt Me 109G. The Gustav went into another vertical climb while executing a left corkscrew. The
palms of his hands moist inside his gloves, Jack
pulled the stick back and felt his eyeballs about to
burst from the Gs. His vision temporarily reddened
and got cloudier while rivulets of sweat tricked down
his forehead, but he did not ease on the rear pressure or power. He followed the Me 109G all the way
up to eleven thousand feet before the Gustav tried
to shake Jack off by executing an inverted dive to
the left.

Jack momentarily eased back the throttle, pushed
the stick hard over to the left, and slammed full
power once more. In the corner of his eye he spotted Natalya on the La-3 getting so close to him that
for a second he thought she was going to ram him,
but she didn't. She executed the maneuver beautifully and stayed slightly behind and to his right.

He had the Gustav in his sights. Jack let go a short
burst of the powerful 37mm nose-mounted cannon.
The Aircobra shuddered with every blow as the all-
aluminum structure absorbed the M4 cannon's powerful recoil once every two seconds. It took six bursts
before the Gustav fell apart. Several rounds pierced
through the rear fuselage, tearing off the tail and

the left wing with a bright flash. The sky in front of
him suddenly filled with fire. Jack pulled left and
noticed Natalya breaking right. The wreckage was
still too thick to fly through.

Jack scanned the skies for Natalya but couldn't
find her. He half rolled the Aircobra to the left and
back in the direction of the fallen Gustav. She had
gone the other way and the sky was filled with . . .
there she was . . . with a Gustav diving toward her!

"Natalya! Break left! Left!"

The Soviet woman did and barely missed the cannons of the Gustav as it leveled off behind her. The
Messerschmitt closed for the kill. Jack saw Natalya
desperately going for a steep climb and turn, but
the Gustav easily imitated the maneuver and opened
fire again.

"Invert and dive right, Natalya! Now!"

She did, and the Gustav followed, and he followed
the Gustav. Natalya completed the dive and pulled
up at less than three hundred feet above ground,
with the Gustav on her tail. Jack closed the gap . . .
so close that he could almost touch the Gustav's vertical fin. The dangerously low altitude at which the
trio had pulled out of the dive didn't sink in until
a few seconds later. Jack's concentration was so intense that he had nearly blocked everything else
from his mind. Natalya's change of direction had
gone from a shallow to a very intense and abrupt
tight left turn. Her wingtip was less than twenty feet
from the treetops. The Gustav was beginning to
have a hard time keeping up, and so did Jack.

He glanced at the altimeter. Fifty feet. Natalya
briefly leveled off, and so did the Gustav, but Jack
already had an angle on the Messerschmitt even before the Gustav's wings became flushed with the horizon.

Another five bursts from the cannon at such close distance, and the Gustav went up in a ball of orange flames.

"Good flying, Natalya!"

"Thank you, Jack. Thanks, really."

She reduced airspeed enough to let him get by and take the lead once more. Jack pulled up and began a steep climb, when directly above him he saw something zooming across the sky at great speed. Whatever it was had come and gone in a couple of seconds.

"What in the hell was that?"

"I saw it too, Jack. Can't tell, but there were two of them."

Puzzled, Jack scanned the skies, and saw Krasilov and Andrei closing in on another Gustav. There were three other pairs in the air, each with their hands full, but they were all normal planes . . . there it went again. This time Jack got a good look at them.

"They're jet aircraft!"

"What?"

"Jets, Natalya. Airplanes without propellers using jet propulsion technology! Sweet Jesus!"

The pair of fighters dashed past a group of scattered clouds and closed in on Krasilov and Andrei.

"Watch out, Colonel! You've got two on your tail!"

Jack noticed Krasilov breaking hard left as the two jets made a quick pass from behind.

"I'm hit! I'm hit!" Jack heard Andrei scream over the radio.

"Andrei, this is Jack. Can you make it to the base?"

"I'm not sure, Jackovich. I still got some power but the smoke . . . I can't see through it."

"I'll tell you what. Don't pull back throttles. We're only ten minutes away. I'll come up on your right side and take you all the way home. Once over the field you can cut back power and glide your way in. The Aircobras float beautifully."

"Thanks, Jackovich."

At four thousand feet, Jack saw Andrei's plane, followed by a river of smoke a mile ahead of him. He was about to add throttle when something zoomed past him. It was the second jet, and it was headed directly for Andrei. A moment later the Russian's plane caught fire.

"Turn the plane over and drop, Andrei!" Jack heard Krasilov scream over the radio as he watched Andrei's craft in a steep climb. The fighter inverted, and the nose dropped a few degrees. Jack held his breath, waiting for Andrei to leave the burning craft, but no one dropped.

"Get out of there, dammit!" screamed Jack.

"I can't . . . the canopy! The bullets bent it! It's jammed . . . it won't give . . . the flames! My back is on fire! My legs!"

Jack watched as Andrei's cockpit filled with smoke first, then with fire. The Aircobra went into a dive, but to Jack's utter surprise, it was not an uncontrollable dive.

"I'm burning! I'm burning! . . . Stick left! Rudder left . . . stick forward!"

Jack was speechless. He could see clearly the inside of the cockpit filled with flames and Andrei's blazing figure talking himself into the last few maneuvers. In his agony, the young Russian had kept his hand pressed on the radio transmit button.

Jack saw the target, a slower Me 110 twin-engine fighter. Andrei's plane, now totally ablaze, dashed across the sky like a comet and approached the Me 110 at great speed. The Messerschmitt tried to break left, but not soon enough. With a final cry of despair, Jack heard Andrei curse the Germans as both planes exploded in a spectacular ball of flames and debris.

Jack saw the two jets depart the area. He didn't even attempt to pursue. Krasilov was in trouble. With all the commotion with the jets, a Gustav had managed to sneak behind the Soviet colonel.

"Hang in there, Colonel. I'm on my way!" screamed Jack as he set the craft in a vertical dive and closed in on the Messerschmitt.

The negative Gs pushing him up against the Aircobra's restraining harness, Jack lined up the Gustav and fired a short burst from the wings' 12.7mm guns. Nothing. He closed in a bit more. Krasilov pulled up and rose to the sky like an elevator. The German did likewise, and Jack and Natalya followed along.

"Take the shot, Captain! Get this Hitlerite bastard off my tail!"

"Trying, Colonel. I'm fucking trying. On my mark break hard right. Hard right. Got that?"

"Got it."

"Three . . . two . . ." Jack broke hard right and cut back throttle. "One . . . now!" Jack was now flying parallel to them.

Krasilov broke right. Jack swung the stick left and caught the German broadside. The pilot realized he'd been tricked just as Jack opened fire with the 37mm cannon at less than fifty feet. The Gustav came apart. Jack and Natalya flew through the flames and emerged on the other side.

The trio climbed to five thousand feet and were soon joined by three more pairs. Behind, they left the still-blazing wreckage of the Me 110 and Andrei's Aircobra, along with five destroyed Gustavs and three Stukas. The remaining Stukas were already out of sight and out of reach. Everyone had barely enough fuel to make it back to base. Not only had they lost Andrei, but they had not been able to stop the bulk of the Stuka force from reaching the Soviet front lines.

KALACH AIRFIELD, TWENTY MILES WEST OF THE STALINGRAD POCKET • DECEMBER 15, 1942

Jack taxied his airplane into the three-sided shelter, turned it around, idled the engine, and cut back the air/fuel mixture. The propeller stopped. He powered down the magnetos and the master switch, unstrapped his upper and lower safety harness, removed his parachute, pulled the canopy open, and climbed outside.

He walked over to Natalya's La-3. She was climbing down with her parachute still on her back.

"Your parachute," he said, pointing to her back.

She nodded, unstrapped it, and threw it inside the cockpit. "What a terrible thing, Jack," she said, jumping on the frozen ground. He noticed the lines down her cheeks. She had been crying. "I was very close to his older brother."

"The one missing in action?"

"Yes. Now Andrei . . ." Natalya lowered her gaze and slowly walked away. Jack was about to follow her, but decided against it. She needed her privacy.

That afternoon, Jack walked inside the briefing bunker and saw a lonely Krasilov behind a half-drunk bottle of vodka. Jack noticed the pad and pencil next to two crumpled sheets on the side of the table.

"Mind if I join you, Colonel?"

Krasilov pointed at a chair across the table. Jack

took it while Krasilov slid the bottle over to his side.
Jack took a sip, letting the liquid warm his mouth
and throat before swallowing it. He took a second
sip and eased back on the chair.

"I'm very sorry about Andrei, Colonel. I understand he was a close friend."

Krasilov's bloodshot eyes stared directly at him.
"He was a good friend, Captain. He has a mother
and three sisters living in Moscow. His older brother
went missing some time back. Now I'm left with the
burden of writing to them, but as you can see, the
words are not there. That poor woman has now lost
two sons."

Jack exhaled and took another sip. His chest felt
warm. He slid the bottle back to Krasilov, who took
a long swig, swallowed it, and took an even longer
second. The Russian set the bottle down.

"Andrei was a fine warrior, Captain Towers."

"Call me Jack, Colonel."

Krasilov grinned slightly. "I go by Aleksandr. Now,
listen, Jackovich . . . about today. What you did . . ."

"You would have done the same for me."

"Probably not before today."

Jack shrugged.

"You fly well, Jackovich. The American Air Corps
has good pilots and good machines."

"Thanks."

"The . . . *Impatient Virgin* . . . why?"

Jack smiled. "Named it after a girl I met while in
flying school. She was pretty wild, as you can imagine."

"Hmm," Krasilov retorted as he drank more
vodka. "Might as well enjoy it while you're young.
Before life hardens your heart."

Jack narrowed his eyes as Krasilov lowered his
gaze and fixed it on the bottom of the bottle.

"The war will be over soon, Aleksandr. After that we shall all be able to get on with our lives."

Krasilov leveled his gaze with Jack and breathed deeply. "Maybe that's something you can do, Jackovich, since there is no war in your motherland, but here there won't be much left for us after the war."

"But surely you must have a family, Aleksandr. A wife maybe, or a brother or sister?"

Jack saw pained expressions brushing over Krasilov's face. The Russian took another swig, set the bottle down, and began to speak, slowly and moderately. Although the context of his words was appalling, his tone never changed. When he finished, he took another swig.

"I'm deeply sorry about your wife and daughters, Aleksandr. I had no idea."

"It happened a long time ago. It's all right now. You have a cigarette, Jackovich?"

Still a bit stunned from the revelation, Jack reached for his pack of American cigarettes and handed them to Krasilov, along with a lighter. The Russian briefly inspected the colorful design of the package before pulling out a cigarette.

"Chesterfields? What does that mean?"

"I have no idea."

Krasilov lighted up and took a draw. He narrowed his eyes, exhaled, and took another draw.

"Something wrong?" Jack asked.

Krasilov stared at the cigarette, tore off the filter, took another long draw, and closed his eyes. "Now, *this* is a cigarette."

Jack stared at the filter on the table before looking back at the burly Russian. "By the way, Aleksandr, you've got yourself one hell of a pilot in Natalya. She is very good behind the stick."

Krasilov exhaled. "But she's a woman. I need someone I can depend on as my partner up there, not some shrinking violet that might come apart during a critical situation."

"Well, I'll have to say that she is *exactly* the type of wingman I would like to have. Someone who would stick to me in all weather. Today she did just that, Aleksandr. You should give her a chance." Jack got up. "I'll leave you to your privacy, my friend. Again, I'm truly sorry about Andrei, and about your family."

Krasilov nodded. Jack walked outside. The morning clouds had broken, and the sun now warmed the airstrip. Jack inhaled deeply. The air was cold, but he could breathe it without much trouble. The thermometer outside the bunker read five below zero.

Pulling up the lapels of his jacket, Jack glanced at the fighters parked along the side of the runway behind the three-sided shelters. He stopped and smiled, spotting Natalya standing with a bucket under the engine of the La-3 she had flown that morning. Jack walked in her direction. Her back was to him.

"You're going to be an ace one of these days, Natalya Makarova."

Startled, Natalya spun around, spilling the contents of the bucket by her feet.

"Jack! Look what you made me do! You scared me!"

Jack smiled. Natalya was indeed naturally pretty. The dazzling hazel eyes inspected him. Jack thought he could look into her soul through them. His physical attraction for her went beyond anything he'd felt before. Jack wasn't sure if it was because she was so pretty, or if it was because she was so different from any other woman he'd ever known. Natalya was a woman of substance, and she also seemed to love flying as much as Jack did. He decided that was a very hard combination to find.

She lowered her gaze and picked up the bucket. "Here, now you'll have to help me."

"Help you do what?"

"Just hold the bucket right under . . . here."

Jack picked up the heavy cast-iron bucket and placed it exactly where Natalya told him, beneath the La-3's radiator drainage plug.

Natalya pulled the plug and let the steamy-hot water pour into the bucket. "Steady, Jack."

"Easy for you to say. You're not the one holding it."

"Hmm hmm, I guess I'm gonna have to get one of my Russian comrades with real muscles to—"

"Just keep pouring."

Natalya grinned. "There. You can set it down now."

"What's this for?" he asked as he straightened his back and rubbed his shoulders.

"You're about to find out, Jack." Natalya tousled her hair and leaned forward. "See that other bucket next to the landing gear?"

"Yeah, what about it?"

"It's filled with snow. Bring it over and pour some hot water into it until it gets warm."

Smiling at her ingenuity, Jack did so. Inside the large bucket was a small pint-sized pot. Jack used it to pour water on Natalya's head as she leaned over.

She pulled out a bar of soap and worked up a lather as Jack poured a little more water over her head. After a few moments, he poured some more to rinse it off.

Natalya stood up, pulled her hair back, and

wrapped it with a towel. "Thanks, Jack."

He smiled. "Thank *you*, Natalya."

Eighty Miles Southwest of the Stalingrad Pocket • December 16, 1942

Firmly clutching a weathered machine gun he had taken from a fallen German soldier weeks ago, Aris Broz moved swiftly and quietly on a dry ravine that bordered the road where he was certain German panzers would soon be crossing through.

His sheepskin-covered boots sank deep in the snowbank as he struggled to keep his balance and move forward for another ten feet before stopping to listen. His trained ears searched for noises other than the howl of the wind sweeping through the trees, yet they detected nothing.

He continued.

Trained in the classic hit-and-run Partisan tactics by his father, who was posthumously named a hero of the Soviet Union for taking out an entire squadron of Germans before turning the gun on himself to avoid being captured alive, and by his uncle, the famous Yugoslav Josip Broz, known by his comrades in arms as Tito, the thirty-year-old Aris considered himself a Partisan in the true sense of the word. He was not Russian by birth. He was Yugoslav, although no one could tell by his accent—something that was useful during recruiting trips. And, of course, he was a Broz. Tito himself had sent Aris to these regions with orders to recruit fresh troops among the men and women of the western Ukraine and eastern Russia, and train them in the art of guerrilla warfare to fight the Germans in the region.

Most of the recruits were peasants, people who

had lost everything to the Germans, including loved ones. They were people who had nothing to lose and an uncompromising will to fight to the death. Aris had seen fifteen- and sixteen-year-old girls turned into women overnight after Germans had raped them, and they had subsequently joined Aris's Partisan force with a desire to learn to fight back that even Aris himself found extreme. Those were his soldiers, his guerrillas, his Partisans. Missions ranged from minor ambushes of German motorcyclists carrying messages to and from the front, to the destruction of bridges, roads, railroads, and anything else that disrupted the flow of supplies to the German forces.

To accomplish these tasks Aris would spread his warriors in small groups of six or seven on the outside. His logic was simple: If the mission backfired, the loss of soldiers and equipment could be easily replaced in a week's time. It also allowed him to strike multiple targets in synchronized fashion to give the enemy the impression of being attacked by a much larger force.

Sometimes, when a mission called for a large number of Partisans, Aris would be careful enough to divide the large group into small subgroups, or packs, each with its own independent escape route.

For Aris and his guerrillas, stealth and surprise meant survival. Capture meant torture, mutilation, and hanging. That was the grim fate of captured Partisans. In addition to the risk of his soldiers being captured, the Germans had recently added another dimension to the Partisan war. They had set a strict set of guidelines that defined how many innocent peasants—women and children included—were to be executed on the spot for a particular type of Partisan crime. The loss of one German soldier usually

meant the hanging of ten or more civilians picked
at random off the streets of cities or villages. The
new German directive was, of course, created with
the hope that it would force the Partisans to slow
down or even stop their attacks, but in the few
months since its implementation the opposite had
happened. More and more peasants had approached Aris with the wish to be trained to fight
the Germans.

Yes, the Germans would butcher captured Partisans, but the opposite held true. Aris had seen many
German soldiers putting pistols to their heads when
surrounded by Partisans, and that suited Aris just
fine.

His Partisans were many in numbers, but none of
them were with Aris on that chilly and humid morning as he continued uphill for another hundred meters before checking for enemy tanks once more.
This time he heard them coming. With a grin on
his face, the Yugoslav guerrilla leader set the machine gun next to a tree and removed a sack hanging from his back. There was a handful of explosives
in there. Not enough to destroy a tank, but simply
destroying a tank wasn't his mission that day. Aris
had chosen something much more dangerous than
that and had opted to do it alone. The risk was too
high, and besides, he moved better alone. He knew
the forest—every square inch of it. He knew where
the hideouts were, sources of food, shelter . . . and
weapons. Aris always had weapons hidden everywhere, and all his soldiers knew of their locations.
It was a contingency that had saved a number of his
guerrillas' lives in the past.

Aris cautiously walked up the side of the ravine
and reached the edge of the frozen road. His heavy
gloves made his work cumbersome, but he had no

choice. At forty below, his fingers would have crystallized and fallen off after a few minutes of exposure.

First, he strapped a grenade to the trunk of a large tree that leaned in the direction of the road. He attached a thin wire to the safety pin and ran it across the narrow road to the other side, where he secured it around another tree. He walked back across the road and slid an explosive pack between the grenade and the tree. He lifted his head and looked down the road. The tanks were getting closer. Any moment now the lead tank would clear the turn in the road.

Quickly, Aris removed two bottles filled with gasoline. He poured half of the contents of the first on the booby-trapped tree, then ran a river of gas toward the middle of the road, where he emptied the second bottle.

Aris quickly stepped around the large puddle of gas and ran to the side. He slid down to the ravine and sprinted away from the trap until he estimated he was a few hundred yards from it. Then he stopped, climbed up to the side of the road, and waited.

He didn't have to wait for long. Bellowing clouds of blue smoke from its harsh engine exhausts, the first panzer tank came sweeping down the road, closely followed by several soldiers on foot, while others clung to the sides of the armored turret. The smoke swirled over the soldiers' heads and soon joined the smoke from two other tanks, along with several open trucks carrying loads of soldiers. Aris could clearly see the rows of steel-helmeted heads behind the truck.

He held his breath the moment the tank got near the wire . . .

The bright explosion had the desired effect. The tree plummeted over the lead tank, rolled in front of it, and caught on fire. The river of gas turned into a river of fire that ended under the tank. In seconds, the entire underside was in flames, along with the burning tree blocking the road.

The driver and the gunner pushed open the hatch and quickly crawled outside. Two of the soldiers hanging on to the sides caught fire. Aris could hear their guttural screams drifting across the frozen woodland while other soldiers threw snow and blankets over them.

Aris smiled broadly and slid back down to the bottom of the ravine. His father and his uncle would have been proud of him.

As he left the screaming Germans behind, Aris heard something overhead. The forest was too thick to make out what it was. The sound definitely was not that of a plane, but of something else.

Aris's smiled washed away the moment a German plane dropped from the sky and cleared the way for the panzer column with its cannons. He was both furious and also surprised. He had never seen a plane like that. Not only did the craft lack propellers, but it had the firepower to slice a panzer in half.

It didn't matter. For Aris, a plane was a plane, and it was coming back down again. Aris pulled up his machine gun and aimed it at the incoming . . . the craft rushed past his field of view at such speed that Aris didn't have time to let go a single shot. What kind of fighter was that? Did the Germans finally come up with some of the revolutionary weapons that their propaganda officials claimed they had for so long? Aris was not a pilot, but he could guess the type of damage a craft like that could have on the Allied air force.

He slid down the ravine and raced back toward his camp. The word would be passed around. If the German propellerless craft were hidden somewhere in the region, Aris had no doubt his Partisans would find them, and destroy them.

THE SKIES EIGHTY MILES SOUTHWEST OF THE STALINGRAD POCKET • DECEMBER 16, 1942

"Stay with me, Natalya!" screamed Jack as he set his craft in a vertical dive. The Me 109G Gustavs were still in formation several hundred feet below surrounding the Stukas.

Information on the German attack had come sooner this time around, giving Krasilov's free hunters plenty of time to prepare. There were a total of five pairs in the air from Krasilov's fighter wing alone, including Jack and Natalya.

The Gustavs scrambled while the Stukas remained in formation. Jack picked a Gustav and closed in. The Aircobra trembled as Jack pushed it beyond four hundred knots. The wail of the engine rang in his ears as the soul-numbing vibrations made it harder for him to get the right angle. The Gustav went for a vertical climb and turn. Jack pulled back throttle momentarily and swung the stick back. The Gs blasted on his shoulders. His vision reddened, and his palms were sweaty, but he remained on the Gustav's tail. At five thousand feet the Messerschmitt went for a dive. Jack almost pulled back throttle to avoid ramming it, but decided against it. *Reduce throttle now and you'll never catch him, Jack,* he told himself as he floated his plane right up to the Gustav's tail and opened fire with the 37mm cannon.

The tail blew up in pieces, and the craft went into a flat spin. Jack broke right. Natalya followed him. He spotted another Me 109G to his left and swung the control stick in that direction. The wickedly tight turn pressed him against the seat with such might that Jack could barely keep his hand on the throttle control valve.

The Gustav's tail was a few hundred feet straight ahead.

"All yours, Natalya!"

"Wh . . . what?"

"Go, go! It's your kill!" Jack pulled back throttle just a dash to let her take the lead. The Gustav went for a dive. Natalya waved as she dashed past him, inverted her plane, and dove straight down on the Gustav. Jack had a hard time following the maneuver, but he remained on her tail. The Gustav went for a turn and climb. Natalya remained locked on its tail but was not firing yet. She got closer. Jack understood. She wanted to take the Messerschmitt in one burst.

She did, and the Gustav's nose was covered with smoke. Natalya broke left and so did Jack. She searched for another target and found it: a Gustav on Krasilov's tail.

"Break left, Colonel! Left!"

Krasilov and his wingman turned in opposite directions, but the Gustav stayed with the Russian colonel, who turned, dove, and abruptly executed a loop-the-loop.

Natalya inched her way toward the Gustav until she was less than fifty feet away. As she opened fire, Jack spotted something in the corner of his right eye. It came and went in a flash, and for a brief second Jack also heard a thundering machine gun.

When he looked down at Natalya's plane, he noticed that smoke spewed out of the front. He shifted his gaze to the sky and saw the German jet again. *Bastard!*

"Get out of there, Natalya!" he screamed as he saw the nose of her craft catch fire. "Jesus! Get out of there! Jump, dammit. Jump!"

They were flying at three thousand feet. Natalya inverted her plane and lowered the nose. Jack held his breath and saw her drop as the jet came back around, this time in Jack's direction.

As her bright red parachute opened, Jack went for a vertical climb to seven thousand feet. The German zoomed past him. Jack undid his restraining harness and turned his plane in its direction, but by the time he had done that, the jet had already completed a 270-degree turn and was approaching from his right. Jack veered the Aircobra to the right until he saw the jet head-on.

Jack's craft shook violently. He ducked under the windshield and continued to press the trigger of the 37mm nose cannon. The glass windshield shattered, and he was showered with it. The firing lasted but two seconds before Jack saw the grayish underside of the German jet dart over him. He sat up and put on his goggles. The windblast from the propeller nearly jerked his head back, and the frigid air numbed his face.

Jack looked for the German jet. He tilted his wings both ways, but the jet was out of sight. He looked down and saw Natalya reaching the woods. He exhaled in relief.

The sky was still filled with planes. "Aleksandr! Aleksandr!"

"Jackovich, I saw what happened."

"She's fine. She made it down."

"Jackovich! Behind you! Break right! Break—"

Krasilov's words were cut short by roaring cannons. Jack ducked again. The rear windshield, rated to sustain a direct hit from a 20mm cannon, was successful in deflecting the first few rounds before it collapsed, taking the overhead glass along. Once more Jack was bathed in crushed glass. The German scurried past him on his right side.

"Son of a bitch!" Jack cursed over the radio. The German had left him with a convertible Aircobra. *His Aircobra.* His *Impatient Virgin.*

Jack saw the jet returning for another pass. This time he had a plan. He put his craft in a shallow dive while pushing full throttle. Airspeed darted past four hundred knots. He let the German get on his tail.

Jack peeked behind him and saw the German approach at great speed. He waited.

"Break left, Jackovich! Break left!" Krasilov's voice crackled through his headset. Jack ignored his Russian friend and remained in a leveled flight. He waited just a little longer . . . *now!*

In the same swift move, Jack pulled back throttle and lowered flaps and landing gear. His airspeed plummeted by almost two hundred knots in under ten seconds. He crashed against the control panel, bounced, and slammed his back against his flight seat. A moment later the German plane's belly scrapped his tail as it pulled up to avoid a midair collision.

Partially disoriented from the blow, Jack tried to turn the nose in the direction of the departing jet, but the rudder wouldn't respond. He threw the stick to the left and forced the nose in its direction with ailerons, but instead, he wound up inverting the plane. For a second, the nose temporarily turned in the German's direction. Jack pressed the trigger and managed to fire a few rounds before the stick slipped away. He was not wearing his restraining harness and the canopy had been blown off. Jack dropped out the Aircobra.

In a flash, the powerful windblast crushed his chest as the craft remained inverted above him. The plane and earth switched positions while Jack, disoriented, struggled to find his rip cord. He slapped his right hand on his back but could not find it. *It has to be back there somewhere, Jack. Reach, reach, dammit!*

The peaceful sound of the wind whistling in his ears, Jack plummeted toward earth at a speed of 150 knots. His right hand was so far behind his back that he thought it was going to snap.

There!

Jack found it and pulled hard.

The canopy opened a few seconds later with a hard tug. He was roughly a thousand feet up and saw his Aircobra slowly arching toward the ground. It disappeared behind the trees, and the orange ball that followed foretold the end of his *Impatient Virgin*.

He tried to search for Natalya's canopy and spotted it about a mile to the north. He steered his parachute in that direction.

EIGHTY MILES SOUTHWEST OF THE
STALINGRAD POCKET
• DECEMBER 16, 1942

Jack untangled himself from the silk parachute and pulled it down. He buried it in the snow and quickly began to feel the effect of the thirty-below weather. To both Krasilov's and Natalya's disapproval, he had not worn the heavier—and therefore bulkier—coat that was standard for all Soviet aviators, but had chosen his standard-issue USAAC leather jacket, which was good for keeping him warm in freezing temperatures, but not in the extreme cold of the Russian winter.

Snow clinging to the sides of his face, Jack began to move quickly to stay warm and headed in the direction where he had seen Natalya go down, but didn't get far. He spotted three figures roughly fifty feet ahead.

Instinctively, Jack dropped to the ground and reached for his handgun, a Colt .45, flipped the safety, and cocked it. The steel helmets protruding over the line of bushes told Jack all he needed to know. They were Germans, and they were probably looking for him.

He remained still as their guttural sounds filled the air. Jack didn't speak a word of German, so he had no idea what was being said, and besides, the German language was so rough that it was even hard for him to tell if the soldiers were shouting or simply talking to one another.

The soldiers got closer. His initial assessment had been accurate. There were three Germans and, to his relief, no dogs. The trio walked fifteen feet to his right. Jack had to move quickly or risk losing his limberness to the cold weather, which stung him hard. His arms and legs were shockingly cold. His hands were stiffening and his fingers losing sensation. A few more minutes and he probably would not be able to move them.

He took a chance. The Germans were thirty or so feet behind him now and their backs were to him. He got to his feet and took a few steps forward.

Snap!

A weathered branch under a thin layer of snow

had given under his weight. The guttural voices intensified.

Jack broke into a run, the Colt firmly gripped in his right hand. He was about to reach a cluster of trees . . .

One, two, three bullets grazed past him and exploded in a cloud of bark as they struck a pine tree to his right. Their zooming sound rang in his ears long after they had lodged themselves in the tree. Jack cut left and kept on running for another hundred feet as the noise behind him grew louder. The trees to both sides of him turned into a solid wall as his boots kicked the snow . . . the snow!

Only then he realized that no matter how fast he tried to get away, the Germans would merely follow his tracks. Sooner or later they would catch up with him.

Jack continued to run, but this time he searched for a break in the snow-covered woods. Perhaps . . . a frozen ravine!

That was it. With three more shots cracking through the frigid air, Jack raced past the frozen underbrush that led to a ten-foot-wide ravine. He could see water flowing under the ice, and there was no way for him to tell how thick the layer was, but he had to take a chance. The Germans were closing in on him.

He jumped over the ice and tried to run over it, but instead he slipped and fell facefirst. The blow stung and momentarily disoriented him. He felt a warm trickle of blood running down his forehead. For a few seconds everything appeared blurry.

Jack struggled to his feet and, instead of running, lunged forward and slid down on his belly for a few dozen feet until his momentum stopped. He stumped his feet against the ice to push himself to the opposite side of the ravine, and managed to reach a branch. He pulled himself up and was about to step on the snow by the edge, but stopped in time. Instead, Jack held on to a higher branch and swung his shivering body a few feet away, landed on his back, and rolled behind a tree as the Germans reached the ravine.

He looked for his Colt . . . his Colt! The last time he had it was when he fell . . .

"Amerikaine? Amerikaine! Hello, *Amerikaine!"*

Jack saw the German raise his Colt .45 in the air. Jack had his name engraved on the handle.

"Captain . . . Jack Towers? I have your weapon, Captain Towers! Come out with your hands above your head, and no harm will come to you! Resist, and you will be shot!" said one of the Germans in a heavily accented English.

In spite of the appalling cold, Jack wiggled his body into the snow, taking time to cover his legs and back. His arms were numb, and so were his legs. His fingers were swollen. The cold had made it into his body and was quickly stripping him of his life-supporting heat. If his temperature dropped any lower, Jack feared he would lose consciousness.

"Very well, then. Have it your way, Captain Towers!"

The Germans split three ways. Two went back to the opposite side of the ravine while the third entered the forest twenty feet from where Jack hid. Slowly, Jack reached down to his boot and gripped his numbed fingers around the black handle of a ten-inch steel blade. The pain from his fingers as he forced them to clutch the handle hurt more than the wound on his forehead from falling on the ravine.

He narrowed his eyes as the German, wearing a

bulky white coat that dropped to his knees, turned in his direction. The muzzle of the machine gun held by the tall and thin soldier was pointed in his direction. Jack didn't move. He remained pressed against the ground as the German scanned the forest in front of him with the weapon before taking two more steps in Jack's direction. The cold was beginning to cloud his judgment. For a second he forgot the threat and simply stared in envy at the German's thick coat. He quickly forced his mind back and prayed that the snow over his legs and back was thick enough to disguise his presence. It appeared that way, because the soldier, after taking two more steps, turned his back to Jack.

The soldier now less than six feet away from him, Jack hesitated about attacking. Would his achingly cold body move swiftly enough to reach the German before he turned around? Jack wasn't sure, but he was certain of one thing: If he didn't move soon, he was going to freeze to death. He had to make his muscles work to get his circulation flowing.

The German remained still. The weapon pointed away from Jack.

Jack breathed the cold air once, exhaled, and breathed it again as he inched his legs forward to see how they would respond. They moved. Jack inhaled once more, recoiled, and lunged.

The German must have heard him, because halfway through his attack, the soldier began to turn around, but it was too late. Jack kept the blade aimed for the neck and drove it in hard. Both men landed by the edge of the frozen ravine. The blade had only gone halfway inside the soldier's neck.

Their eyes locked. Jack jammed his numb right hand on the soldier's mouth as he fiercely palm-struck the knife's handle. The blade cut deeper into the German's throat until the handle met the soldier's windpipe. Jack knew that his palm should be hurting from the blow against the handle, but it didn't. Although he could still move his hands, he had lost sensation below the wrists.

The German went limp. Jack stood up and dragged him away from the ravine. His lips were trembling, and his cheeks twitched out of control. Hypothermia was slowly setting in. Jack needed protection quickly before he froze, before the cold seeped deeper into his core.

He leaned the dead German against a tree and pulled out his knife. The jagged edge cut a wider track on its way out, jetting blood over Jack's legs. He ignored it, set the bloody knife on the side, and undid the straps of the soldier's heavy woolen jacket. He removed it and quickly put it on. Next he slung the machine gun and . . .

"Hans? Hans?"

Jack's head snapped left. The other two Germans were back on the ravine. Jack got caught in plain view kneeling in the snow. One of the Germans looked straight at Jack and waved for a moment before realizing what had happened, and leveled the machine gun in his direction.

Leaving his knife behind, Jack jumped away as the slow rattle of the German's machine gun thundered in the woods and was followed by fierce explosions of snow. He got to his feet and reached a thick cluster of trees. The firing subsided. His back crashed hard against the trunk of a tree, and breathing heavily, he clutched the machine gun and glanced over his left shoulder. Gunfire erupted once more, shaving off the bark of the tree.

Son of a bitch!

His face was bleeding from the flying bark. Trying

to control his quivering hands, he dropped to the ground, rolled away, and blindly opened fire in the Germans' general direction. It had the desired effect. Both Germans ran for cover, giving Jack enough time to reach a fallen log.

On his belly, Jack spread both legs, set the muzzle over the log, and waited. And waited. Minutes went by. Jack kept the gun trained on the trees protecting the soldiers. His face felt so cold, he couldn't feel it.

The German's jacket wasn't helping much either. Enough heat had escaped his body before he put on the jacket to keep him from getting warm again. Jack understood what that meant: He had lost the ability to warm himself back up. He had to get to a source of heat fast. His body was falling deeper into hypothermia.

One of the Germans ran to an adjacent tree. Jack tried to fire, but his index finger didn't respond fast enough. He missed the soldier by a few feet.

The second soldier now ran. Jack fired and missed again. He tried to shift the gun toward the new German hideout, but his arms wouldn't respond; his body wouldn't respond. He was convulsing.

One of the Germans came into plain view. Jack tried to fire but couldn't. He pressed his lips together and forced his index finger against the trigger, but it wouldn't move. It was frozen stiff!

Jack found it harder and harder to breathe now. Every gulp of air that entered his lungs felt like a hard, cold hammer squashing his chest and forcing the last remnants of heat out of his exhausted body. His vision became foggy, cloudy. The shadowy figures loomed in front of him.

Jack heard laughter mixed with the dreaded guttural words he couldn't understand, but this time he decided they were screaming, and in the middle of all the shouting he picked up the only word that his ears recognized: Hans, Hans! Jack had killed their comrade in arms. He knew the Germans would not be merciful.

His thoughts became fuzzy, irrational. His ears picked up several shots, and he tried to brace himself, but his arms only moved part of the way. His body was too rigid. Jack didn't feel any impact, and he couldn't feel most of his body. He could be bleeding to death at that moment and not even know it. He tried to find the shadows of the Germans, but they were gone. They had shot him and left him to bleed to death.

A shadow came up over him and began to lift him to his feet. Were the Germans dragging him away? Why not just let him die in the freezing woods?

Jack tried to open his mouth to say that he didn't care anymore, but his body was past the brink of exhaustion and would not respond to his commands. A sense of desolation took him over as he felt life slowly escaping him.

Slowly, very slowly, Jack surrendered himself to the Russian winter. Then all went dark.

"Is he alive?" Natalya asked while Aris Broz dragged Jack's body toward a pair of horses next to the ravine. Natalya rode on one with a heavy blanket thrown over her shoulders.

"Barely," he responded, hoisting Jack over the horse's mount, which was made of thick blankets. "I don't think he is going to make it."

Natalya looked at the craggy Partisan who had rescued her from a German patrol less than thirty minutes ago. "How far do we have to go?"

"It all depends. The nearest place where he could

get any type of medical attention is over two hours away. I can tell you for certain he's not going to last that long."

"Dammit, Jack," Natalya cursed as she lowered her gaze to Jack's hunched-over figure. "I told you to wear warmer clothing!" She exhaled and looked back at Aris. "Where is the closest place that's protected from the elements?"

"The caves, but again. There is no medical . . ."

"How far away is that?"

"Just minutes away."

"Let's go!"

EIGHTY MILES SOUTHWEST OF THE STALINGRAD POCKET • DECEMBER 16, 1942

With the help of three Partisans, Natalya Makarova quickly dragged Jack's freezing body inside one of several huts built against the side of a rocky hill.

"Get me some vodka!" she screamed as she set Jack down over some blankets next to a gas lantern.

Aris ran outside, leaving the door open. A gush of cold air entered the hut. Natalya cursed out loud and rushed to close it.

Jack was still unconscious and extremely cold. She removed both his jackets, his boots and pants, and began massaging his stiff legs and arms, trying to get some blood to his purplish feet and hands.

Aris came in and closed the door behind him. He handed Natalya a dark bottle. She removed the cork, took a sniff and brought it to Jack's lips.

"Drink it, Jack."

She got no response. She put a few drops on his lips and saw his tongue move.

"He needs immediate medical attention. A fire

would probably help him, but I'm afraid it's out of the question. There are too many German patrols around," said Aris, feeling Jack's pulse. "There is, however, another option to get heat into his body fast, but that's really up to you, Natalya."

Aris turned and left the room. Natalya knew what she needed to do if she was to save his life. Jack's body was so cold that his core was not able to produce enough heat on its own to bring his body temperature back up. Jack needed another heat source to radiate warmth back into his body.

Natalya quickly removed the rest of his clothes. Jack braced himself and shivered. She covered his body with blankets before removing her clothes. First the wet boots, thick aviator pants and jacket, followed by her undergarments. The nipples on her breasts shriveled the moment she snapped off her brassiere.

Natalya maneuvered her pale, thin body under the blankets and pressed Jack against her. Her body tensed the moment his cold chest came in contact with her breasts, but she forced herself to remain like that. The skin of her stomach was against his; his face buried in her neck as she breathed heavily over his face to smother him with warmth. She parted his cold thighs and wedged her right leg in between his while rubbing her arms up and down his back. Heat radiated from her onto him.

Minutes went by. Natalya didn't stop. She continued to rub her entire self against him, until slowly, very slowly, Jack began to respond. His body became soft, still cold, but soft, relaxed. His breathing steadied. She could now feel his heartbeat pounding against her chest. She felt his arms pulling her tighter against him. She was his heat source. His body needed more of her to survive.

Time went by. Natalya saw Jack open his eyes, inhale deeply, and close them again. He was obviously drifting in and out of consciousness. Their body temperatures became one. She felt his fingers move on her back, and his toes against her legs.

Jack felt as if he was dreaming. The harsh cold wind had been replaced by a rhythmic warm breeze that caressed his neck. There was heat around him, and it felt good, cozy, intimate. He opened his eyes and realized where he was, and was instantly comforted by a familiar pair of hazel eyes a few inches away. He tried to speak, but she put a finger to his mouth.

"Shh . . . rest, my dear Jack. Rest."

Jack stared at Natalya's eyes as they reflected the flickering light of the gas lantern, which cast a yellow glow on her white Slavic face. The high cheekbones, full lips, and small chin looked majestic in the twilight of the room. Her powerful embrace was the most intimate Jack had ever felt. He never thought he could feel such complete union with a woman, and yet there was no sex involved, just the thrust of her lifesaving heat into him.

Slowly, all faded away. The face, the yellowish light, the eyes. Jack Towers quietly surrendered himself to the warm and soothing comfort of Natalya's nearness.

KALACH AIRFIELD, TWENTY MILES WEST OF
THE STALINGRAD POCKET
• DECEMBER 16, 1942

Krasilov jumped out of his plane and raced for the communications bunker. The German jet craft was no match for their Aircobras or La-3s. The Soviets had not been able to stop the advancing Hitlerites.

The jet had taken two of his planes while the Gustavs took care of three more. Krasilov himself had been pursued by two Gustavs once, but had managed to escape their cannons by remaining close to a third Gustav.

How ironic, Krasilov thought. He had actually used one Gustav to shield himself from two others. The tactic worked beautifully. The pursuing Messerschmitts did not fire a single shot while he kept his Aircobra glued to the side of his German shield. But in spite of all that, the day had been a defeat for his free hunters. More than half his pilots didn't come back. The Germans had effectively prevented Krasilov's squadron from reaching the front lines.

Without air support, the Sixty-second Army of General Vasily Chuikov had no choice but to retreat. General von Hoth's panzers were now only forty miles from Stalingrad. If a corridor was established, he knew that Paulus's 250,000 soldiers would get enough supplies to keep the city through the rest of the winter.

Krasilov inhaled the relatively warm air inside the communications bunker. They needed additional planes if they were to provide any type of air support. More planes and also a way to get rid of the annoying jets, although Jack had found a way that seemed to work . . . *Jackovich.*

Krasilov frowned. He also needed to make two more calls. One to the U.S. Army Air Corps advisor in the Kremlin, and a second to Major Chapman, who was currently training another air regiment one hundred miles north of Stalingrad.

Captain Jack Towers had been shot down. Krasilov knew the Americans would not react well to that. Jack's training role had been clear from the start. Krasilov felt responsible.

EIGHTY MILES SOUTHWEST OF THE
STALINGRAD POCKET
• DECEMBER 16, 1942

That evening Jack Towers sat next to the fire outside
the hut where he had slept most of the day. As Natalya had explained to him, German patrols were no
longer in the area, making it safe to start a small
fire. His body was rested, and to Natalya's amaze-
ment, he had survived without the need for an amputation. His fingers and toes were all pinkish. Jack
had indeed been lucky. His mother had warned him
about the Russian winter. Jack now understood her
fears.

Jack took another draw from the strongest cigarette he had ever smoked in his life. At first, Aris
and Natalya had smiled when he nearly turned
green while smoking one earlier that afternoon, but
as the day went on, he'd grown accustomed to the
locally made unfiltered cigarettes.

"You're going to be all right, Jack," said Natalya,
sitting next to him and smiling.

"Thanks, Natalya. I mean it."

She looked away and frowned.

"Hey, hey. What's the matter?"

Natalya didn't respond. She simply gazed down at
her boots. Jack gently pulled up her chin. She was
in tears.

"Look, Natalya. I'm really sorry you had to do
that. I just want you to know that . . ."

"You were wonderful, Jack. You didn't take advantage. That's what makes it so hard . . ."

Now Jack was really confused. "I don't understand
then, Natalya. What . . ."

"I promised myself I wouldn't fall for another pilot, Jack. Don't you see the kind of life we live? I

lost a loved one once. I'm afraid to get close again!"

Her face disappeared in her hands. Jack put an arm around her and pulled her close. There wasn't much he could say. Natalya's fears were well-founded.

"Look, Natalya. The way I see it is that you must live life today, now, because there might not be a tomorrow. You're absolutely right. What we do up there is dangerous. Don't kid yourself about it. It's right damned dangerous, but someone's gotta do it, and for some reason that I still don't understand, you and I are among the lucky ones who get to do it. That's our fate. Our destiny. And fate will happen regardless of what you do today. So live for the day, Natalya. Worry about the future after the war is over."

Natalya lifted her head and kissed him on the cheek. "Thank you, Jack Towers. You are a decent man."

She got up.

"Where are you going?"

"To get some coffee."

Jack nodded and turned his head toward the fire. Natalya was a fine woman, Jack decided. A fine woman . . . and a fine pilot. Jack had a totally different opinion of Russian pilots. Unlike American and British pilots, who got to go home after a certain number of missions, the Soviets—and also the Germans for that matter—continued to fly until they either were shot down and permanently disabled, or killed. There was no minimum number of missions or a fixed-length tour of duty. Here you fought until it was over or you died, whichever came first.

"How are you feeling, Jackovich?"

Jack turned his head and stared at the thin—borderline emaciated—Aris. The Yugoslav held a bottle in his hands. He offered Jack a sip, but Jack kindly declined. Aris sat next to him.

"It's going to be another cold night, comrade Jackovich."

Jack nodded.

"That was a good job you did with the knife on the Nazi pig."

Jack frowned as he remembered the quick but brief battle. "Can't say that I'm very proud of it. I did it because I had no other choice."

Aris smiled. "You have a lot to learn about the Hitlerites. They are not humans, you know? They are . . . I don't know . . . animals? Beasts?"

"I'll just call them the enemy, if you don't mind."

Aris took a long swig from his bottle, rolled it inside his mouth for a few seconds, and swallowed it. "Whatever you say, comrade Jackovich. Oh, Natalya told us how you and she got shot down. I saw the jet, too, you know."

Jack narrowed his eyes. "Oh, really?"

"Yes. It has no propellers, and it's very fast."

"Tell me what you know, Aris. It could be important."

In a tone that lacked emotion, the Yugoslav told him about his encounter with the panzers. He described how he saw two German soldiers burn to death, and how upset he had been when the jet blew away the roadblock.

"That's a very hot plane, Aris."

"Yes, and my people are trying to find it."

"I've seen two so far. I wonder how many more there are."

"One of our contacts thinks he saw one landing at a German field around seventy miles southwest of the Stalingrad pocket."

Jack's eyes narrowed. "Hmm . . . how far away is that from here, Aris?"

"About a day's walk northeast. Less, if we drive, but that could be dangerous. This is no-man's-land. There is no telling what we'd find on the roads."

"Could you take me there?"

"Take you where, Jack?" said Natalya from behind. She sat next to Jack with a cup of coffee in her hands. She pressed her shoulder against his. He smiled.

"Aris here tells me he thinks he knows where there might be one of those German jets."

Jack stared into her eyes. He didn't have to say anything else. Her eyes blinked understanding.

"You are crazy, Jack Towers. You are absolutely crazy."

KALACH AIRFIELD, TWENTY MILES WEST OF THE STALINGRAD POCKET • DECEMBER 16, 1942

Krasilov stood by the side of the runway as the Aircobra came to a stop, turned around, and headed for the bomb shelters. He walked up to the craft as the propeller stopped and the pilot pushed the cockpit open.

The pilot, a tall heavy man with broad shoulders and a square face, climbed down the side of the plane. He removed his helmet and scanned the base. Krasilov approached him.

"Major Chapman?"

"That's right, I'm Major Kenneth Chapman. You must be Colonel Krasilov."

"Yes, Major."

"Well, Colonel, I gotta tell you. I wasn't pleased

to hear that you've used one of my bilingual trainers to fly in your sorties."

Krasilov did what he could to contain his temper. He simply stared back at Chapman for a few seconds. "We all make our mistakes, Major. And we all learn to live with them."

"What in the hell happened? You were running short on pilots?"

"Something like that."

"What do you mean? The Kremlin's not sending you enough men to fly the machines we're giving you?"

"I must make do with what I have at my disposal, Major. Unlike your country, we don't have unlimited resources available to us at a moment's notice. We have to fight back and use whatever is available at the time. Jack Towers was available, and I used him. You may include that statement in your report of the incident."

The two pilots stared at one another for a few seconds.

Chapman exhaled. "Do you have a place where I can get a drink, Colonel? I nearly froze my ass off tonight trying to get here."

Krasilov nodded. "This way, Major."

SEVENTY-FIVE MILES SOUTHWEST OF THE
STALINGRAD POCKET •
DECEMBER 17, 1942

Jack and Natalya followed Aris and a dozen other Partisans as they made their way northeast. The sun had already broken through the horizon, casting enough light inside the murky woods for Jack to get a better feel for where he was.

Following Aris's advice on proper breathing in

forty-below weather to avoid excessive heat loss, Jack
kept a scarf around his mouth and nose, forcing
himself to breathe slowly. Under no conditions was
he to open his mouth unless he had to talk to someone, and even that was kept to a minimum to keep
warm and also to maintain their stealthiness.

The group walked single file, with ten or so feet
in between, preventing an enemy grenade from
hurting more than one or two of them. It would also
allow them to have ample time to seek cover if someone in the group spotted a German patrol.

The road narrowed as it began to wind its way up
the side of a hill. Jack struggled with his balance.
His aviator boots lacked the necessary traction for a
smooth ascent. As the path turned ninety degrees,
Jack slipped, landed on his back, and began to slide
down the hill.

Flapping his limbs to find anything to hold on to,
he crashed against a tree, stopping. He looked up
and noticed the Partisans looking at him with grim
faces. Jack understood the reason for the silent rep-
rimand: Aris believed there were German patrols
nearby. Jack's noise could have easily given away
their position. He shrugged, struggled back up to
his feet, and continued moving uphill under the
watchful eyes of the guerrillas.

Only after reaching the edge of the bluff did Jack
realize how high they were. From where he stood
he could see several miles of white, desolate countryside extending beyond the jagged edge of the frozen rimrock.

As they approached the summit, Aris, who was the
lead, abruptly raised his hand. The caravan stopped,
and the Yugoslav dropped to the ground and
crawled forward to take a glimpse at the other side
of the hill.

The group remained still. Jack heard a shouting or screaming of some sort.

Slowly, the team crawled up and took a spot at the edge of the hill. Jack lay down next to Natalya and shoved aside enough snow to get a clear view of a small village below. It took Jack but a few seconds to realize what was happening.

Like most villages in the region, the people there were probably Partisan sympathizers. Jack saw one truck and a dozen German soldiers gathered at the center of the village, where the villagers, whom Jack estimated at around thirty, were all kept in a tight group to the side.

One of the Germans, who by now Jack had guessed as their leader, took an old woman to the side and pushed her onto her knees. He then screamed in Russian for the Partisan collaborators to step forward.

None did, but most of the women in the village began to scream, cry, and plead with the Germans. That had no effect. The German officer unholstered his pistol, pressed it against the old woman's head, and fired.

"Jesus! What in the hell—"

Natalya squeezed his hand, hissing, "Keep it down, Jack."

"But that son of a bitch just—"

"This goes on every day, Jackovich," said Aris as he knelt next to Jack and put a hand over his shoulder.

"Are you going to let them get away with that?"

Aris smiled. Jack saw the Yugoslav's eyes burning, but the smile remained. "Justice will prevail, Jackovich. Partisan justice."

Aris then signaled his men to follow him. Jack and

Natalya were about to get up, but Aris motioned them to remain put.

"We can't afford for either one of you to get hurt," said the Partisan leader. "You are air warriors. We belong to the land battle."

Jack wanted to go along anyway, but Natalya pulled him down. "We might be more burden than help, Jack. They have trained together. Let them do what they do—"

Jack heard something, like the muffled cry of a woman, but it did not originate from the village. His head turned toward a road just below them, snaking its way down to the village in the valley. Jack crawled back until he was out of sight of anyone in the village, raised to a crouch, and, weapon in hand, began to move down the side of the hill.

"Jack? What are you doing?"

"Shh . . ." Jack motioned Natalya to follow him.

She looked down at the village, back to Jack, then reluctantly crawled toward him.

"What is going on?"

"Trust me. Come."

This time Jack was careful when making his way toward the road below. He had seen Aris and the other Partisans using the land to their advantage by selecting their next foot or handhold before moving, and avoiding hesitation in midstride. The terrain was slippery, but as Jack quickly realized, as long as he remained in slow but constant motion, he could make reasonable and controlled progress. After the first hundred yards his confidence built up to the point that he started coaching Natalya. His breathing also slowly became one with his moves. He inhaled prior to moving, held his breath during transition, and slowly exhaled as he reached his next rest point.

The sound—a sound of struggle—got louder as Jack approached the frozen, unpaved road, but with trees in the way, he still could not get a clear view. The slope changed to almost forty-five degrees, forcing Jack to change his strategy. He opted to slide on his back, always using his arms and legs to hold on to roots and branches to control his descent, until he reached the edge of the trees, where the thick underbrush prevented him from seeing what Jack felt certain he would see. The struggle was indeed with a woman. It was a muffled moan while men laughed. He looked up hill and watched Natalya catching up with him and kneeling by his side.

Jack parted the foliage enough to see two German soldiers on the open bed of a truck, parked just around the corner from the village. One soldier had a girl, who couldn't have been much older than fifteen or sixteen, pinned against the flatbed while the second, the trousers of his uniform down to his knees, forced himself into her from the top. The first soldier held her arms and kept a piece of cloth over her mouth as the girl's head snapped back with every thrust.

"Fucking bastards," Jack hissed, glancing over to Natalya. There were tears in her eyes, which Jack promptly brushed away.

He holstered his pistol and grabbed the double-edge knife. "Cover me, Natalya, but don't fire."

"But, Aris . . . he said not to . . ."

Natalya's eyes were leveled with his. Jack put a hand over hers. "It's gonna be all right. Trust me. Now cover me," he whispered.

Natalya pulled out her pistol as Jack moved down the hill until he reached a spot directly above the German kneeling down holding the girl steady. With the fingers of his right hand curled around the

handle, Jack jumped over the side and landed on
the German, with the knife directly in front of him.
The blade entered the base of the neck at an angle,
the sound of bones and cartilage snapping as he
crashed against the soldier and pushed him to the
side. His limp body rolled away.

The second German jerked in surprise. He was
still inside the girl. He jumped off and reached for
his pants, but his fumbling hands never made it past
his knees. Jack lunged, slitting his throat. The soldier whipped both hands up as blood jetted from
his neck. He tried to scream but couldn't, finally
dropping to his knees while staring at Jack, at the
bloody knife in his hand, before collapsing.

The girl was in obvious shock. She had not moved
during the entire incident. Misted by the blood of
his victims, Jack pulled up her heavy pants and
waved Natalya over. She climbed into the rear of the
truck and got to the girl's side while Jack walked up
the road to see if someone had heard him.

A hair-raising scream made Jack rush toward the
village, hidden around the corner, his eyes narrow-
ing in anger at the sight.

The German officer had taken another woman
from the group. This one looked fairly young. The
officer had ripped off her dress and tore down her
undergarments. Her chest was exposed. From behind, the German pressed a pistol to her head as
she braced herself, shivering. Jack exhaled. If the
German didn't kill her, then the Russian winter
would.

More shouts came from the villagers, whom the
soldiers were now shoving back with the butts of
their rifles.

"Partisans! Enemies of the Reich! Come forward
and spare the life of this woman!" the officer

screamed to the mob of crazed villagers.

"Butchers! Butchers!" came the unanimous response.

A gunshot splattered across the frozen tundra.

The girl stood alone, screaming while hugging herself. The German officer lay on the ground, his face smeared with blood. The soldiers appeared momentarily confused.

Jack unholstered his Colt, flipped the safety, and lurched around the corner while the Germans raced for cover behind their truck. Half of them never made it. They fell victims to Aris's sharpshooters. The others made it to the rear of the truck and began to exchange fire with Aris's men.

Jack approached the Germans from behind. He knelt, cocked his weapon, and fired. The first German jumped up in shock as his hands tried to reach behind his back, where Jack's bullet had entered. Before he fell to the ground, Jack already had a second German lined up in his sights, firing twice, the reports deafening. The German crashed against the side of the truck.

The other three Germans swung their machine guns in his direction. Jack jumped behind a tree as bark and snow exploded all around him, but it didn't last long. As he placed both hands over his face to protect himself from wooden chips stinging him, fire ceased.

Slowly, warily, Jack got up and looked around the tree trunk. Aris stood over the bodies of the Germans. Jack picked up his gun and walked in his direction. He noticed that two of the Germans—their chests covered with blood—were moving their heads from side to side. Aris shoved the muzzle of his weapon inside the mouth of one of the Germans and fired once. The German jerked for a second, then remained still. The Yugoslav did the same to the second fallen German. Jack felt no compassion for the soldiers, who on closer inspection appeared to be not older than twenty years.

An hour later, with all the corpses buried under the snow behind the village and the trucks driven into the woods and covered with branches, the villagers brought out loaves of bread and bottles of vodka for Aris and his rescuing band.

The men ate outside in front of the fire, while the women, Natalya included, tended the assaulted girls. Aris took a long look at Jack.

"Animals, Jackovich. Animals."

Jack stared back at his bearded friend. The Yugoslav stuffed a large chunk of bread in his mouth and washed it down with a gulp of vodka. Jack's view of the Germans had definitely taken a turn for the worse during the day's events. He no longer saw them as the mere enemy, in the classic sense, but more like common criminals.

"Jesus. What kind of war is this anyway?" he muttered, extending his hands toward the fire.

Aris took another swig of vodka and passed the bottle to Jack, who took a sip.

"Their plans have been clear from the start, comrade Jackovich. The Hitlerites seek the total destruction of this country. They have no regard for Slavic lives and take them without a second thought. See that boy over there?"

Jack spotted a kid, probably fourteen, biting into a large piece of bread he held with both hands.

"Yeah. What about him?"

"He saw his entire family get executed as he returned from the forest with a pile of firewood. The Germans raped his mother and two older sisters before hanging them. And the worst part of it was that they weren't Partisan collaborators. They were simply picked at random and executed."

Jack narrowed his eyes. "Why?"

"To create terror. The Germans have created this law that for every German killed by Partisans, ten innocent peasants will hang. The rule, of course, is aimed at trying to force the people to do what the Germans themselves have not been able to do: stop us."

Jack couldn't think of anything to say to that. Aris continued after he grabbed the bottle from Jack and took the last swallow.

"We see that as an act of desperation. The Germans are resorting to reckless measures to try to bring the situation under control, and it's not working. That frustration, of course, drives them into committing more and more atrocious acts of violence, but it will all end soon."

Jack stared at the fire. "How can you tell for sure? I mean, there are still, what? More than two million German soldiers in Russia. I call that far from being over."

Aris smiled. "And there will be two million dead Germans when this is all over, comrade. Justice will prevail. The German High Command will regret the day they decided to attack Russia. Soon, the thought of Soviet reprisal will haunt every living German. It will be their nightmare."

Jack didn't know how to respond to such harsh words, so well-spoken, and coming from a man who had just shot each of the fallen Germans in the head once to make sure there were no survivors.

"Justice will prevail, Jackovich. Justice will . . ."

Suddenly, a young boy came running to Aris's side, leaned down, and murmured something into the Yugoslav's ear. Aris lowered his gaze and exhaled before his expression turned stone cold.

"What was that all about, Aris?"

The Yugoslav guerrilla looked at Jack. "Come. I want you to see for yourself the agony that our people must endure." Aris got up and started walking toward one of the shacks at the edge of the village. Puzzled, Jack followed him. So far he'd seen plenty of despicable acts of cold murder. His skin shivered at the thought of anything worse.

Jack walked a few steps behind Aris. The leader of the Partisan band reached the shack—a round, fragile-looking structure made of stone, clay, and straw. It had an opening at the top, where he could see a trail of smoke from the burning stove, probably also used as a heater.

Aris pulled the canvas flap hanging at the entrance and held it open to let Jack in. Through the yellowish light, Jack saw a man in his early twenties lying in bed. Two older women sat by his bedside as a child held his hand.

Aris turned to Jack and whispered in his ear. "We were about to engage in a joint ambush of a German detachment of soldiers two weeks ago. He was a commando from another group of guerrillas. As we planned our attack in this village, he and three others were in an adjacent shack readying the weapons. It appears that a grenade slipped from one of the commandos' hands and went off by his feet, lightly injuring the others, but mangling his right leg.

"Because we knew the Hitlerites were coming, we all fled and left him in the care of the villagers. We hoped that maybe the Germans would bandage the wound, but they didn't. Instead, they tortured him for information, and when he refused, instead of just killing him, the bastards rubbed horse manure over the open wound and left. The villagers tried to clean the leg as best they could. I got a report on his condition every few days, and from what I heard it seemed that his leg had stopped bleeding and was healing fine. I saw him an hour ago, and he claimed to be feeling better, but that boy just whispered in my ear that he saw his leg without the bandage, and it looked blue and smelled like rotten cheese."

Jack nodded solemnly. Aris approached the young commando.

"Hello, Ivanovich."

The women and the child moved to the side of the room.

"Hello, Aris."

"You don't mind if I take a look at that leg, do you?"

A half smile appeared on Ivanovich's face. "Wh . . . why? It's all right. I already told you it's healed. I might even walk back with you tomorrow."

Aris's expression became harsh. "The leg, Ivanovich. Let me see it."

The young man turned his head to the side as Aris lifted the cover. Aris removed the cloth wrapped around most of the leg. Jack took one look and closed his eyes. The child had been right. The leg was blue with gangrene from the foot all the way up past the knee.

"Call the others," Aris said to the child, who promptly ran outside. "That leg has to go, Ivanovich."

If Jack could ever describe what fear looked like, it was definitely what he saw in that young man's eyes. His lips quivered, and his face contorted with anguish.

"No, Aris, please. No. Look, I can move the foot and the toes and . . ."

"I'm sorry, kid. It's either that or you'll be dead in a week. That gangrene is going to eat you alive, and you know it. It has to be done."

Three other Partisans arrived. One carried a black case. Aris opened it and removed a green bottle, two small rags, a thick piece of leather, and . . . and a hacksaw!

Jack felt sick and stopped breathing, turning around the moment the Partisans held down the trembling commando while the women and child ran outside in tears.

"Comrade Jackovich? Jackovich, please help us!"

Jack felt light-headed. He inhaled deeply and exhaled. He breathed in once more and turned around.

"Hold his leg!"

Hold his leg? You have to be fucking kidding me, he thought, but Aris's face looked as serious as the life-and-death decision the Yugoslav had made for the young commando.

Jack gripped the decomposed foot in his hands, lifted it up, and wedged it in his armpit while pressing his arm against his side to hold it taut. Then he used both hands to force the knee against the bed while fighting the nausea induced by the rotten smell that assaulted his nostrils.

Jack's gaze met with the young Yugoslav's for a brief moment. His pleading eyes reached Jack's soul, but what could he do? The damage had already been done by the Germans. The manure had created an infection that could have been stopped had Ivanovich been given some type of antibiotic, but just a rudimentary cleaning of the leg had not been enough to avoid infection.

Jack felt his sense of compassion about to burst the moment Ivanovich lifted his head and stared at his leg one last time before one of the Partisans pressed the young man's face down against the bed with a rag saturated in vodka while jamming the piece of leather in between his teeth.

Aris soaked the serrated blade with vodka and brought it to the fire. Jack watched the blade burn for several seconds before looking down at Ivanovich's chest rapidly swelling and deflating as the young man mentally prepared himself for the amputation.

The blade cooled. Aris brought the saw down next to the leg and used his other hand to feel the skin on Ivanovich's thigh, seemingly looking for the safest place to make the cut without robbing the young man of a healthy section of his leg. His finger stopped feeling on a spot roughly six inches above the knee, almost two inches from the last section of decayed skin.

Aris lifted his head and scanned the room. "Keep him steady! He must not move no matter what happens, or he might bleed to death!"

"I'd rather die, Comrade Aris!" Ivanovich screamed as he managed to free one hand and remove the piece of leather from his mouth. "Please, just shoot me. Please!"

"Quiet! Everyone quiet!"

"What is the use of living if I can't—"

"Keep that leather in his mouth! What's the matter with you, men? Can't hold one man down?"

The Partisans brought him under control once more as Aris pressed the disinfected blade over the selected section of flesh. The American pilot clenched his teeth, pressed the leg down and against his side hard, and closed his eyes.

The scream came, followed by sudden jerks and by a warm spray that showered Jack's face. Jack kept his eyes shut while the liquid trickling down his face and neck was accompanied by the revolting noise of rupturing skin, cartilage, and bones pounding against his eardrums.

Natalya ran outside when she heard the bloodcurdling shriek. Then she heard another one, and one more. She ran to the back of the village and saw two women crying into each other's shoulders in front of a shack. One held a child in her arms.

"Hold him steady! Steady!" came Aris's voice from inside.

More screams followed. It was the sound of a man in agony. She ran inside, froze in horror at the sight, and raced back out, staggering across the village, falling to her knees in the snow, hands covering her mouth. She tried to control her convulsions, but couldn't. Her body tensed, and her throat and mouth filled with bile.

The horrifying screams ringing in her ears, Natalya vomited until she was left with nothing but dry heaves. She breathed in and out for seconds. The screams had stopped. They had been replaced by a light moan.

She turned her head to the entrance and saw Jack and Aris carrying something wrapped in a bloodstained sheet. Jack's face had been splattered with blood. The American pilot looked different. It was in his eyes. He looked . . . older? Natalya wasn't sure.

She followed them to the rear of the village, where they had buried the Germans earlier. She helped them bury the amputated leg.

"Will he make it, Aris?" Natalya asked.

"Hard to tell, Natalya. I cauterized the arteries and disinfected the wound as much as I could. The rest is out of our hands."

Aris looked at Jack, who remained quiet, staring at the snow.

"Justice will prevail, comrade Jackovich."

Jack closed his eyes as pure white snow now covered everything, the dead Germans, the slain villagers, the infected leg . . . the sins of war.

SEVENTY MILES SOUTHWEST OF THE
STALINGRAD POCKET
• DECEMBER 17, 1942

Jack Towers lifted his gaze and saw the crystalline, star-filled sky. The majestic view was in sharp contrast with the desolation and suffering below it. This was Jack's first war, and the romance had long been lost. The glorified posters of fighter squadrons flying into the sunset seemed like a masquerade on a voracious wolf with an insatiable appetite for young men. There was nothing to be gained by war—Jack was now certain of that. Not for the soldiers who fought it, anyway.

An end to a brutal war was the reason Jack pushed himself harder up the hill even after marching for eight straight hours with minimum rest. The war had to end. The German killing machine had to be stopped.

Jack reached the top of the hill and crawled next to Aris. The Yugoslav scanned the airfield with the set of binoculars he'd stolen from the German truck earlier that morning. He passed them to Jack, who slowly searched the edge of the forest outlining the German airstrip. He carefully looked at every plane, then continued to the next when he spotted its propeller. The unpaved airstrip was roughly two thousand feet long by seventy wide. The Germans had done a fairly good job of keeping it clear of snow, and the surface appeared reasonably flat. There were tents to both sides of the airfield.

"You're sure about this place, Aris?" Jack asked as he finished searching one side and saw nothing but six Gustavs and two of the larger Me 110s.

"Our contacts tell us this is where they saw one landing yesterday afternoon. Maybe they moved it to another airfield."

"Maybe . . . then again, maybe not."

Jack smiled and passed the binoculars to Aris and pointed to a spot directly behind a tent halfway down the airfield.

Aris pressed the binoculars against his eyes. "Is that it? The one without the propeller in the nose?"

"Yep. That's the one, Aris," Jack responded, taking the binoculars back from the Partisan guerrilla and studying the plane once more. It was dark, but there were enough lights by the edge of the clearing for Jack to see the streamlined outline of the German jet clearly. It looked like something out of a science fiction magazine, but it wasn't. The plane was for real, and Jack had already witnessed what it was capable of doing.

"Are you sure you want to do this, Jack?" Natalya asked as she leaned down next to him. He passed the binoculars back to Aris, who used them to scan the rest of the field.

"I have to. There is no other way." He stared into her pleading hazel eyes and put a hand over her cheek. "Look, I know what I'm doing. I can handle it. Trust me."

Without waiting for a response, Jack got the binoculars back from Aris and stared at the German jet once again. An officer came out from the tent right next to it. Jack put down the binoculars and looked at Aris. "Let's do it."

Firmly gripping his double-edged hunting knife, Aris approached the base from the east side—the side where they had spotted the jet. Jack, also clutching a knife, remained a few feet behind him. Their weapons were slung across their backs.

Natalya was not with them. She had reluctantly agreed to head back to the nearest Soviet air base the moment she got the signal that Jack's plan had worked. Aris had placed two Partisans on either side of the runway. The rest were with Natalya at the top of the small hill.

Hit-and-run, Jackovich. Stealth and surprise are your main weapons, he recalled Aris telling him ten minutes before. Jack felt much more comfortable in the woods now. He felt he blended well within its protective cover. He moved only when Aris moved, and stopped when he stopped. He used the same foot- and handholds as the Yugoslav guerrilla, and managed consistently to pace himself so that he could sustain his body's oxygen needs by slowly breathing through his nostrils.

He was about to take another step when Aris abruptly stopped. The bearded Yugoslav didn't have to say or point to anything. Jack nodded the moment he spotted the German sentries some fifty feet ahead. It wasn't very hard to notice them, Jack decided. Even in the murky woods. The soldiers were smoking.

Smoking while on guard?

Jack tilted his head. Given the forty-below temperatures, he couldn't blame them for doing that, although if it had been him, he would have chosen hot coffee—or anything else that wouldn't give away his position.

Aris pointed at Jack with his index finger and made a circle in the air with his hand. Jack nodded.

The two men split. Aris's tactic was both simple and clever: attack from an unexpected angle and surprise the enemy from the place it would least expect an assault to come.

Jack made a wide semicircle to the right of the guards, while Aris made one to the left. Now Jack had to be extra careful. He didn't have Aris to guide him through the forest. He was on his own, and well aware that one false step could blow everything. The Germans were too close. Jack developed a new rhythm. He moved only when the gusts of wind swept through the trees, stopped the moment the breeze died down, and moved forward once more with the next gust. After a few minutes the rhythm was perfected to the point that Jack could almost anticipate when the breeze would come again, and how long it would last. That allowed him a few extra seconds of motion by moving just before the wind started and continuing a second or two after it died down. The feeling of control was exhilarating.

The sounds of branches and leaves moving in response to the cold Siberian wind, Jack struggled toward his objective foot after agonizing foot, reaching it five minutes later fifty feet on the other side of the guards, so close to the edge of the clearing that Jack could see the tail of the jet about forty feet away. Aris was already waiting for him.

The Partisan leader pointed to the sentry on the left. Jack nodded and moved forward as quietly as his heavy garments allowed him. Once more, he mimicked Aris's every move, advancing and stopping when he did until slowly closing the gap to twenty feet. The guards continued to smoke while their weapons hung loosely from their shoulders.

The constant whirl of the wind through the trees

masking their sounds, Jack and Aris dropped to a crouch and quietly—

The guards turned in their direction and began to walk. Jack froze. Aris had to drag him down to hide behind a thick pine.

The guards stopped. Jack looked at Aris, who brought a finger to his lips. Jack nodded and remained still. He didn't even breathe.

The guards, holding their weapons in front of them, moved closer until they were directly on the other side of the tree. Aris motioned Jack to go around at the count of three.

Aris's extended his index finger. Jack recoiled. The Yugoslav extended his middle finger. Jack leaned his body forward. *Now!*

Jack shot around the tree and caught the German broadside. The knife went in through the side of the neck at an angle. Jack drove it up with all his might, nearly lifting the soldier off his feet. By the time the German dropped, Aris was already wiping his own blade clean of his victim's blood. He smiled at Jack, who felt sick. It was one thing to pull a trigger and watch the enemy go down in a smoking plane. It was a different story to watch them roll on the ground gasping for air with a severed windpipe.

He shifted his gaze toward the clearing and saw the long cylindrical turbines hanging beneath the wings of the German jet.

"It's all yours, comrade Jackovich."

Jack carefully walked by the tail while Aris, left hand clutching his knife and right hand on the handle of his machine gun, warily surveyed the deserted airfield. Most pilots were inside their—

Another German approached the jet.

Aris stopped Jack from squeezing the trigger of his machine gun. Instead the Partisan grabbed his knife by the blade and waited until the officer was almost out of sight of the clearing.

The German stopped next to the wing and froze. He had recognized them, but before he had a chance to turn around and yell for help, Jack watched the glistening shape of Aris's knife streak across the chilly air and embed itself in the German's chest. The soldier dropped to his knees, but not before he let go a loud shriek, which Aris quickly stopped by jamming a hand over the German's mouth while he finished him off.

"Go, Jackovich! Do what you must! Hurry!"

Jack climbed on the wing and walked up next to the cockpit. He opened the canopy, crawled inside and closed it, locking it from the inside.

He spotted three Germans racing across the field. Jack pulled off his heavy gloves and scanned the cockpit. The basic instrumentation was as it should be. The artificial horizon to the left, next to the airspeed indicator and above the slip/turn indicator. On the right side were the directional gyro, clock, and dual engine gauges. The jet's controls were standard stick and rudder with a built-in trigger and radio buttons on the upper section of the control stick. The landing gear lever was to his right above the small elevator trim wheel.

His head snapped up the moment he heard gunfire, quickly followed by a loud scream. Jack glanced to his right and watched Aris's body tossed by the enemy gunfire.

Jack turned around and watched Aris dragging himself into the forest, but the Yugoslav guerrilla didn't get far. Another burst across his back killed him.

Gunfire erupted from both sides of the hill as the

Partisans began their coordinated attack to draw fire away from Jack.

Natalya knew something had gone wrong the moment she'd heard a scream and gunfire, but no sign of jet engines.

"Stay down!" one of the Partisans shouted moments before a loud explosion caused three of Aris's men ten feet behind her to arch back and fall faceup. The remaining two opened fire on the squad of Germans coming from their rear. Natalya reached the fallen guerrillas, but in a moment she realized there was nothing she could do for them. Their chests had been ripped open with shrapnel. Somehow, the Germans had flanked them.

She pulled out her pistol and was about to get to her feet when the remaining two Partisans flew over her head riddled with bullets. She was trapped between the airfield and the advancing squad of Germans. As steel helmets loomed behind a line of bushes twenty feet away, Natalya rushed down hill toward the clearing. She was well aware of the fate fighting Soviet women faced at the hands of the Germans.

Jack saw five soldiers less than fifty feet in front of the plane, but for some reason no one would open fire. Three were busy returning fire from the hills. The others simply stared at the jet.

Jack threw what he guessed were the electronic switches to power the avionics. He was right. The cockpit came alive, giving him readings on fuel, oil, and turbine temperatures.

He pressed the dual set of buttons above the engines' gauges, and the turbines began to make a high-pitched sound. Jack let go and the turbines died down.

He pressed them again until the turbines engaged. The jet briefly jerked forward. Jack pushed the dual throttle controls forward, but they didn't move. Puzzled, he pulled them back some and the craft lurched forward.

"Shit! This thing works backward!"

The Germans took a few steps back as the jet inched forward. One of them leveled his machine gun at him, but before he could let go a single shot, Jack lifted the trigger guard casing and fired for three seconds. Actually he had wanted only to fire for one second, but the powerful recoil almost stopped the craft's momentum. Jack crashed against the control panel, bounced, and slammed his back against the seat while his finger remained on the trigger.

"Jesus!"

Half-startled, Jack leaned forward, and all he could see was a pile of human refuse where the five Germans had been. In disbelief at the kind of power stored in the nose cannons, Jack pulled back the throttle handles and the Messerschmitt lurched out of its hideout and onto the frozen runway. He quickly reduced throttle, deciding that it would take some time to get used to the volatile engine response.

The airstrip blared with sirens. Pilots ran for their craft as Jack slowly added more throttle. Two of them tried to climb onto the wings of the jet, but with additional power he left them behind and quickly taxied to the end of the runway and turned the jet around. The craft's tail almost touched the trees. Jack needed every single inch of runway available to him.

Now this is when the real test begins, Jack, he told himself. He had no idea what the takeoff speed for this jet was, or the stall speed. Furthermore, Jack had no idea what was the takeoff run. He had already estimated the runway was two thousand feet long. Did such short runway require him to perform a special takeoff technique? Jack decided he would try a modified version of his Aircobra's short takeoff maneuver, and searched for the flaps' handle. *Flaps? Flaps? Where?*

He spotted a vertical lever with three different settings. He lowered it to the first, and watched in satisfaction as the hydraulically driven flaps lowered. Suddenly, a spotlight blinded him. It came from his left.

Jack pressed left rudder and let go another burst the moment the nose lined up with the source of light. The light blew up in a bright flash. He recentered the nose and began to pull . . .

Jack briefly glanced at the Me 262's built-in rearview mirror and saw Natalya running in his direction.

Natalya! What are you doing?

She reached the tail of the plane. Jack turned his head toward the runway and saw a truck loaded with soldiers bustling toward him. He lined it up using rudder and throttle while stepping on the brakes, and let go another burst. The guns were impressive. The truck stopped dead in its tracks, flipped, and went up in a ball of flames. Once more, Jack lined up the craft with the runway.

Natalya made it up the wing and began to bang on the canopy.

Jack unlocked it and she pulled it up.

"Are you crazy! You want to get us both killed?"

he screamed. "You were supposed to have gone with—"

"They're coming, Jack! The Germans!"

"Wh . . . what are you . . ."

"They got the Partisans . . . oh dear! It was a massacre! They're right behind—"

He pulled her by the collar and sat her between him and the stick over his left leg. He closed and locked the canopy as more machine-gun fire erupted from the front.

"Get out of the way!" He pushed her head farther to the left as several bullets ricocheted off the bulletproof glass. Jack pressed the brake pedals, pushed full right rudder, and added throttle. The Me 262 pivoted clockwise at great speed. Jack pressed the trigger.

The whole world seemed to catch fire around him as the Messerschmitt showered everything in sight with 30mm rounds.

Jack lifted his finger off the trigger. Gunfire ceased. He lined up the nose with the runway once more and, while pressing on the brakes, pulled back the dual throttle handles.

"Hold on, Natalya!" Jack placed his face over her shoulder to get a better view of the runway. The jet trembled as Jack gave the throttle handles a final pull. Full throttle. The engine whirl became deafening.

The craft plunged forward the moment he released the brakes. He felt Natalya's body crushing him against the seat from the powerful acceleration. Jack tried to get a glimpse of the airspeed indicator, but Natalya's head was in the way.

"Read out the airspeed!"

"Seventy knots . . . eighty . . . Jack! There's a tank blocking the runway. Slow down!"

Jack shifted his gaze directly ahead and saw a panzer rolling onto the center of the runway.

"Just read the airspeed!"

The tank and a number of Germans were roughly one thousand feet ahead. The massive turret turned in his direction. Jack lined up the tank and squeezed the trigger. The thundering cannons shook the entire craft.

"Airspeed!"

"Ninety knots . . . one hundred . . ."

The soldiers were cut to pieces by the guns, and the tank caught fire but it remained there, blocking the way. He estimated no more than seven hundred feet away.

"One hundred ten knots!"

Jack pulled back on the stick, but the craft didn't climb. He decided they were too heavy and were not accelerating fast enough. He needed a way to reduce drag . . . the landing gear!

"One hundred twenty knots . . . Jack, the tank!"

Jack let go another burst. The tank exploded, but he could not see if it was out of the way or not. "Speed's down to one hundred ten knots . . . fifteen . . ."

The tank's turret was gone while the bottom half burned, but Jack decided that enough of it was still there to spoil his takeoff run. Using guns, however, was out of the question. The brutal recoil would only slow him down even further.

"One hundred twenty knots."

The scorching wreckage rapidly grew in size. In the corner of his eye, Jack noticed the muzzle flashes of Germans on the side of the runway emptying their machine guns on them.

With bullets bouncing off the glass, he reached for the landing gear lever and pulled it up as he eased back the stick. The jet trembled but left the ground. The landing gear lifted and locked in place.

"One hundred thirty knots!"

Flames filled his windshield. Jack pulled on the stick hard, and the Messerschmitt bolted up a few feet. The bottom of the fuselage scraped the wreckage, but he'd cleared it.

"Ninety knots, Jack! We're gonna stall!"

The stall buzzer went off. Jack lowered the nose and regained some airspeed, but the craft dropped a few feet. A cloud of sparks engulfed them the moment the jet's belly bounced off the runway before coming back up. Jack lowered the nose even more, keeping the plane just a couple of feet over the runway.

"One hundred forty . . . fifty . . . sixty."

Jack waited. He couldn't afford another stall. A wall of trees rapidly approached. He was running short of runway.

"One hundred seventy . . . eighty! The trees, Jack!"

A dark green wall nearly engulfing him, Jack pulled back on the stick and the jet sprang upward at a steep angle. He waited for the impact of branches against the underside, but it never came. He had somehow cleared the forest. The stars were the only thing visible through the armored glass— the stars and the tiny cracks left by the rounds that had struck the sides of the bubble-shaped canopy. Jack quietly thanked the engineers at Messerschmitt for making the canopy bulletproof. There were over a dozen cracks in all.

As he watched the altimeter reach five hundred feet, Jack eased the stick forward and reduced throttle, but the plane continued to climb. He reduced throttle once more, and the plane leveled off at a thousand feet. He trimmed the elevators and re-laxed the pressure on the stick.

The craft now felt very smooth. Only the quiet whirl of the turbines told him they were airborne. There was no trembling, no engine-induced vibra-tions, no turning propeller or black smoke coming out of the exhausts. The jet was indeed a work of art. The elevator trim worked perfectly. He briefly let go his hand off the stick, and the artificial hori-zon confirmed his suspicion. The craft remained perfectly leveled.

Natalya rested her head against his shoulder as Jack briefly closed his eyes. "You're crazy, Jack Tow-ers. Absolutely crazy."

"We're not out of the woods yet, Natalya. We got to land this thing somewhere."

She turned her head and smiled. "Leave that to me."

KALACH AIRFIELD, TWENTY MILES WEST OF
THE STALINGRAD POCKET •
DECEMBER 17, 1942

Krasilov and Chapman sat inside the briefing bun-ker and read the official report of the attempted surprise bombing of the German airfield that intel-ligence claimed housed two jets.

The Red Air Force colonel pounded his fists on the table and stared into Chapman's bloodshot eyes. Neither of them had slept much in the past twenty-four hours.

"Damn! The bastards have probably moved them to another field by now. We lost our chance to blow them to hell!"

Chapman sat back on the wooden chair and qui-etly studied Krasilov through the smoke of the cig-

arette hanging off the side of his mouth. "We'll find
the jets again, Colonel."

"Yes, but every extra day that those infernal craft
remain in the battlefield costs the lives of my people, not yours."

Chapman stared into Krasilov's weathered eyes.
"Really, Colonel? Your people only."

Krasilov frowned. "Sorry. For a moment I . . ."

"Look, you have been under a lot of stress. Why
don't you take a break for a few hours and get some
sleep."

"I can't. I need to prepare the reports of today's
sorties for Moscow, and plan tomorrow's sorties."

"You're burning out, Colonel, and you know it.
You better take it easy."

Krasilov leaned forward and put both elbows on
the table. "I'm burning out, Major? Well, I've got
news for you. My *country* is burning, major. *My country*. Do you understand that? Those Hitlerite bastards have taken everything from me. My wife and
daughters; my home; everything, except for my will
to fight. If Russia loses, Major, you'll go back home
and perhaps prepare for an invasion of the main-
land, but we, Major, lose everything, our home, our
dignity, our lives, our traditions, everything. The Nazis have sworn to tear this nation into small pieces
and use the people as slaves. So if I'm burning out,
Major, then I'll just burn out." Krasilov reached for
the bottle of vodka next to him, took a swig, and
handed it to Chapman, who turned it down.

Krasilov abruptly stood. "Sound the alarm! Sound
the alarm!" He raced outside. Chapman followed
him.

"Hear it, Major?"

"That's a jet engine, Colonel. Looks like the bastards have decided to pay us a visit after hours!"

"Why can't we just contact them and tell them it's us?"

"Because, Jack, all radios are off. Radio silence is essential to the night bombers."

Jack frowned and reduced throttle even further. He couldn't see much. Below, the ground was pitch-black. There was not a single ground reference he could use to guide his craft. On top of that, without a moon, there was no horizon to tell Jack if his wings were leveled. He had to depend fully on the craft's artificial horizon—something he was not particularly used to doing. The Aircobra was a day fighter. Jack had flown at night before, but only when he had no other choice.

"Where is the damned runway?"

"You'll have to drop below one hundred feet to see the approach lights. We set them very low so enemy fighters can't spot the airfield at night unless they know to fly this low. Something very unlikely."

"Below a hundred? At night? I'll say that's *very* unlikely, Natalya. If the altimeter isn't properly calibrated, we're gonna run right into the ground!"

"Do it, Jack!"

Jack exhaled and dropped the nose by a few degrees while shifting his gaze between the darkness below him and the altimeter's needle. One hundred feet.

"There. Now all I got to do is sneeze and we're dead. What's next?"

"We look for the lights. They should be around here. Blue over green, Jack. Look for them."

Jack felt the wings tilting to the right. Instinctively, he inched the stick a bit to the left to compensate.

"Jack! What are you doing?"

Jack shifted his gaze to the artificial horizon and

noticed he was flying at a twenty degree angle of
bank. He had allowed spatial disorientation to take
over his judgment. Spatial disorientation came in
when the brain, confused from lack of visual inputs,
decided on its own which way was up and forced
that false reference on the pilot. The only way to
fight back was by forcing his brain to accept the
artificial horizon as the real reference.

Feeling the nausea induced by spatial disorientation, Jack clenched his teeth and eased the stick
back until the artificial horizon told him his wings
were leveled again. It felt awkward, but he did it
anyway. His instincts were lying to him.

"Sorry, I had vertigo."

"There, Jack. See them? See the lights?"

Jack squinted and spotted the bluish lights in the
distance, but since it was night, it was hard to judge
distance—at least for him.

"How far away is that?"

"About three thousand feet away. I know where I
am now, Jack. Turn left for about thirty seconds,
and then right to one-seven-zero. The nose should
be lined up with the runway."

"How do you—"

"We do this every night, Jack."

Jack eased back throttles and inched the stick to
the left.

Krasilov was about to order the searchlights on, but
decided against it. It had been over two minutes
since he first heard the jet engines, and he could
still hear them, but they had faded away some.

"Alarms off! Turn off all the lights, including the
approach lights!" he shouted. The siren died down,
and the only sounds left were that of the jets in the

distance and the wind swirling across the concrete runway.

"What are you doing?" asked Chapman.

"Trust me, Major. The bastards won't be able to find us. Besides, I don't feel like losing more fighters to those damn German jets."

"There, Jack! See them?"

Jack completed the right turn, narrowed his eyes, and saw the dim bluish lights a few thousand feet ahead. The lights suddenly went off.

"What happened to them? Damn!"

"They turned them off, Jack. Krasilov thinks we're the enemy."

"Lower flaps, Natalya!"

She reached for the lever on her side, and pulled it down to the second setting.

"I did this once without lights, Jack. At least we got to see the general location."

"Great," he said while squinting to see anything. "Airspeed?"

"One hundred fifty knots."

Jack Towers decided that if the jet took off at around 140 knots and stalled close to ninety, an acceptable approach speed should be somewhere in the middle. He cut back power and lowered the landing gear.

"One hundred forty . . . thirty-five . . ."

Krasilov was puzzled. The jet engines became louder, but still did not appear to sound as high-pitched as they did during his two encounters with the German fighter.

"Look, Colonel! There it is!" shouted Chapman.

Krasilov pulled out his gun, and so did most of the pilots on the field, Chapman included. Krasilov leveled it at the incoming craft, but stopped the moment the landing lights flooded the concrete runway.

"Hold your fire! Hold your fire!"

"What are you doing, Colonel? The bastard—"

"Is trying to land, Major! The German is trying to land!"

The runway quickly came up to meet him. Things were getting out of hand. Because of his unfamiliarity with the craft, Jack realized he was fighting the controls. For every adjustment in power and stick, he found himself readjusting in the opposite direction. He simply couldn't get the right response from the German fighter. Always too much or too little.

"One hundred twenty knots, Jack . . . fifteen . . . ten . . ."

Jack added just a dash of power to maintain one hundred ten knots.

"One hundred twenty knots, Jack."

"Dammit! This plane!" Frustrated, Jack reduced power again and eased the stick back, trying to descend and slow down at the same time.

"One hundred ten knots. Holding at one-ten."

Jack exhaled, but the brief surge of confidence was washed away by a gust of crosswind that brushed the craft to the side of the runway. Jack swung the stick in the opposite direction.

Krasilov felt something was wrong. Either the craft was damaged or the pilot was an incompetent. The craft drifted over the side, back over the runway, over to the other side, and finally back on the wide runway.

Someone panicked and opened fire.

Jack momentarily lost control of the stick as three rounds bounced off the armored canopy.

"Damn. Someone's firing at us!"

His left wing got dangerously close to the trees by the side of the runway.

"Right rudder, Jack! Quick!"

Jack pressed the right pedal and eased the stick to the right, bringing the craft back over the concrete.

"Hold your fucking fire!" Krasilov ran toward the young pilot who had his pistol leveled at the German fighter, and pushed his hand up in the air. "You idiot! All of you hold your fire! Now!"

Krasilov grabbed the weapon from the pilot and shoved him to the side. He shifted his gaze back to the craft.

Jack had consumed half the runway's length and still had not landed. He tried to cut back power, but instead of pushing the throttle controls, he automatically pulled them back. He realized his mistake the second after the jets kicked in full power and pushed the craft back up.

"The other way, Jack. It's the other way! Airspeed one hundred sixty . . . seventy . . . eighty . . ."

Jack was about to reduce throttles but it was to no avail. The end of the runway was too close.

"You idiots!" shouted Krasilov. "You have scared him off! The next man that opens fire will have to deal with me!"

He shifted his gaze back toward the plane slowly floating, seemingly out of control, over the runway.

———

Jack pulled up, climbed to one hundred feet, made a 180-degree turn, and came back around for another pass.

He kept the stick dead centered while decreasing power steadily. Once again, the runway came up to meet him. Jack felt the light crosswind that was the cause of his drifting over the runway on his first pass. This time around he had a better feel for the finesse required to control the craft during the last phase of the landing approach. He decided to change landing tactics, and eased the stick to the right to fly into the wind while applying left rudder. The conflicting commands tilted the jet's wings a mild fifteen degrees, but with the payoff of keeping the nose aligned with the runway.

This time instead of overcorrecting, Jack's hands over the throttle handles and stick barely moved. The adjustments were minimal. He felt in control.

The right gear touched down first. Jack centered the stick, and the left wheel bounced against the concrete runway once before it settled. The tail dropped as Natalya read seventy knots indicated airspeed.

Krasilov, Chapman and the other pilots ran behind the German jet, which managed to stop at the end of the runway, turned around, and came to a full stop next to the fighter shelters.

Krasilov was the first to reach it. He jumped on the wing with his pistol in his right hand, and was about to bang on the canopy for the pilot to push it open when he froze.

Jack and Natalya waved at him from inside the cockpit.

Krasilov remained silent for a few seconds before bursting into laughter.

KALACH AIRFIELD, TWENTY MILES WEST OF
THE STALINGRAD POCKET •
DECEMBER 18, 1942

Jack was exhausted. The debriefing with Krasilov and Chapman had gone well, but had lasted a couple of hours longer than Jack would have liked. He went over everything from the time he got shot down to the moment they landed. Everything.

Both Krasilov and Chapman took extensive notes, particularly of Jack's description of the strong points and weaknesses of the German jet. Even before he had completed giving them his impressions of the powerful fighter, Chapman had already made the decision of getting the plane flown to England, where it would be thoroughly inspected by a joint USAAC and RAF team. Jack had been assigned as the pilot, and he was to leave at dawn. Refueling stops were already being set up along a route worked out by both Krasilov and Chapman.

"Well, so much for my little tour of the Eastern Front," he murmured as he reached his tent behind the fighter shelters by the edge of the trees. Things were moving too fast for Jack. Much had happened in the four short days since his arrival there, and now he was being requested to leave for England.

He opened the canvas flap and quickly closed it to keep some of the heat still trapped inside the tent from last night's fire. Each tent had a small wood-burning stove and ventilation pipe.

He walked to the stove in back, reached for a few logs, piled them up, soaked them with kerosene, and threw in a match. He remained kneeling in front of the fire for a few seconds while his face thawed. Jack removed his gloves and cap, and began to unbutton his coat when a gust of wind nearly put the fire out. Convinced that he had closed the canvas flap, Jack turned around.

"Hello, Jack."

"Natalya. What are you—"

"I heard you were leaving tomorrow to fly the German plane to England. I came by to wish you luck, and also to say thanks. What are your plans after England?"

"Sit down, please. And close that flap, please."

The Soviet pilot snapped the canvas shut and removed her furry hat. Her hair hung loose over her ears.

"I'm not sure what's going happen to me after I deliver the plane. Chapman mentioned something about training another group of pilots. There are three shipments of Aircobras on the way."

She lowered her gaze. Jack knelt down next to her and lifted her chin. "I'm going to miss you, too, Natalya Makarova."

She tried to move his hand away, but he softly cupped her face. "Look at me, Natalya. I want you to look at me."

Slowly, she raised her gaze until it melted with his. Jack smiled. "I knew it."

"Please stop, Jack. You know there can never be anything between—"

"Says who? Our governments? The hell with them. Something has happened to me in the past few days, Natalya. I've never felt this way about anybody else. I—"

"Please don't say it, Jack . . . please?" She got up to leave without waiting for a response.

"Natalya. I might not see you for some time."

She stopped. "I can't, Jack."

"You can't or you won't?"

"Jack, please. You won't understand."

"Try me, Natalya. Is it differences in cultures? Religion maybe? What? Tell me, please."

She slowly turned around. Tears rolled down her cheeks. "His name is Boris Nikolajev. He was a pilot with another air wing and was reported shot down eight months ago during the Battle of Moscow. We were married the same day that he was sent to defend Moscow, Jack. We never even had a honeymoon. After several months, I decided to get on with my life, and then you came along and . . ."

"And?"

"A letter arrived from Moscow while we were gone. It said that he was found in a liberated POW camp west of Moscow. It was a miracle, Jack. He and a dozen others were the only survivors out of hundreds of prisoners taken there. He was promptly taken to a hospital, where he is right now struggling to recover from the subhuman conditions in which the Nazis kept him for all those months."

Jack was confused. "Boris *Nikolajev?* Is he . . ."

"Yes, Jack. Boris is Andrei's brother. He needs me. Please understand."

Jack closed his eyes and searched for the words, but there weren't any. He lifted his gaze and stared into the hazel eyes that had somehow taken possession of his feelings. Now those same eyes told him that it could never be. They had been promised to someone else long before he'd gotten here.

Natalya leaned down and kissed him on the lips.

"Good-bye, Jack Towers. You'll always have a special place in my heart. Thank you for giving me my life."

Jack softly pulled her face close to his and inhaled deeply. "Thank you for giving me mine," he responded as he tried to bring her lips next to his. Natalya gently pulled away.

"Please, Jack. Please understand. I can't . . ."

Jack lowered his gaze. She turned around and reached the entrance flap.

"Natalya . . . that day in the hut after we got shot down, when you . . . did you feel what I . . ."

"I will treasure that day for as long as I live, Jack. Good-bye."

A gust of cold wind blew inside the tent as she left. Jack felt the bitter air cut through his soul.